100 Days of Cake

100 DAYS of CAKE

Shari Goldhagen

atheneum

NEW YORK LONDON TORONTO
SYDNEY NEW DELHI

An imprint of Simon & Schuster Children's Publishing Division
1230 Avenue of the Americas, New York, New York 10020

For information about special discounts for bulk purchases, please contact Simon &
Schuster Special Sales at 1-866-506-1949 or business@simonandschuster.com.
The Simon & Schuster Speakers Bureau can bring authors to your live event. For more
information or to book an event, contact the Simon & Schuster Speakers Bureau at
1-866-248-3049 or visit our website at www.simonspeakers.com.
The text for this book was set in ITC Esprit Std.
Manufactured in the United States of America
First Edition
2 4 6 8 10 9 7 5 3 1
Library of Congress Cataloging-in-Publication Data
Names: Goldhagen, Shari, 1976– author.
Title: 100 days of cake / Shari Goldhagen.
Other titles: One hundred days of cake
Description: First Edition. | New York : Atheneum Books for Young Readers, [2016] |
Summary: "Molly suffers from depression, and when she finds out that the
exotic fish store she works at is closing down, her whole life, which is already
hanging on a thread, starts to crumble"— Provided by publisher.
Identifiers: LCCN 2015033431 | ISBN 9781481448567 (hardcover) |
ISBN 9781481448581 (eBook)
Subjects: | CYAC: Depression, Mental—Fiction.
Classification: LCC PZ7.1.G63 Aah 2016 | DDC [Fic]—dc23
LC record available at http://lccn.loc.gov/2015033431

For my family

DAY 12

Cherry Berry Bundt Cake

It's been summer break for four hours, and Alex McDermott and I are already on our third *Golden Girls* rerun and our second container of house special lo mein.

Sitting cross-legged on the counter at FishTopia Saltwater Fish & Supplies, we're staring at the ancient TV above the register, passing the carton of noodles between us, and basking in the thin wave of air from the oscillating fan that blows our direction every few seconds.

"Molly, you're hogging all the good air." Alex scoots closer to me, near enough that our shorts and thighs are practically touching, and I'm thankful I was motivated enough to shave my legs this morning; some days it's a stretch.

"Shouldn't you be sweeping or something?" I nudge his shoulder with mine, and he rolls his eyes. Since the place opened two years ago, I don't think anyone has ever taken the broom out of the supply closet in the back, much less attempted to use it. The handful of customers who come in never complain, and the owner, Charlie, pops in only once a week to do inventory and drop off our checks.

"If Chuck graces us with his presence, I'll point out that he's violating just about a thousand labor laws for not having AC in this place." Alex gives this cute crooked smile, and a dimple pops into his cheek. "Seriously, this *cannot* be good for the fish."

Like me, Alex is a junior (technically we're seniors now, I guess), but he goes to Maxwell—Coral Cove's other high school, across town. When we started working here after school and on weekends, I wasn't sure we'd have much in common. He's in a band, and there was this steady stream of girls with inky dyed hair and Hot Topic graphic T-shirts who used to come in here and flirt with him. But it turns out *Golden Girls* and take-out noodles are some kind of universal language; Alex and I were fast friends from the first time we stumbled upon an episode and he said Betty White was the bomb.

We've seen this episode at least four times in the past six months alone. It's the one where Blanche, Rose, Sophia, and Dorothy put on a production of *Henny Penny* at an elementary school, and they're all wearing these ridiculous leotards and feather headpieces. Knowing when the jokes are coming only makes it funnier; sometimes I crack up just seeing Rose on screen.

In my perfect world I'd spend the rest of the day (maybe the rest of the summer; maybe the rest of my life) right here at FishTopia just like this . . . but in the pocket of my cutoffs, my cell phone rings.

"Your wife again?" Alex asks, and I scrunch up my face in mock annoyance, but it *is* the third time Elle has called in the past ninety minutes, and Elle and I *have* been best friends since kindergarten, which is a lot longer than either of our parents were married, if you think about it that way.

I wander into an aisle of clown fish and guppies for moderate privacy.

"Hey."

"Mrs. Kamp next door can watch Jimmy, so that's taken care of." Elle picks up the conversation in pretty much the exact spot where we left off half an hour ago, when she was trying to find a babysitter for her little brother. She's still trying to convince me to be her wing woman at Chris Partridge's end-of-the-year party tonight. I don't want to go any more than I did the last time she called.

"Come on, Mol. How often do we even get invited to stuff like this?"

Ah, never. It's not like Coral Cove High is a John Hughes film, where you never talk to people outside your clique, but Elle and I have always spent most of our time with the other dorks in advanced classes and on the swim team (before I quit), while Chris plays baseball and is the president of our

3

class; there's just not a lot of overlap. So it was doubly weird this afternoon when Elle and I were emptying out all the crumpled notebook paper and stray pen caps from our locker, and Chris sauntered over and specifically invited us. "Bring whoever you want," he said, "friends, family." I thought that Elle's head might explode. She's had a crush on Chris since he offered her a Life Saver one time in study hall freshman year.

"Chris probably just invited the entire class or something," I say.

"*See*, everyone will be there; we have to go."

That makes the prospect even less appealing. I haven't been to a single *anything* party since my massive freak-out at the divisionals meet a year ago. A ginormous party with everyone talking about senior year and college and who's getting engaged and all that other BS seems a horrible place to dive back into the CCH social scene. But . . .

Even though I'm reasonably sure Chris and Elle never spoke again after the Life Saver incident (technically I don't think he actually spoke to her then, just kind of held out the pack and grunted), it would still be pretty crappy if I didn't go with her.

"I promise I won't say anything if people aren't recycling," Elle says, which is a big deal for her. Then she threatens to invoke BFF law—this modified version of the Girl Scout Law we came up with way back when we were in Brownies. "Pleeeeeeease."

"Will you drive?" I ask, and I can almost see her weighing the environmental damage of using the old gas-guzzling Jeep Cherokee her dad gave her, against the off chance that Chris might go all *High School Musical* and fall in love with her.

"Can we do windows instead of AC?" she asks.

"Elle, it's one hundred thousand degrees out!" Technically 103, but it has been that way for three days, which is ridiculous even for central Florida.

"Fine, we'll turn it on low. I'll pick you up at the store in an hour."

"Deal."

When I hang up and turn around, Alex is standing at the opening of the aisle, staring at me like I've grown additional heads. Automatically my hand goes to the mouse-poop-colored frizz on my head; with this humidity it's more of a lost cause than usual. My mom—who wouldn't hesitate to tell you she owns the most successful hair salon in Coral Cove *and* the surrounding areas—would be horrified.

"What?" I ask defensively.

"Sorry, I was totally eavesdropping, but were you guys talking about Chris Partridge's thing tonight?"

Hesitantly, I nod.

"Dude, Chris and I have been buddies since Little League." Alex is nodding excitedly. "How did I not know you guys were friends?"

SHARI GOLDHAGEN

"More like acquaintances." I shrug. More like nothing.

"But you're going?"

"For a little. . . . You?"

I probably see Alex more than any human being on the planet who doesn't physically live in my house (and honestly, more than I've seen my sister lately), but we only ever hang out at FishTopia. Sometimes he suggests we go grab dinner or coffee or he'll ask if I want to see some show, but I can never tell if he's serious or not or if it would be a date-date or not, and then I start thinking about those Hot Topic girls and all the weird stuff that's been going on with me this past year, and it gets hard to breathe. So I always kind of brush him off. It's safe to be with him *here*—like our own little aquarium.

But maybe it *would* be okay if we saw each other at this party? Then there'd be at least one person other than Elle who I know I like. Although, it's already a little screwed up, since Alex thinks I'm all buddy-buddy with Chris.

"I've got band practice after we close up here." Alex is still talking. "But I'll come after that." He takes his phone from his pocket and unlocks the screen. "Gimme your digits, and I'll let you know when I'm on my way."

Reciting my phone number, I have this flash to winter sophomore year when T. J. Cranston asked for my number after swim practice; suddenly my stomach feels all oily.

"Cool," I say. I have no idea if this is actually cool. All

I know is, I'm nervous enough that it's hard to follow the rest of the *Golden Girls* episode.

In her ancient Jeep Cherokee, Elle pulls up in front of the store and honks. She refuses to enter FishTopia, because she thinks it's a prison for marine life or something. I push off the counter, gather my backpack, and throw my container of lo mein into the garbage. Alex waves to Elle through the store window. They've never actually met, but Alex has heard me tell enough stories that he could probably write a dissertation on Elle Lovell.

"So I guess maybe I'll see you tonight?" I say.

"Definitely." Alex holds the door open for me, and the little bell that alerts us to new customers dings. "Let me help you with your bike."

"I got—" I start, but then I just nod, and he follows me into the soupy air that is Coral Cove this summer. Motioning for Elle to pop the rear door, I unlock Old Montee—this green Murray Monterey Beach cruiser that my mom used to ride around when she was growing up here—from a handicap-parking sign. Alex hoists it over his shoulder and slides it into the back of the Jeep. Even though I'm still pretty twisty about tonight, I take a minute to appreciate just how easily he lifted my bike. Alex is a little on the short and slender side, and I had no idea he was that strong. . . . Duly noted.

7

In the driver's seat, Elle spins around and introduces herself, her dishwater-blond curls still in springy ringlets, despite the heat and lack of animal-tested or ozone-destroying hair products. "And I'm guessing you're Alex."

"Guilty as charged." He gives that crooked grin again. "Nice to finally meet you."

"Same. You need a ride?"

"Naw, I got a car." Alex gestures toward his Ford Fiesta with the rusted undercarriage. "But it looks like I'll be seeing you girls later tonight at Chris's."

Elle shoots me this laser-focused What's-going-on? eyebrow lift.

"Yeah, it turns out Alex and Chris go way back," I offer.

"Sweet," Elle says, even though she doesn't normally say things like "sweet."

Alex says he'll text me when he's en route, and goes back inside to finish closing up. I barely make it into the passenger seat (the AC is totally *not* on, BTW) before Elle is bombarding me with questions about how Alex knows Chris and why I never told her.

"I swear I had no idea until today."

"Are you excited he's coming? He's so cute," she says. "And I kept telling you he was into you."

This is true. Despite having never actually met Alex—that whole not-entering-the-store thing—Elle has long been convinced that Alex and I are destined to get married and have a million babies and live happily ever after. I guess I do talk about him a lot.

"I don't know." I bunch my shoulders. "It's weird."

"It'll be fine, and your mom will be thrilled you're finally going out again."

"True."

We've never been to Chris's house, but we know where it is. There are only thirty-two thousand people in Coral Cove (up seven thousand souls from a decade ago, before J&J Plumbing moved its headquarters here), so you pretty much know all the subdivisions and who lives where. His place is only a few streets down from the model home where my mom and sister and I moved a few years ago.

The street is packed with the cars of kids from school. Half of them are new and shiny sixteenth-birthday presents, the other half hand-me-downs from parents and even grandparents—that's new/old Coral Cove for you. My mom has promised me "any car within reason" if I'm ever motivated enough to sign up for driver's ed; I'm probably the only seventeen-year-old in the entire county without a license.

We park and follow the line of cars to a big new house (Chris's dad is J&J corporate), and we make it to the driveway before I start wondering if maybe I should have put on something other than my summer uniform of cutoffs and a tank top, or if I should have at least put on a *fresh* tank top instead of just keeping on the one that I've been sweating in all freaking day.

Elle is wearing one of her oatmeal-colored shapeless cotton T-shirts and a pair of drapey pants that cost a lot because they're made without any of the bad chemicals and don't exploit cheap labor. There are probably hip eco-chic models wearing them all over San Fran, but Elle weighs ninety-eight pounds soaking wet, so the getup just looks frumpy on her. Obviously too late to say anything now.

Since the bright blue door is wide open, Elle and I exchange shrugs, let ourselves in, and follow the music out to the backyard.

I guess I was expecting some crazy TV party scene, but honestly it doesn't look all that different from the swim team parties Elle and I used to go to back when I did stuff like that. There's a bunch of people from our class clumped around deck chairs or sitting by the inexplicably drained swimming pool. On a folding table there are plastic containers of cold cuts and a pink bucket of beer and soda cans, as well as an enormous punch bowl. A few of the girls are wearing slightly dressier tank tops, but Elle and I don't look horrifically out of place.

Meredith Hoffman—a cheerleader from my sophomore year health class—is giving off this first-lady vibe, scurrying around straightening the table and adjusting plastic cups.

I wonder if she and Chris are dating, wonder if Elle has picked up on that.

Seeing us, Meredith gives a little wave. "Hey, ladies!"

We nod back.

"You've got to try this punch," she says, ladling out two glasses. "It's a sacred recipe from Chris's brother's FSU frat."

The color of a flamingo, it smells like pure gasoline. It must also be about ninety proof, because I feel totally loopy from one swallow. To be fair, even when I did used to go to parties, I was never a big drinker. Elle starts coughing on her first sip and mumbles something about not being able to drive home.

Informing us that she has already "broken the seal," Meredith jogs off to the bathroom.

Gina and Tina, these freckled identical twins from our AP English class (the only advanced class I was able to keep this year), are sitting on the diving board with their feet hanging over the empty pool. So maybe the entire school was invited. Elle leads us toward them, and within minutes they're all talking about the summer reading list and whether they're going to take the SATs again in the fall—as if we hadn't gotten out of school less than six hours ago.

"A scholarship is my only shot at paying for Columbia, so I've got to," Elle is saying.

We were supposed to take the test at the same time in May, but I had such a panic attack that not even the Xanax helped. My mom and Elle ended up suggesting that I just wait until the fall.

Gina or Tina is saying something about applying early decision somewhere. These are the conversations that make me want to gnaw my arm off. "Are you thinking FSU or UF?" "You're going into the army even though your dad was a navy man?" "Did you plan out every minute of the rest of your life already?" Vomit.

I'm just staring into the pool. Generally I haven't been a big fan of pools ADF (After my Divisionals Freak-out, which was a year ago), but the missing water makes it much less intimidating. The bottom is painted this nice blue that's probably supposed to look like the ocean.

"Your dad went there, right, Mol?" Elle asks.

"Wha?"

"Your dad went to the University of Miami, didn't he?"

"Oh yeah," I say. "He was always talking about how this one biology professor changed his life." Other than the Miami part, I don't know if any of this is true. My dad died when I was three, and sometimes I just make stuff up because I don't remember, which is weird and sad, but at least all conversations don't come to a screeching halt the way they do when you say you have no memories of your own father.

"Yeah, I'm definitely doing early decision," Gina says, as if someone asked a question; someone probably did.

Eventually Gina and Tina go get more chips, and Chris Partridge catches my eye and starts jogging over. Since we've hung out all of never, it's surprising that he looks so completely psyched to see us.

"Molly, Elle." He nods. "Thanks for coming to chez casa."

Elle might burst into a million happy bits because he remembered her name. She doesn't even mention that he just welcomed us to his "house, house."

"Thanks for asking us," I say, and hold up my still-full glass. "Awesome punch."

"Yeah, it's from my brother's fraternity. He could get banned for life for sharing it."

"His secret is safe with me," I say.

Elle stands there like someone hit her pause button, and I can see Chris kind of looking off to my right.

"So, got any big summer plans?" I ask, because it's my duty as a wing woman, not because I want to get into another discussion about SAT prep.

"Well, the pool should be fixed by the end of the week." Chris gestures to the big empty hole. "Total bummer it wasn't ready for tonight, but we'll definitely get that going."

"If you want an alternative to chlorine, they have natural enzymes you can use to keep it clean." Elle finally says something, albeit a completely face-palm-worthy something.

"Huh?" Chris looks genuinely confused.

"An alternative that's a little more earth friendly . . ." Elle trails off, as absolutely none of this is registering for Chris. "Is the bathroom this way?" she practically squeaks and points to the house, like the bathroom would be any other place. "Whoa, I had a lot of punch."

And then she darts off.

Does a good wing woman run after her, or stay behind and explain why she's acting like a total spaz?

"She okay?" Chris asks.

"Yeah, uh, she just broke the seal already." This is so not something I would ever say, and it sounds ridiculous, but Chris bobs his head empathetically.

"That's the worst, man. No wonder she was talking all crazy about chemicals."

I bite my tongue.

"So, um, did you come with Ronnie—I mean Veronica?" he asks, and it takes me a good second to realize he's talking about my younger sister.

"No, I didn't even know you guys knew each other," I say, wondering how Chris Partridge became this weird epicenter of my universe, secretly connected to everyone in my life.

"We had a study hall together. She said she might stop by." He looks really dejected that I didn't know this.

"Oh, she's probably coming. I just haven't seen her since this morning. After school I went right to work."

He nods again, still looking like someone filled his pool with natural chemicals, so I tell him that it turns out we also have Alex in common.

"Shut up! You're Alex's Molly?" he asks.

Alex's Molly. Chris looks as shocked as I feel. *Alex's Molly.*

"He's talked about me?"

"I mean, he said he worked with this really cool girl. I just didn't put two and two together."

Even though it's already a million degrees out, I feel myself blushing.

"Is he coming tonight?" Chris is asking.

"Yeah, when he's done with band practice."

"Sweet. McD is a good dude."

From the table of snacks by the screen door, Meredith calls out to Chris that they need more beer.

"Duty calls." Chris smiles and trots off.

This really cool girl. Alex's Molly. Everything is all jumbled in my head. Is Elle actually right about Alex being into me? What about the Hot Topic girls? What about the way he always seems to be joking when he asks if I want to hang out?

My phone chimes that I've got a new text, and I jump a little, thinking it must be Alex and that he can somehow magically read my thoughts.

The message is from Elle: *Hiding in upstairs linen closet. Mortified.*

I write back: *Told C u were drunk.*

Thanks I guess??!!! Have to use b room for real now. BRB

I really don't want to hear Gina and Tina go on and on about college anymore, and I don't have strong connections to any of the other clumps of people, so I sit on a deck chair a little away from everyone and wait for Elle. To avoid looking like a total loser, I pretend to do something extremely important on my phone. When this slobbering adorable golden retriever comes over, I treat it like a long-lost relative.

Before he died, my dad always used to promise we'd get a dog. That's one thing I actually do remember.

"Molly Byrne." A familiar voice, and my stomach drops.

T. J. Cranston, all tall and tan and good-looking in this cheesy, Captain America way that your mom thinks is super-handsome—at least my mom did when he picked me up for our first date.

He was a couple of years ahead of me, but when I got bumped to the varsity swim team sophomore year, we were in the same practice lane, and sometimes he'd tell me he liked my suit or joke about how I was attacking him with my flippers. Then one day he asked me out. My mom and Elle and V were all excited, so I got a little excited. He took me to an Olive Garden knockoff, paid the check, and kissed me good night. We started going out like that maybe once a week, or we'd watch something on Netflix or go to a team party together, and he always gave me rides home after practice.

He was a nice enough guy—he never pressured me to have sex or do drugs like bad boyfriends always do in sitcoms—but it was right around that time when everything started to really pile up. I've always been kind of obsessive about grades and art class and big meets and stuff, but it got to the point where little things like having to pee when I'd already put on both practice suits could bring me to tears, and it just became easier to give up on stuff.

Finally T.J. asked why I was so mopey, but it wasn't like anything was actually wrong, and when I told him that, his face scrunched up into this fake sympathetic look like he'd stepped in dog crap. So I never said anything again, but I started to dread seeing him and having to pretend I was this ray of sunshine, when in reality it didn't even feel like I was there. It was like I was floating above, watching this undeserving girl with blue-green eyes and mouse-poop hair holding hands with Captain America dude, and French-kissing him at the end of the night. Then I'd go inside to my model-home bedroom and cry. Pathetic.

And then, the day before the divisionals meet, T.J. drove me home after practice, pulled into my driveway, turned off the ignition, and sighed. "You're a great girl, Molly," he began. "You're just kind of different from what I thought before I got to know you."

Oddly, out of all the appropriate times to start bawling, I didn't—I actually felt sort of relieved. But then when I saw him the next day at divisionals talking to this blond junior, something inside me just broke . . . which led to my infamous freak-out at the start of the freestyle relay. For the entire rest of the school year I managed to avoid him—which is pretty impressive, since our school has only seven hundred people total—and then he was off to Florida State.

But I guess he's back now, and apparently he's also BFFs with bloody Chris Partridge! WTF!

"What's up?" I hear myself asking him.

"Well, FSU is awesome." T.J. gestures to Chris's older brother, who I hadn't noticed before. "I pledged Kappa Sig with Robbie."

"You guys make good punch." I hold up my glass.

"Thanks. How 'bout you, Mol?" He tilts his head a little like he's trying to be extra sincere, the stuff that annoyed the crap out of me when we were dating. "This year go okay?"

The panic is circling in my throat.

"Yeah, it was peachy."

I need to get out of here.

I can't have Alex come here and see this. See me. Can't let these people tell him that I'm not this really cool girl he works with. That the real me is a girl who randomly cries in the bathroom between classes. A girl who got hysterical on the starting block before the freestyle relay and ran away, disqualifying the team from the race and ruining the divisionals meet for everyone.

"Look, for a while now I've wanted to say something about what—"

"No, it's all good." I cut him off before he can say any of this out loud. "Actually, I gotta hop. Great seeing you."

Then I'm hurrying away, back into the house, the golden retriever following after.

I try to text Elle that T.J. is here and I have to leave. But I'm so screwed up that I fat-finger half the letters, and it's auto-corrected to: *The hart O gave to hp.*

What? Elle writes back.

Where r u? Have to leaf.

To what?

TJ HERE!!! Meet me at car.

OK

I'm nearly at the front door, but the dog is still following me, so I try gently pushing his face back, indicating that he should stay, but he just licks my arm. I try throwing an imaginary ball into the living room, but he's clearly on to me.

Ugh. I *need* to leave; already I can feel tears in the corners of my eyes. I can't be that girl, not again.

In the kitchen someone opens the refrigerator, and Lassie immediately loses interest in me and trots off. I make a run for the door, but my phone dings. I look down to read it and smack into a sheet of shiny dark hair smelling of lilacs . . . my sister.

Veronica is two years behind me at CCH, but she's with a group of older girls she works with at Jaclyn's Attic, a trendy boutique in the "revitalized" downtown. Some of the girls I vaguely know from school; the others must go to Maxwell with Alex. They all have perfectly applied eye makeup and smudge-proof lips. All of them are pretty in sundresses or designer shorts and tops that show off shapely shoulders. But even among the gorgeous girls, my sister is the standout.

V got the good genes from Mom—the razor-sharp cheekbones and gravity-defying boobs, the legs that go all the way up.

"Molly?" she asks, part terror, part straight-up confusion. "Why are you here?"

"Great to see you, too, V. "

"No, I mean, I thought you didn't do stuff like this anymore. Go to parties?"

"I don't." I nod. "I'm leaving."

Glancing down, I see a text from Alex: *Heading over now.*

I *need* to get out of here.

"Wait. Why don't you just stay?" V grabs my arm and holds it. She sounds like she might actually mean it, even if her friends are giving these WTF? looks. "We'll, like, bond or something."

Just a few years ago we were super-close. But things have been weird since ADF. Since she started in high school too.

Another text. Not from Alex but Elle: *Finishing up here; there in a few.*

"I gotta go. I'll see you at home."

"Yeah, okay." V lets me go, and I practically run to the door.

Behind me I hear one of the Jaclyn's girls snarl, "What was that all about?"

Closing my eyes, I try not to let it bother me too much. My shrink—Dr. B.—says that sometimes it helps just to take a couple of deep breaths, but it was like breathing through clam chowder. So I do.

How is it still so freaking hot out?

When Elle gets to the Jeep, she doesn't even object when I crank up the AC knob as soon as I climb in.

"Sorry I made you go," Elle says. "I had no idea T.J. would be there."

I shake my head and try the breathing thing again.

"Are you okay?" she asks.

The answer is probably no. I want to scream or cry or go to bed for a week. But it's almost worse to be honest and have people—even people like Elle, who's been my best friend for longer than our parents were married—look at me like I'm broken. So I try to rein it all in.

"Yeah, that was fun," I say flatly. "We should definitely go to more parties."

When Elle drops me off and I make it upstairs to my room, all I want to do is fall into the huge sleigh bed and pass out, but there's a piece of horribly dilapidated blue-and-red-stained cake on a plate by my nightstand, along with a note in Mom's chunky handwriting.

> *Hope you had a great time tonight! Figured I'd*
> *leave this for you in case you're hungry. I have a*
> *good feeling about this one!*
>
> *—Mom*

Bunching the note into a ball, I hurl it across the room and miss the garbage can by at least a foot.

DAY 13

Ooey-Gooey Butter Cake

*A*fter seeing T.J. last night, and all the weird confusion over being *Alex's Molly*, I want to never leave the house again. But if I stay home, Mom will ask a million questions about everything, and that will just make it all so much worse. Plus, I have an appointment with Dr. B. in the afternoon, and I always look forward to those.

Without incident, I manage to get out of bed, throw on clothes, and bike to the store in the oppressive heat. Since I'm free to work days now that school's out, I'm supposed to handle the swing shift today—half with Alex in the evening and half with JoJo Banks in the early afternoon.

During the school year JoJo opens the place and is gone by the time I get there, so she's just initials on the schedule to me. Based on the name, I thought she'd be some gray-haired soft woman like my grandma, but it turns out she's maybe four or five years older than me with a streaky orange tan. Who fake-bakes when you live in Florida and it's a thousand degrees out?

Strike one against JoJo is that she has Maury Povich's show blaring on the TV so loud, I can hear it outside the store.

The little bell on the door dings when I come in, and she briefly looks up at me.

"Molly?" she asks.

"Yep."

"Cool. I already checked the tanks," she says, then turns back to some guy on *Maury* doing a "You're Not the Father" dance.

Strike two is that she gets vocally angry when the next guy insists he isn't the baby daddy, despite the paternity test results.

"Why can't these A-hats man up?" she yells. "That's your child!"

It doesn't seem like she's talking to me, so I don't feel any pressing need to respond. On the back of someone's discarded receipt, I sketch Maury, making his hair extra crazy. Art class was always my favorite before I dropped all my electives.

A commercial comes on the screen for some antidepressant. There's an attractive thirtysomething blond woman sitting in a rocking chair in a dark room, watching through the window as her attractive husband, attractive kids, and equally attractive dog are having the time of their lives playing catch outside in the yard. As the announcer is reading off the laundry list of side effects—dizziness, drowsiness or tired feeling, upset stomach, dry mouth, changes in appetite, constipation—the woman heads outside, a little hesitantly, and starts playing with her family.

It's a different med than the one I'm on, and it seems to be working much more effectively for the Attractives than mine does for me.

I study my Maury sketch and hope JoJo doesn't have any commentary on the commercial, too.

"You go to CCH?" she asks.

"Yeah."

"I'm class of 2011," she says.

"I just missed you," I say, hoping to avoid that awkward conversation where we try to figure out if we have friends in common. She doesn't know Elle, and I hardly talk to anyone else anymore.

"Demarco still teaching geometry?"

"I think so."

A look of righteous indignation falls across her face. "That A-hat sent me to detention at least once a week. For piddly shit too, like chewing gum."

"Sucks." I try to sound sympathetic. "I had Swinton; he was okay."

"Lucky." She turns back to the TV, where The *Jerry Springer Show* is starting. Apparently today's episode features a woman who wants to marry her husband's grandfather. I take a lap through the aisles to double-check the tanks in case she may have missed something. I even contemplate digging out the broom and sweeping.

I took the job here because Chuck thinks minimum wage is two bucks higher than it is, and that's what he's paying. But the fish really *are* beautiful. All the bright colors of the mandarin fish and the parrot fish, and the crazy shape of the nudibranch, the way that the tasseled angelfish can disappear in its surroundings. I totally get why people (well, not people in Coral Cove, who couldn't care less that we're here, but people in general) might get a tank to try to calm themselves down.

"Yo, CCH," JoJo calls from the front. "I'm grabbing lunch from Wang's. You want in?"

All strikes against JoJo are erased. Any fan of Wang's Palace (yes, that is the actual name) is my sister from another mister.

Wang's opened a few months ago. It's this confused mishmash of different Asian cuisines—Chinese, Thai, Japanese—run by a family originally from Brazil. Inside it's decorated with black-and-white head shots of celebrities, like some of those famous places in LA and Manhattan, only none of those celebrities have ever actually set foot inside. (Not counting Jim and Joe Johnson from J&J Plumbing, the only famous person from Coral Cove is the guy who played the killer in the *Murder Island* movie. He hasn't been back in years, despite numerous city council efforts to have him as the grand marshal in the Founder's Day Parade.)

Despite all that sketch, Wang's is actually crazy delicious, and their house special lo mein is clearly made up of whatever food in their kitchen is about to go bad. Sometimes it's beef and roast pork, sometimes it's unidentifiable seafood and veggies. Once it was broccoli rabe, a vaguely Mexican sausage, and cashews. *That* was a good day.

When JoJo comes back with the steamy clamshell containers, it looks like today is an indistinguishable protein—maybe duck?—and water chestnuts. JoJo and I eat behind the counter, and she gets worked into a lather about a "surprise proposals" *Jerry* episode, where men pop the question to girls they aren't even dating, with mixed results.

Her cell phone rings, and JoJo groans and hands me the remote. "This might be a while; it's my A-hat ex."

I wonder if she means ex-boyfriend or ex-husband. In Coral Cove plenty of people get married right out of high school, so you never know. She's still in the back room yelling at the ex two episodes of *Family Ties* later (*Golden Girls* doesn't start until three), when Alex comes in to relieve her.

Immediately JoJo materializes in the front of the store and collects her stuff from behind the counter. "Audi, kids." She gives a wave, and the bell on the front door dings her exit.

"You finally got the full JoJo experience firsthand?" Alex smiles, and I laugh. "I've had that pleasure a few Saturdays."

"It was definitely something, you freaking A-hat."

Alex smiles. "Yeah, JoJo's cool, though." He shoves his hands into his pockets. "So, what happened last night? You guys run out to avoid me?" he says nonchalantly, but I still feel a flicker of panic.

"Elle wasn't feeling great, so we cut out early. Sorry, I should have let you know, but we left kinda quick."

"No worries. She okay?"

It takes a half second before I realize he's asking about Elle and the illness I invented for her. "She's good now."

We throw a nod back and forth.

"Next time, I guess," I tell him.

"Sure."

More nodding.

"Oh, I have something for you." He reaches for his backpack.

Alarms start wailing in my head.

We're seventeen—hell, he isn't even my boyfriend—this can't be a surprise proposal, can it?

Nope. He pulls out a gray T-shirt with orange-and-yellow flames on the front and the words "The Flaming Dantes" printed above them.

"The band's got a new name," he says. "Our drummer just realized he was super-inspired reading *The Inferno* last year."

"Ohhh, I likey." I'm totally touched, but I also can't help wondering how many of these shirts they had made.

In the past two years his band has changed names at least five times. They've been Cyanide Six-Pack, Approximate Proxy, Bad Times for All (which they really liked but eighty-sixed when they discovered there was already a group in Chicago called that), Baggage, and something I can't remember, other than that it had to do with cell phones and elephants, maybe Celo-phant or Ele-o-phone. They've never actually played a show under any name, but sometimes Alex will bring his guitar to the store, and if it's really dead (pretty much always—it turns out that Charlie was wrong, and Coral Cove wasn't really clamoring for saltwater fish), we'll go to the roof deck on top of the building, and he'll fool around with some chords and lyrics. It always sounds pretty good.

"Thank you much," I say.

"Now you're ready for our first show."

"Absolutely." I wonder if a bunch of the Hot Topic girls will be there in these tees too.

The *Golden Girls* block starts with the one where Blanche, Dorothy, and Rose accidentally book a Valentine's Day vacation at a nude beach resort and spend their entire trip staring out the window at the nakeds, trying to work up the nerve to strip down and go out themselves. The fourth season wasn't my fav, but this episode always slays me.

With chopsticks he found somewhere behind the counter, Alex sneaks into my leftover lo mein stash, and smiles up at me when I catch him.

On-screen the girls finally decide to go to dinner in the buff. Hiding behind giant heart cutouts, they drop everything when they make it to the dining room. Even though I've seen this episode a thousand times, I still laugh when the snooty waiter tells them, "Excuse me, ladies, but we always dress for dinner here. And in your case, we'd appreciate it if you'd do that for all three meals." Alex is laughing too, and things feel normal and good, even if I still can't shake all of last night away.

We watch another episode and give directions to a guy who comes in completely lost, trying to get to the Disney parks in Orlando. That happens at least a few times a month. Just to be nice, sometimes people will buy one of the fish magnets we have up front.

When the dude leaves, Alex points to my carton of lo mein and makes a face. "Not Wang's best work, was it?"

I shrug. "Definitely wasn't the broccoli-rabe-sausage day."

"After we close, maybe I can take you out for a real dinner somewhere. No offense to Chuck, but this dump isn't all that romantic."

That greasy pull in my stomach, and the uptick in my chest. Lowering my chin to my shoulder, all I can see is freaking T.J.'s annoying Captain America face. *You're just kind of different from what I thought before I got to know you.*

The sigh escapes before I can stop it.

"So I'm guessing that's a no?" Alex sounds more amused

than disappointed, which just makes me wonder if he even means any of it at all.

Luckily, I don't have to flat-out shut him down.

"I can't." I try to sound breezy. "I have to get my head shrunk."

When I first started therapy ADF, I tried to hide it from Alex, but after the third week in a row when I left early for a doctor's appointment, he got worried I was dying of cancer or something, so I had to tell him. Never even fazed him.

"Right, it's Thursday," Alex says. "Some other time, I guess."

"Yeah," I say, but don't offer up an alternate day/month/year, and he doesn't push. Better this way, in our little aquarium without all that outside stuff.

We watch more TV, and he eats my just-meh noodles until it's time for me to leave.

"Same time, same place tomorrow?" Alex says.

"You're on, A-hat."

It's only a fifteen-minute bike ride to Dr. Brooks's office in a converted old house downtown, but it's so hot that I'm a liquefied version of my former self by the time I arrive. My tank top is soaked through with sweat, and even in the blurry reflection from the big picture window, my face is the exact shade of a ripe tomato. I'm a few minutes late already, but I don't want Dr. B. thinking I'm any more of a whack job than I am, so I duck into the bathroom and change into Alex's band shirt—which actually fits pretty well—splash some water on my face, and run my fingers through the knots in my nuclear-winter hair. I'm not a huge makeup person, but looking at myself in the mirror, I wish that I knew how that stuff worked, like V and her friends. I wish I could put on mascara without stabbing myself in the eye with the wand, or apply blush in a way that didn't look clown-y. Finding a tube of tinted ChapStick in my back-pack, I dot it on.

Dr. B. is waiting for me at his office door, perfectly fresh in a light-blue polo shirt and khakis.

"For a minute there I was worried you were standing me up," he says, and I giggle.

"Never!"

Okay, I admit, I *may* have a teeny tiny crush on Dr. B. The guy has a jawline like a cliff and these little depressions by his temples that give him this seriousness with a dash of vulnerability. Obvi, nothing is *ever* going to happen. Beyond the ethical no-no's that he's my doctor and probably thirtysomething, he's got a lovely strawberry-blond fiancée who works in TV news in Miami. (There's a framed picture of the two of them on his desk.) But, hey, a girl's allowed to look, right?

He ushers me in and closes the door, and I take a seat on the leather couch across from his chair.

I *am* sitting BTW, not lying down the way they do on TV. When I came in for my first session a year ago, I saw the chaise longue and asked if I was supposed to get vertical. "Some patients do," Dr. B. said. "Whatever makes you the most comfortable." As if anything about the situation was going to make me comfortable.

To say therapy wasn't my idea is a colossal understatement. When things started falling apart for me on the end of sophomore year, my mom dismissed it as typical teenage stuff at first. But then ADF the high school guidance counselor called Mom and me into her office and explained that, nope, there was nothing garden-variety about my running out of a swim meet after months of training, or about dropping advanced art, or my GPA tumbling from a 3.7 to a 1.7. Mr. Walton used the D word—"depression"—and that hurled my mom into this completely uncharacteristic panic. Mom is a go-getter, not a panicker. If I hadn't already been totally lost and scared, seeing my put-together, perfect mother clutch her chest and blather hysterically about how she'd had no idea—well, that certainly would have done the trick.

Mom took me to my geriatric pediatrician, Dr. Calvin (who'd been old when he was *her* pediatrician), and he wrote me scripts for a low-dose antidepressant and some anti-anxiety meds, offered me a toy from the chest of plastic trinkets for the little kids, and told us I needed therapy.

Mom got Dr. Brooks's name from one of her regular highlights clients. Apparently Dr. B. had helped the woman's
son, and the kid had gotten his act together enough that
he'd been able to turn things around and had gotten into
Florida A&M. This impressed Mom. My mother may not
have gone to college herself, but it's a very big thing for her
that V and I go. I think it has to do with proving something
to her own mother.

Anyway, the first couple of sessions with Dr. B., I just
sat there, arms and legs crossed (sitting was, it turns out,
slightly less uncomfortable than lying down), and gave
one-word answers to the questions he asked about my
family and school and what might have changed for me.
So much of what was going on was stuff I couldn't even
begin to explain to myself, even if I'd wanted to. Then one
day Dr. B. noticed me tucking my earphones into my backpack, and he asked about what kind of music I listened to.
We started talking about some of the nineties bands that I
knew about from Alex or my mom, and it turned out that
Dr. B. had actually seen a lot of them when he was in high
school and college. For the next session he brought in some
Stone Temple Pilots bootlegs, and we talked about those,
and gradually, talking about other stuff got a little easier.

Now I'm a total convert. The dude is awesome. And
even though he knows all this crazy stuff about me, he
doesn't treat me as if I'm a Fabergé egg. ADF a lot of people

in my life either cut me off or started talking to me in a syrupy voice, as though I would crumble into a billion pieces if they said something to upset me. But Dr. B. acts like I'm an actual human, not something that's going to shatter.

"What's a Flaming Dante?" He points to my shirt.

"Oh." I blush. "It's Alex's band."

"Your friend from work, huh?" he asks, and I nod. "I take it he just read *The Divine Comedy*?"

"Well, his friend did," I mumble. "You'd like the band; they sound kind of nineties."

"You talk about him quite a bit, and now you're wearing his shirt; is he becoming more than a friend?"

I shrug. Even though I couldn't wait to talk to Dr. B. about all of what happened with Alex and T.J., now it just sounds like high school drama.

"Molly." Dr. B. cocks his head. "You know this only works if you tell me what's going on."

"I don't know. I feel bad because I think he wants us to be more than friends, and I've been blowing him off."

"He asked you out, and you said no?"

"Technically."

"And this has happened before?"

"I think. It's hard to tell sometimes."

"So you say, 'Thanks, but no thanks,' and he still keeps asking you out, and then he makes you feel as though you've done something wrong by rejecting him?"

"It's not exactly like that—" But I'm not sure how it is, the whole thing is such a swirl.

"Molly, you don't have to go out with anyone you don't want to. You don't owe any one that," Dr. B. says. "At the very least his behavior sounds extremely immature. The fact that you feel bad about it just shows what a thoughtful person you are, but these are his issues."

I know it's pretty crappy that I threw Alex under the bus like that, but I'm fighting a smile. What Dr. B. just said is a compliment, right? Am I supposed to thank him? Feeling myself turning tomato again, I look down, and suddenly, all that stuff with Alex and T.J. doesn't seem like that big a deal anymore.

So I change the subject. "You know, I think the reason I work at FishTopia in the first place is because of my father."

"How so?" Dr. B. leans in. He always seems really interested in talking about my parents.

"When we lived in Miami, he used to take me to the aquarium all the time and show me the fish. It was very important to him." For the rest of the session, I tell him stories about how my dad used to point things out to me—how he loved to talk about all the bright colors and weird shapes. "He always said he could spend days there."

"Does that make you happy, that you have that connection to him?"

"Definitely. It's great to feel connected like that."

At the end of the session, I hand him my co-pay, and he asks if we can meet on Monday instead of Thursday next week. "It's my fiancée's birthday, and I was hoping to get down to Miami and surprise her."

"That's so sweet; of course."

Like I said, me crushing on Dr. B. = utterly harmless.

I stop in the bathroom again on the way out, and Dr. B. must finish up a few minutes later, because he's on his way into the parking lot when he sees me unlocking Old Montee.

"You rode your bike here?" He points at Old Montee. "In this heat?"

Shrugging, I tell him, "I'm a driver's ed dropout."

He chuckles and asks if he can give me a ride home. "If you died of heat stroke, it would probably reflect poorly on my skills as a healer."

We put my bike into the trunk of his Honda Accord and slide into our seats. It's a little weird, and I'm kind of jumpy, being alone with him in such a small space, but when he starts the engine, of course the nineties radio station starts blaring, which makes me laugh.

And we talk about how he used to listen to all these songs on CDs and (gasp!) cassette tapes.

"Those rectangles with the two holes in the middle?" I joke. "I think I saw one in a museum once."

"I'm telling you, Molly, you're missing out." Dr. B. shakes

his head. "Making a mix tape for the girl you had a crush on was like a rite of passage in junior high."

"Did you make one for your fiancée?"

"I *might* have burned her a CD when we first met."

We're having such a good time, I almost forget to tell him when to turn onto my street of new houses, and into the circular driveway of the biggest one. It was the model home for the subdivision—the one builders show to potential home buyers, to demonstrate how great their house could be—and it has all these crazy upgrades, like a huge door and a three-car garage.

"Now, that's a house," Dr. B. says, which is funny, since he's the doctor and Mom is a single mother who cuts hair.

"Thanks," I say, even though I had absolutely nothing to do with it.

After my dad died, Mom moved V and me back to Coral Cove so my grandma could help out (weird, considering most of what Mom and Gram do is bicker). We stayed with her for a while, and then got a little house on the same street as Gram's while Mom worked at someone else's salon. Eventually Mom started her own place—Dye Another Day (yeah, I know). Despite the cornball name, it really took off, and she moved to a larger, shinier location, hired more stylists, and added spa stuff like mani-pedis and massages. She even started a product line. Then she read something about needing your home to outwardly "reflect your inner success" or whatever. So she bought *this* five-bedroom monstrosity a few years ago.

I thank Dr. B. for the ride, and he helps me lug my bike out of the car.

"Good work today, Molly," he says, and I smile, even though I realize that I didn't even mention all the stuff with T.J. "I'll see you next week."

"It's a date," I say, and then feel weird because I used the word "date."

Giving me a wave, he drives off, and I head in through the garage.

Even after two years the house still feels strange. Since it was the model, the developers had it staged with custom furniture and decorations, a lot of it specific to the house. Most of the furniture in our old place was the type of semi-disposable stuff from Ikea that you assemble with that L-shaped wrench, so Mom got the developers to throw in all the furniture with the house.

Now it's like we're living on a movie set or in a glossy add in a lifestyle magazine. Everything is beautiful and well coordinated, but clearly designed for people not us. Curved couches with mounds of throw pillows, sleek tables with brightly colored vases or bowls as "accent pieces," neutral artwork that we don't have any stories for. One of the extra bedrooms is set up as a sewing room, with a fancy Singer machine built into a table. (None of us would even know how to thread it.) Another bedroom is a really whimsical playroom for little kids, with murals from classic children's books painted on the walls. There are giant stuffed animals and a cute wood dollhouse. Great stuff for some model other family.

The second I park my bike next to Mom's Audi and come in through the laundry room, I'm bombarded with the overwhelming smell of confectionary sugar, and I have to fight back the need to hurl. Apparently my mom is baking again . . . for the thirteenth day in a row.

Our model-home kitchen appears to have been the loser in a confrontation with Chef Godzilla: cracked eggshells in the farm-style sink, a dusting of flour on the granite counters and hardwood floor; something that might be butter congealing against the subway-tile backsplash between the cabinets (a pricey upgrade). All of it tastefully illuminated by the recessed lighting in the ceiling (another upgrade).

"Oh, sweetie, you're just in time!" Mom hands me a giant slice of some golden-yellow cake that looks paradoxically burned and undercooked.

"Hey, Mom. This is . . . interesting."

As much of a mess as her surroundings are, my mom is in the middle looking absolutely beautiful, because she's always absolutely beautiful. Perfect shiny hair like V's that somehow isn't curling up in the humidity, perfect barely there makeup, perfect boobs—even the smudge of sugar on her high cheekbone is perfect. She looks like someone in a commercial who is supposed to sell you cake—not necessarily the defeated-looking cake she's holding up, but some Hollywood version of it. If we didn't have the same blue-green eyes and full lips, I would seriously question whether or not I was adopted.

Forcing a smile, I ask, "So what's on the menu today?"

Up until thirteen days ago, the extent of my mom's "cooking" was picking up sandwiches from Chubby Joe's Sub Shop or sliding a frozen pizza into the oven. But she's a big fan of self-help books and empowerment message boards. She has learned all seven steps of those highly effective people, she knows all about the different planets men and women are from, and she's mastered the life-changing magic of tidying up—well, maybe she could use some help with that one right now.

About two weeks ago, the wormhole that is the Internet led her to a website about spreading happiness with desserts. This lady in the English countryside blogged about baking a different cake every day for one hundred days and how much joy that brought people. Naturally, she got a book deal—*How to Bake Friends and Ice People.* (Okay, I made that up.) I suspect that the blogger was probably taking the cakes to nursing homes or hospital waiting rooms and not trying to fix a teenage daughter with depression, but Mom really latched on to this idea and decided to "put her mind to it" and recreate *A Baker's Journey: 100 Days of Cake* (the real title). My mom is kind of like a one-woman cult.

Today's cake is Ooey-Gooey Butter Cake. It does not smell good, and I wonder if the blogger used another English expression that didn't translate quite right for an American baker. (This led to an indelibly salty Caramel Sass Cake last week.)

"Now, I know you thought the double chocolate was too rich, and the pineapple upside-down thing was too sweet, but I think that we might have a winner here." Mom is talking in that singsongy voice she started using when my guidance counselor first uttered the *D* word. "It's supposed to have some savory notes to it. I went ahead and tasted it, and I thought it was really different."

"Sounds great," I say, and make a show of taking a bite.

She just looks at me, eyes wide.

And waits.

You know those moments when you realize you're going to spectacularly disappoint someone who's trying really hard? Welcome to my life.

It tastes like a heart attack on a fork—undercooked butter with a side of more butter, and burned butter on top for kicks. I try to move my mouth into something happy or at the very least not disgusted, but I'm a crappy actor, and Mom's whole face sags in defeat.

"No good?" she asks.

"It's great." We both know that is a huge lie. I mean, she did taste it, after all.

"Should we even bother saving it for Elle and Jimmy?" she asks.

"Yeah, I'm sure they'll love it."

"Well, I'm really excited about carrot cake tomorrow. Maybe a little bit of spice is what we need." She is sort of talking to herself as she spins around to start cleaning.

Sure, there is a part of me that wants to scream, "Explain it to me again how I am the crazy one in therapy?" But I don't, because she's my mom and she's only trying to help. And honestly, there's a part of me that wants so, so much—maybe more than she does—for her to be right about this. All those self-help books and empowering websites worked for her—they helped her get serious about the hair salon and find a dweeby boyfriend with a good job, and live in a house that outwardly reflects her inner success—so maybe this could work for me too? Maybe there *is* some combination of sugar, eggs, and flour that can make me care about school dances and four-hundred-meter relay times and college applications. If there is, I will gladly eat piece after piece every day for the rest of my short type-2-diabetic life.

DAY 14

—◆◆◆—

Good Morning Carrot Cake

E lle wants ice cream, but it can't be just any old Mister
Softee truck; don't be ridiculous. No, it has to be locally
sourced ice cream with no GMOs. She'd prefer vegan, but
that's not a deal breaker. (Also, we don't have that in Coral
Cove.)

For as long as I've known Elle, which has pretty much
been forever, she's always been into various causes. I'm really
hoping this environmental crusade ends soon, so she'll use
her car when it's another million-degree day like today.

We bike past the original downtown with its Baskin-
Robbins ("An eco nightmare!"), and then by a Dairy Queen
("Warren Buffett doesn't need any more of our money!")
to this crunchy little food stand in the park, where all
the employees always reek of pot and nothing ever looks
remotely clean. It's hot enough that none of this matters.

There's a line wrapped halfway around the baseball diamond. Elle and I lock our bikes and get into the end of the queue.

"Okay." Elle looks sort of pained, but it might just be the heat. "I don't want to upset you, but I saw Gina from English at the library yesterday."

"That doesn't upset me."

"Obviously I wasn't finished." Elle threads a still-perfect curl behind her ear. "Anyway, they stayed at Chris's party a little longer than we did, and she said that Meredith Hoffman was all over this guy from Maxwell. It had to be your Alex."

Meredith Hoffman? She isn't artsy or into music or anything other than the latest issue of *Us Weekly*. What would Alex possibly do with her?

"He's not 'my Alex.'" I try to sound nonchalant. "And Meredith's okay."

"Dude, Meredith's life ambition is to become a Hooters girl."

"At least she has an ambition. I can't even bring myself to shower most days," I say. Elle doesn't laugh.

"Stop beating yourself up like tha—" Elle stops midsentence.

A few feet from the line a little girl—maybe eight or nine—is licking a cone of free-trade chocolate ice cream, and drops a clump of dirty napkins on the ground. The man with her, who hasn't stopped yakking away on a cell phone the whole time we've been here, looks directly at them and walks away. The girl bounces after him.

Uh-oh.

Before I can stop her, Elle scoops up the offensive napkins and pounces on the girl and her dad.

"Excuse me, sir," she says, thrusting the paper into his face, "but I noticed you left these."

Cell Phone Dad doesn't respond. His daughter, utterly confused, reaches out to take the napkins from Elle, but her father swats the girl's hands down. The girl looks to him, even more baffled than before. I can almost hear Elle boiling over internally.

"I guess it's safe to assume that you meant to drop these and just leave them there," Elle continues, with this growing mania in her wide-set eyes. "So while you and your daughter are out enjoying this lovely day, you're carelessly poisoning the earth so her children and their children won't ever have that opportunity and will have to live in a dome."

Cell Phone Dad gives Elle a dismissive once-over and then turns away. "Just some bat-shit hippie," he mumbles into his phone.

"Yeah, a hippie who is trying to keep the world beautiful for your grandchildren!" Elle fires back.

By this point everyone in line or at the picnic tables is

staring at us; even the stoned employees have snapped into focus and are sizing up the situation.

I'd like to hop onto Old Montee and ride away before someone calls the 5-O on Elle for disturbing the peace, but we've been best friends since the third day of kindergarten, when she shared her crayons with me after Jeffrey Meyers murderously broke mine in half. She's a good person like that.

"Let's just go." I grab her arm and pull her away. "We have to save room for Mom's latest misadventure in baking."

"Yeah, the ice cream's not certified organic, anyway."

Unlocking our bikes, we make the most graceful exit we can under the circumstances.

We're riding up to the model home, when my sister bops out the giant front door in this flowy sarong-type skirt and a string bikini top. She looks like a Victoria's Secret model, which would be cool . . . if she were a Victoria's Secret model and not my fifteen-year-old sister.

"Are you the bait for *To Catch a Predator*?" Elle asks by way of a greeting.

V offers the withering glance to end all withering glances. "Actually, I'm going to a pool party at Chris Partridge's—you know, the president of *your* class," V says. "If you weren't so busy harassing people to save the dolphins, maybe he would have invited you again."

For a moment Elle looks upset; I wonder if Alex will be there with Meredith Hoffman.

"Well, don't wait until you're twenty-five to get your first PAP smear. Remember, HPV kills," Elle snaps. I'm not sure if she means this as an insult or as legitimate advice.

"What-ever!" V says as a Mini Cooper full of the Jaclyn's Attic girls pulls into our driveway.

And then V turns to me, as if she just remembered that I'm there, that I'm her actual sister and the one who should probably be giving her a hard time about her kiddie-porn ensemble. Her tone is kind of sad and serious. "You don't want to go, do you, Mol? Chris said it's totally cool to bring whoever."

Unadulterated relief floods her face when I shake my head, and she climbs into the backseat.

Watching the car disappear around the corner, I feel that pull of sadness. Veronica used to follow Elle and me around everywhere and do everything I did; she was practically my minion. Now she's the one inviting me places. The irony is not lost.

Inside, the house smells sweet again.

Sure enough, Mom has every piece of kitchen equipment on the center island and is holding a plate with a giant piece of unnaturally orange cake with cream cheese icing.

"Hi, Mrs. Byrne," Elle says, and takes the plate right out of my mom's hands.

Mom's *Baker's Journey* challenge might just be the best thing that's ever happened to Elle. Since I'm too bummed and Veronica is too weight-conscious to make any real headway on each baked blunder, Mom just boxes up the leftovers for Elle and her brother. With all the butter and eggs, nothing about the cakes is remotely vegan. And none of the ingredients are locally sourced or organic or anything good for the planet, but when I pointed this out to Elle, she said that she's a "consumption environmentalist" and that it isn't hurting the world to eat the cakes, because the damage was already done. You gotta give her points for creativity.

Between forkfuls, she gushes to my mom, "Ohmygod, this is your best work to date."

"Glad you like it, hon." Mom smiles. "What about you, Molly? You like this one?"

I tell her it's really nice, even though it's cloyingly sugary and I can't force myself to take more than a few bites. Mom sighs and says she's got "high hopes" for tomorrow's cake.

"Hot date tonight, Mrs. Byrne?" Elle asks, and I notice that Mom is wearing a flowing yellow maxi dress and has her hair tied in a knot on her head.

"You seeing Thom?" I ask. About two years ago Mom started dating this divorced divorce attorney with an office in the same building as her salon. He's actually one of FishTopia's few regular clients, so, you know, not the world's hippest guy. But other than his horrible blond hairpiece (we're talking so bad that it's probably not good for business for Mom to be seen with him in public), he's pretty nice, and he is always taking V and me on these cheesy activities—bowling, an aviation show—to try to get to know us better.

Mom says that she's just meeting one of her clients-turned-girlfriends for a quick coffee. Her eyes flutter to the right, and I get the sense that she wants to say something else, but doesn't.

"I shouldn't be gone more than an hour or so," she says, pauses, then adds, "unless you girls want me to stay." Because clearly ADF me can't be trusted to be alone.

"Mom, we're fine."

When Mom leaves, Elle suggests we move into "the sa-lon," stretching out the word so it sounds ridiculous. It's not really a salon but a bonus room (another upgrade) that the model-home stager had set up like an old-timey parlor, with heavy velvet curtains and French-empire-inspired furniture. It always looks as though some lesser royal might be dropping by for tea. At the old house, we spent most of our time on this splintery wooden swing in the backyard. The salon chairs are way more comfortable, but it's still kind of weird.

My house has always been kind of a second home to Elle and her little brother. Until they got divorced, her parents were constantly screaming at each other. Now they're still constantly screaming at each other from across state lines. While not having a dad sucks, it's probably still better than having Mr. Lovell. And even when she's not ranting at or about her ex-husband, Elle's mom is hardly ever around in any real way either. Because our old house was kind of Elle's place too, she might be even more weirded out by the model home than V and I are.

"So seriously, what was up with V's hoochie mama getup?" Elle asks. "Was she going cock shopping?"

Elle has never kissed *anyone*, and that bothers her a whole lot more than she lets on.

"It *was* kind of like a nip slip waiting to happen."

"Not to be a sexist troll—obviously a woman has the right to wear whatever she wants." Elle remembers she is an outspoken opponent of rape culture.

I shrug and wonder if maybe V was going "cock shopping." Wonder if she's sleeping with any of the guys at the party. As the big sis, I always figured I'd lose my virginity first (in my head it was always with some Zac Efron/ Channing Tatum hybrid in a hotel in Venice or one of those other romantic places from the movies), and then I used to imagine telling V about it when we were cuddled under the blankets on Mom's bed, watching old sitcom reruns like we used to do in the old house.

Before T.J. decided I wasn't who he thought I'd be and broke up with me, we got to about second base. (At least I think it was second base; everyone I talk to uses a different scale. Like, some people think that first base is kissing, but someone else says that's more like the on-deck circle. And no one seems to know if third base is a handy j or a blow job.) There was over-the-bra groping, but no crucial pieces of clothing were removed. By the time we'd started doing that, I didn't really feel like talking to anyone anymore. I didn't tell V or even Elle. If V *is* sleeping with someone, she probably wouldn't tell me either.

"It's obviously her prerogative"—Elle is still talking—"but it was like your sister was ready for a *Girls Gone Wild* audition."

"I thought she looked kind of pretty," I say, which is the truth.

"If that's your thing." She looks serious. "Do you think Chris really didn't invite us back because of what I said about natural pool cleaners?"

"Naw, he probably just figured V or Alex would let us know."

She nods, but we both know it's not true.

"Are you worried Alex might be there with Meredith Hoffman?" she asks.

I remember Dr. B. saying the whole dating debacle was Alex's issue, not mine, and I brighten a little. "I don't know. Dr. Brooks thinks Alex sounds kind of immature anyway," I say.

"Oh, he does, does he?"

"Yeah, and he gave me a ride home yesterday. Isn't that sweet?"

Elle practically chokes on her cake.

"Mol, that is so not appropriate." She says this in the same voice she used to chew out Cell Phone Dad at the ice cream stand—as if this is something that everyone should know and it's an insult to the planet that I don't.

"It was hot out, and he was being nice." All at once I'm angry with Elle. She was one of the people hounding me about "getting help" when everything started to fall apart, and now she's inexplicably annoyed that my shrink is a nice guy. "What's the big deal?"

"It crosses a line."

"What line? The common courtesy line?"

"It's just not kosher."

"How do you know? Because you always know how everything is 'supposed' to be?"

"Well I know you're not supposed to cruise around town with your shrink."

"V is right; it's no wonder you never get invited to parties."

I regret it the minute I say it. Elle's whole face collapses, and she looks like she used to in gym class when no one would pick her for their softball team because she was really skinny and small and had the hand-eye coordination of a drunk penguin with an old-fashioned medicine ball.

My heart breaks, and I realize how much of a jerk I am.

Without saying another word, she gets up, walks back to the kitchen, puts her plate and fork in the sink, and reaches for her hemp-weave eco-friendly bag.

I grab her arm. "Look, I didn't mean that."

"That was a really shitty thing to say."

"I know. It's just . . . I really like Dr. Brooks, and I'm doing a lot better than I was, right?"

Elle shrugs. "I guess."

"And maybe he doesn't do everything like some Dr. McHottie you saw on *Grey's Anatomy*, but he's honestly kind of great. So can we maybe lay off him for a bit?"

She pauses and then sighs. "Sure," she says.

But it still feels weird. And even though it's not even nine o'clock yet, I want to go upstairs to my model-home bedroom (with its upgraded window seat and stylish blinds) and fall into bed.

DAY 17

⚭

Red Velvet Cake

The high school swim team practices in the mornings before classes, which means getting up at five thirty a.m.—a bushel of laughs, I know. But freshman year, Coach Hartley and I were really obsessed with getting my split times down, so I didn't even mind. Just to make sure I never slept late, I had Mom get me one of those old-school alarm clocks with the two bells on top. Back then I was so pumped to please Coach that I'd usually spring out of bed a few minutes before it went off anyway.

It's crazy that that was only three years ago. In the time before the model home, V and I would sometimes get into bed with Mom and have these marathon sessions watching sitcom reruns like *Who's the Boss?* and *Family Ties*. One of our shows was *Roseanne*, and we all did this double take one season when they recast the oldest daughter. The new girl was blond like the first one, and they were about the same age, but other than that, the second Becky was nothing like the original. I'm pretty much the second Becky of my old life—an entirely different person.

Last night I set the alarm clock for ten fifteen so I could make it to my appointment with Dr. Brooks at eleven. It's been going off for about ten minutes, and even though I've been lying awake in bed for hours, I can't bring myself to reach across the nightstand and turn it off. So I let it gong and gong, the little bells on top going crazy.

Maybe it was the fight with Elle or the whole thing with Alex or the trauma of seeing T.J. again, but it's one of those days when the world feels like this expansive ocean and I'll drown if I get off the life raft of my bed. The kind of day where I weigh ten thousand pounds and lifting my head would require one of those cranes at construction sites.

Outside my room, Veronica is screaming at me, probably about the alarm clock; I bury my head under the covers.

The door bursts open with so much force that the knob (a brass upgrade) smashes against the wall, and V charges in, all shiny hair, platform sandals, and righteous anger.

"Seriously, you couldn't just reach over and turn this off?" she says as she smacks the alarm clock's off button. "Pathetic."

Then she's gone, the door rattling the frame when she slams it shut.

Of course she's right; I am pathetic. But it's not like I want to be this way—the heaviest 120-pound girl in the entire state of Florida.

A minute or an hour passes, and my phone rings. It's in the pocket of the shorts I wore yesterday, which are slung over the back of my desk chair, which is miles and miles and miles away from the safety of the bed.

Probably Dr. B. calling to ask where the hell I am.

Gut punch of guilt. Mom will probably have to pay for the session, and even though Dye Another Day is going, like, gangbusters, we're not one-percenters or anything. Plus, Dr. B. had promised to bring in some of his favorite old mix tapes for our session. Feeling *that* much worse for disappointing all these people yet *again*, I roll over.

Time is kind of gooey on the life raft of my sleigh bed, and I sleep on and off. Our old house had those popcorn ceilings, and sometimes V and I would stack chairs on our beds and pinch off the little plaster balls between our fingernails. But in the model home, the ceilings are smooth and free of cracks. Just blank nothingness. I wonder what it would feel like to blend with the ceiling, become one with that.

Elle—except she looks like Miley Cyrus—and her kid brother are chomping up a line of cakes like Pac-Man. Alex and T.J.

are doing "I'm Not the Father" dances, and Mom and V are performing a mother-daughter tap number with feather boas. I'm just standing there.

Not participating.

Because even in my dreams I'm pathetic.

When I wake up, I'm sort of hungry. Mom and V are both at work, so I head to the model kitchen to see if we have any non-cake food. The best I can find is a couple of string cheeses and half a tuna wrap Mom must have had for lunch a few days ago. It has that too-cold-fridge taste.

The formal dining room isn't on the way back to the stairs and my bedroom, but I go there anyway, and have a seat on one of the plush chairs.

One of the few things we did bring from the old house is this framed ten-by-twelve family photograph of all of us that hangs over the sideboard. In the picture I'm in an OshKosh jumper holding this little doll that the photographer gave me; baby V is just blue-green eyes (like Mom's and Gram's and mine) peeking out from a swaddle of embroidered blankets; Mom, not even thirty, and so achingly beautiful; and Dad with his high-sloped forehead, wavy mouse-poop hair like me, and these giant hands as big as catcher's mitts. He's got one on Mom's forearm, the other protectively on my shoulder—so large that his fingers reach all the way down to my elbow.

I was three (well, almost three—the accident happened the day before my birthday) when he died, and there isn't much I really remember besides those hands and his voice, which was this incredibly deep cannon, like a DJ's on a classic rock station. A voice that made everything, even Dr. Seuss books, sound important.

As much as I love my mom and her misguided attempts to cure me with baked goods, I wonder—a lot, actually—how things might have been different if Dad hadn't gone out that day. If he could have offered a different perspective to balance things out. Wonder if he could have shared stories about his own childhood and filled in all those blanks. Wonder if maybe, just maybe, his hands would have been big enough that they could still hold me up even now.

I'm back in the sleigh bed when Mom knocks on my door around six. She asks if I'm okay and if she can come in.

"I kind of just want to be alone," I say.

"Are you sure?" She's got the nervous syrupy voice again. "I was thinking maybe you could help with today's cake."

I tell her I'm pretty tired, which is somehow true, despite the fact that I've been sleeping for hours and hours.

"Okay. I think that you're really going to like it; it's red velvet."

"Mom, maybe we can skip it today—"

"Nonsense." She makes it sound like I'm suggesting that she not show up for my wedding day.

An hour or two passes, and then there's another knock on my door, Mom announcing that she's finished baking. I don't say anything.

"Okay, sweetie?" she asks. "You awake?"

I say nothing and hope that's enough of an answer. "Maybe I can just slide it under the door," she says. Then she's trying to shove a three-inch-high plate of cake through the inch and a half of space between the bottom of the door and the floor.

"Oh, shoot," she says. On my side of the door there is now a plate with red crumbs and a smear of cream cheese frosting. I can only imagine what kind of mess happened on her end.

It's actually really funny, like something that Rose might try on the *Golden Girls*. I should get up, open the door, hug my mom, and tell her that I love her. I *want* to.

But I don't do that.

And I hate myself for it.

DAY 18

Buttermilk Cake

It's still a million degrees outside, but from the way Alex and Elle are yapping on and on about the ACT versus the SAT, you'd think that it was fall and we were all back in school already. (To be fair, it will probably still be a million degrees then; central Florida is really freaking hot.)

We're sitting on the steps of Elle's front porch, while her eight-year-old brother repeatedly rams his bike into the mailbox post as if he's stuck on a difficult level of a really lame video game. When the force is enough that Jimmy actually falls off the bike, Alex turns nervously to Elle.

"Um, should we maybe do something?"

"My mom's free-range when it comes to parenting," Elle explains. "She believes that we should let him discover things on his own."

I'm pretty sure that Mrs. Lovell hasn't put that much

thought into it and just doesn't care, but I would never say that. Elle can get sensitive about stuff with her mom.

"That's cool, I guess." Alex doesn't look convinced.

The three of us have never hung out like this before, but when Alex and I were closing up FishTopia for the night, he asked where I was headed. When I told him Elle's, he kind of invited himself along. Under normal circumstances I would have protested hanging out outside the aquarium of FishTopia, but it was literally 104 this afternoon, and his Ford Fiesta is air-conditioned. And I still feel bad about blowing him off the other day, no matter what Dr. B. says. Also, with Elle there I figured it wouldn't be a date-date so things couldn't get too weird.

Of course Elle was all excited when Alex and I showed up together, and the minute Alex went to the bathroom, she asked if we were together. She looked genuinely bummed when I told her no.

But now the two of them are talking and talking and talking about school and college applications. They're so animated and alive, they don't notice that I haven't said anything in forever.

Alex is going on about how he really wants to go to a music conservatory program, but his father is this macho guy who would never be okay with that. "I'm trying to see what places have okay music schools so I can double major," he says. "I might be able to slip that one past my dad if I got an econ degree or something, but everything is just so expensive."

Elle is nodding. "I hear you. Like, Columbia has a great environmental studies program, but unless I win the lottery, there's no way. So I'm probably going to FSU like everyone else . . ."

I'm really glad they are getting along so well, but it's like I'm watching them from above, like they're on a TV show, playing the roles of optimistic teens excited about the next phase of their lives. Everything they're saying is from some script that no one bothered to send me.

This past spring I gave up Facebook cold turkey because of all my senior "friends" posts. *I'm a USF Bull! Just signed up to be all that I can—go army! Don't hate, but I got into Georgia! Karla said yes!!!* Like everyone had to decide everything about the rest of their lives by June 5.

"Have you looked into student loans?" Alex is asking Elle in their TV-show conversation going on beneath me. "It might be worth it if that's really your first choice."

"My dad might make too much money—"

A crash. Metal on concrete.

Jimmy has knocked over the big silver garbage cans on the curb and has somehow managed to get his head and upper body stuck in one of the bins. From the opening, his summer-scabbed legs jut out.

"Ugh." Elle sighs. "This is the second time he's done that this week."

She heads over to unstick Jimmy, and Alex turns to me, laughing.

"This just a normal day for that kid?" he asks.

"Yeah, he is pretty much a rabid possum," I say, and Alex laughs harder, and then I start laughing. The floating/ watching sensation is gone; I'm a part of this world again.

Until Alex asks, "What about you, Mol? What are your big college plans?" *Crap.*

"I'm just waiting to see how the year goes," I say, which isn't a total lie. I'm definitely waiting for something. To change the subject, I tell him about JoJo going totally ballistic a few days ago when a woman on *Maury* broke up with her man because she found a tooth in the house that he couldn't explain.

"The best part? JoJo actually said the same thing happened to her! Like how is this a thing that actually occurs in real life."

Alex starts cracking up. "This is why I only cheat on my girlfriends with toothless women; significantly cuts down on the chance of getting caught."

"All I know is, I've worked with JoJo three days, and I'm already having nightmares about *Maury*. You were even in one."

"You're dreaming about me now?" Alex moves his eyebrows up and down suggestively. "Exactly what kind of dreams are we talking about?"

Feeling heat on my cheeks, I swat his shoulder. "It wasn't *that* kind of dream."

"Are you telling him about your dream where I was eating

all your mom's cakes?" Elle asks, back from a successful Jimmy extraction.

"I was entertaining both of you ladies in Molly's dream?" Alex puts an arm around each of our shoulders. "Nice!"

"It WAS NOT that kind of dream!" I say, but I'm laughing now too. "Freaking Jimmy was in it!"

Alex pulls back his arms and crinkles his nose in faux disgust. "Now, that's just sick."

The two of them tease me about my stupid dream for a solid five minutes.

"Can we please talk about anything else?" I ask. "Alex, how's the band?"

Clearly this was the right question. He bursts into the kind of radiant smile usually reserved for toothpaste commercials. "I've got a whole newsletter for you. First off, we've changed our name. We're now Headless Naked Ken."

"I love it!" shrieks Elle. "It's a complete dig on our plastic culture and unrealistic standards of female beauty."

"Eh, something like that." Alex tilts his head; clearly none of that had anything to do with the name change. "The other day we were playing in our drummer's garage and found some of his sister's old dolls without their heads. We thought it sounded pretty badass."

Elle looks tremendously disappointed.

"But even bigger, we have a gig on Thursday night!"

He explains how the manager at McCloud's Music and

Coffee called this morning to see if the Flaming Dantes (the manager wasn't aware of the name change) would be able to fill in, because both the drummer and the bassist for Sinking Canoe (some local band I've never heard of) have mono and had to pull out of the show. "I mean, I know it's not the Viper Room, but it's kind of a big deal for us."

"What? That's awesome," I say.

"We are so there!" Elle gushes.

"Seriously?" Alex says, but he's looking at me, not Elle.

The thought of McCloud's and people like Chris and the Hot Topic girls and maybe Meredith Hoffman makes me itchy. But Alex is looking at me with these big wounded-puppy eyes, and I don't want to hurt his feelings one more time. And who knows, maybe Thursday will be a good day? Maybe all the therapy will work, or maybe Mom's cake tonight will be the magic bullet and I'll wake up and be back to the old me?

"Sure," I say. I remember Dr. Brooks telling me that I shouldn't waste my time feeling bad about Alex and his issues, but I still feel really crappy about it.

That nervous tic starts, where I twist my fingers all together.

Alex puts a hand on top my finger ball, and I feel this little pulse of electricity, like something from physics class. I look up at his face.

"Promise?" he asks.

"Yeah. I promise."

DAY 20

Tunnel of Fudge Cake

I do actually intend to go to Alex's gig.

I'm not on the schedule at FishTopia today, so I spend pretty much the entire day in the model-home family room bonelessly slumped on the couch, watching reruns. *Roseanne* episodes with both Beckys; *Three's Company* with all three of the hot blond roommates (they were never recasts like Becky, but different characters written in when one actor would leave because of a contract dispute); and finally the *Golden Girls* block starts. They air this one weirdly sad episode where Dorothy's brother—who happens to be a cross-dresser—dies, and Sophia has a hard time grieving for her son because he wasn't what she thought a son should be.

The antidepressant commercial with the attractive family and their dog comes on again. *Ask your doctor about...*

Maybe I should.

Maybe I will . . . if I'm motivated enough to go to my next appointment.

An hour before Elle is supposed to pick me up for the show, I go upstairs and shower under the big brass rain showerhead (another upgrade). Everything is going okay-ish until I pull open the double doors of my bedroom closet (yep, an upgrade) and realize I have absolutely nothing to wear.

There are a few dressy-ish sleeveless tops and a couple of long flowy skirts, which I guess would be okay, because Elle is driving, so I don't have to worry about anything getting caught in Old Montee's spokes, but when I take them down, they look all wrong, too froufrou, like I'm trying too hard. Maybe my uniform of shorts and a tank top would be okay since it's just a coffee shop? But my favorite cutoffs have crossed that line from worn to just dirty. And what if those Hot Topic girls are there all cool and judgey. Or Meredith Hoffman?

Stupid tears sting my sinuses. A part of me knows I'm being ridiculous, but it's like this loop in my head that I can't stop. How can I not own anything appropriate?

The panic ratchets up to the point where it's hard to breathe.

Still wrapped in a towel, water droplets skiing down my hair onto my shoulders, I sink down to the floor of the closet. Hanging clothes tickle the bare skin of my back.

The ring of my cell phone in yesterday's shorts pocket startles me. Checking the screen, I see it's Elle.

Man, she is going to be pissed.

"I can't go," I say when I finally answer.

"What do you mean?"

"I don't feel well." This isn't really a lie. My head hurts, and my digestive system seems to be digesting itself. Plus, I still can't breathe that great.

"Are you kidding?"

"No."

"Come on, Molly. Alex will be crushed," she says, and I can hear just how disappointed she is too. "We promised— *you* promised—him we'd be there."

"You can still go; you should go."

"Alone?" she scoffs. "Besides, he's *your* friend. You're the one he's totally in love with."

Tears of frustration. That grapefruit bunched in my throat. I channel Dr. B.

"That's his issue, not mine," I croak. "Can we just drop it?"

After a second she sighs. "Fine."

"Will you just tell Alex I'm sick or something?"

"Sure." Her tone is softer.

An hour later, when I'm still in the towel in the closet, Elle comes in.

"You didn't go to the show?" I sit up and make sure I'm mostly covered, even though Elle has seen me naked a million times in the locker room after swim practice.

"I guess it's not really our summer to party." She shrugs. "Your mom said we should come down and try the cake."

I put on the dirty cutoffs and tank top, splash cold water on my face so I look less puffy, and we do.

The cake part is very rich and weirdly sticky, but the fudge in the middle is pretty solid. Elle eats a good half of the cake herself, and Mom is practically glowing because I don't hate it—even if I can't seem to get it off my fingers.

"Crazy good!" Elle is saying, reaching for another piece from the kitchen island.

"I'm glad you like it." Mom smiles. "Maybe it would be better in winter when you want something warm."

"Yeah." Elle shrugs. "Right now I kinda want to chop off all my hair."

She points to this cool braid that my mom has snaking around her head. "I wish I could do something like that."

"We can definitely do that." Mom touches Elle's curls. "That would be really pretty, I think."

With fingers as quick as sewing machine needles (I'm guessing), Mom twists up Elle's hair. She doesn't even need rubber bands or spray or anything to keep it in place; she's that good. She leaves a few spiral tendrils out around Elle's face, which looks sweet and feminine. Elle practically squeals when she sees it in the mirror.

"Can I do yours too?" Mom asks me.

She used to do this for V and me all the time—try out new conditioning rinses or give us fun cuts from pictures we picked out of the magazines in her reception area, but it's been forever. If it helps with the heat, I'm willing to try. So I shrug, and she goes to work on my head.

As Mom finishes, Elle sucks in her breath. "Wow, Molly, you look amazing."

I blush, and when I go into the powder room to check it out in the mirror, I can see that it *is* nice. But it makes me look really different. Without the mouse-poop frizz all crazy, you can see a little more resemblance between me and Mom and V.

Gingerly dotting the braid with my fingertips, I wonder if this is who I am.

DAY 21

—∞—

Angel Food Cake
with Cherry Sauce Topping

Alex looks kind of like Joseph Gordon-Levitt. But he so doesn't have JGL's acting ability. It's sparklingly clear that he's really hurt that I didn't make it to his show, but instead of just saying something about it like a normal person, he's doing a comically bad job of trying to act as though nothing is wrong.

"Byrne in da house," he calls out when I pull open the FishTopia door, even though no one has ever called me by my last name and he never uses hip-hop-y phrases. Then he immediately starts sweeping the floors, like it's some ultra-important time-sensitive task—like anyone ever comes in or Charlie cares. He barely even looks at me.

Car keys and purse in hand, JoJo appears at the front door. "Ohhhh, love your hair, CCH!" she says, and I briefly feel Alex's eyes flicker to the braid Mom did last night.

"Thanks."

"Okay, kids. I'm off to meet my man," she says on her way out, the little bell on the door dinging after her.

"Wonder if that's the guy with the tooth collection?" I joke, but Alex doesn't hear or, more likely, pretends not to hear.

The whole bike ride over, I thought about how to apologize, but really I've just got to grow some lady balls and do it. Rip off the Band-Aid.

Following him into the aisle of coral beauties and butterfly fish where he's cleaning, I start to explain, "I wanted to tell you how so—"

Before I can get any further, he's over by the side windows, running his finger along the dusty sill.

"Ew, these are gnarly." Holding up his pointer, he shows me the dark film of greasy schmutz. "I should definitely tackle this today."

He starts toward the back room, and I follow, hoping he'll slow down enough for me to get a word in edgewise. But then he's got his head buried in the storage cabinets, and he's humming to himself as he looks for cleaners that no one has used since the place opened.

I kind of want to leave him to it, but, you know, lady balls, ripped Band-Aids.

"Can you slow down for a sec?" I reach for his arm. There's that shock of my skin on his that I felt when he touched my hand on Elle's porch.

For the first time since I came in, he actually looks at me, and before I say anything, his face goes back to normal.

"About last night." I'm still holding on to his arm, so I let go. "It's not that I didn't want to come; it's just . . ."

So many ways I could complete this sentence. I went through tons on the bike ride over: ". . . just that I'm pathetic and would have ruined the show for everyone else anyway." Or ". . . just some days the thought of leaving the house feels pretty much on par with scaling Mount Everest in flippers." ". . . just that hearing one more conversation about the future makes me want to rip off my arm and jump on it."

"Just that you were having a kind of cruddy day?" Alex mercifully finishes for me. Shaking his head, he adds, "I'm sorry for making things weird lately."

"It's fine," I say. "I did totally want to go, and I *am* sorry."

Alex smiles (which makes him look even more like Joseph Gordon-Levitt). "You'll come to the next one. If you really want to make it up to me, you can pick up the Wang's today."

"You're on."

I'm about to ask him if he wants the house special lo mein, when I notice a new tank by the stacks of extra fake coral. It's not filled with water but with rocks, and inside are two dozen hermit crabs. With their spiny pink legs and big black eyes on stalks, they are the cutest things that have ever happened in the history of FishTopia.

"Ohmygod, where did these come from?" I ask.

One little guy at the front of the cage has a bright green shell. He lifts up a mini claw at me, like he might be trying to wave.

Scooping him up in my hand, I pet his shell with the pad of my thumb.

"I'm totally keeping him," I announce. "We can call him Pickles."

"I wouldn't get too attached," Alex says. "Turns out hermit crabs don't live in salt water, and they were sent here accidentally. Charlie threw a hissy fit when he saw them this afternoon. The distributor is picking them up tonight."

"No! These are seriously the best things we've ever had in this place!"

Pickles crawls hopefully along my palm, and I pat his front claw. There is no way I'm letting anyone take him back to Crabland, or wherever our fish supplier got him from. He's just so little and helpless. I *love* him.

"It's okay; you're going to stay with me." I hold him up for Alex to examine. "What do you think?"

"Pickles, huh?" Alex shrugs. "I guess no one is going to miss one crab."

We spend the rest of the afternoon on our iPhones, Googling how to build a "crabitat," and then setting up the rocks and extra shells in one of the little handheld plastic tanks that parents sometimes buy for their kids, even though they're horrible for more than a couple of fish. When we're finished, we set Pickles on the counter so he can watch *Golden Girls* with us. If anyone walked in right now, we'd look completely crazy, but really what are the chances of *that* happening.

They play the episode where Dorothy decides to fulfill her lifelong dream of doing stand-up comedy, after one of her friends from high school dies. Pickles seems to really enjoy it—definitely a crab after my own heart.

He can totally join Alex and me in our private aquarium club.

DAY 22

―∞∞―

Everyday Wedding Cake with Faux Fondant

When we first moved into the model home, Mom said that we should probably convert the playroom into something else. But every time she goes in there, she gets all wistful and says how much she and Dad would have loved to have been able to give V and I stuff like that when we were little. Yeah, the playroom isn't going anywhere. It's just too precious, with the Beatrix Potter murals of Peter Rabbit and Tom Kitten on the wall, and the giant plush stuffed bears and tigers, the built-in bookcases with all the classic children's stories, and beautifully photographed National Geographic books.

And the dollhouse is perfect—not the super-intricate kind that they have in museums, but one that looks like a little kid would actually be allowed to use it. Brightly painted wood with mini furniture and lacy drapes. There are even little metal plates for the dining room table.

Today it's finally getting some use. Elle, Jimmy, and I are letting Pickles explore the various doll-furnished rooms. The kitchen, with its tiny appliances, doesn't hold much interest for him. And he immediately crawls back into the house when we set him on the terrace. Guess he's not the outdoorsy type. Honestly, he's most comfortable on the velveteen couch in the living room, which kind of makes me wonder if depression is a thing in the hermit crab community.

"You should give him a Twitter account," Elle says as she snaps cell phone photos of Pickles kicking back in his shell on the sofa. "You'd probably get a book deal—*The Everyday Hermit Crab* or something."

"*A Hermit Crab's Journey: One Hundred Days of Shell*?" I laugh. "My mom would buy that."

"I would buy that one!"

"You guys are weird." Jimmy looks up from a three-quarter-size table, where he's pitting classic tin soldiers against plastic jungle animals. "When is Veronica coming back?" He may be an eight-year-old rabid possum, but he's not blind; naturally, he has a ginormous crush on my sister.

"I have no idea," I say. It's true; I don't think I've even seen her since she slammed off my alarm clock and called me pathetic.

Jimmy looks momentarily bummed, then brightens. "Do you guys have scissors?"

I tell him they're in the sewing room across the hall, and he scampers off.

"You *cannot* try to stab Carly again," Elle calls after him.

Elle and Jimmy have to spend a few days with their dad and stepmom in Jacksonville, and Mr. Lovell and Carly are picking them up here because it's just best if Elle's parents don't interact . . . *ever*. This way it's much less likely to result in property damage.

From downstairs Mom calls that she finished today's cake a little early, in case Elle and Jimmy want to take a few pieces on the road.

"We'll be right down," Elle yells, and I raise my eyebrows. "What?" she says. "I'm starving."

Since Pickles likes the couch so much, I put it in the crabitat so he can have his own lounging area, and Elle and I head downstairs.

Mom and the kitchen are back to their model states. The same cannot be said about the Everyday Wedding Cake. I'm not entirely sure what real fondant is supposed to look like, but the faux fondant icing is all spikes and unseemly lumps that remind me of the scene in *Alien* where the baby monster punches out of the guy's gut. It also tastes as though Mom might have forgotten some crucial ingredient, like salt.

Elle doesn't mind; that girl would eat a tennis shoe if you sprinkled enough sugar on top.

"Amazing, Mrs. Byrne," she says. "Really great stuff."

From upstairs there's an eardrum-busting shriek from V, who must have been home all along. "Elle! Get up here now!"

Elle and Mom and I look at each other, and then race up the spiral staircase (a somewhat impractical upgrade). The hallway hardwood floors are spattered with wisps of cotton and feathers. We follow the mess to V's room, where she's standing on her bed, hands raised in the universal sign for *Stay the hell away from me*. Stripped down to his Superman underpants, Jimmy has the hollowed-out exterior of the white tiger stuffed animal from the playroom draped over his shoulders like a hard-won pelt. The plush white face is perched on top of Jimmy's own head, as if he's a tribal hunter from one of the National Geographic books that came with the house.

"Jimmy!" Elle shrieks.

"I wanted to impress my love with my kill," he says to V, as if this makes total sense.

It takes every ounce of self-control not to bust out laughing. I have never loved Jimmy more than at this moment.

"Sorry, kid. I'm not a plushie," V mutters, but she actually seems less annoyed now, or at least less scared.

"I'm so sorry, Mrs. Byrne." Elle reaches out for the slain tiger. "It's completely ruined."

"Don't worry about it." Mom shakes her head, and then smiles. "You know, it's actually extremely creative."

Jimmy lights up, apparently excited that someone isn't simply fed up with him, for a change.

"It would make a pretty cool Halloween costume," I say, and Mom and Elle agree.

"Honestly, we could probably sell something like this at Jaclyn's." V climbs off the bed and sizes up Jimmy. "You know, market it as kind of a fun fake fur, for save-the-planet nuts like Elle." She nods at Elle. "No offense."

"None taken," Elle says. "But if you really wanted to appeal to the eco-conscious consumer, you'd need to use certain materials."

As the four of us circle around Jimmy, his face changes from pride to frustration or maybe terror.

"You guys are weird." Throwing off his tiger pelt, he runs out of the bedroom.

DAY 24

Banana Split Cake

Y ou stood me up last week," Dr. Brooks says when I come into his office for my rescheduled appointment. "Everything okay?"

"Yeah, I just wasn't feeling well," I say, and feel bad all over again. "I'm so sorry."

I try to give him the co-pay for the missed session, but he waves it away. I guess stuff like this probably happens in his line of work all the time.

"No worries. Next time just let me know as soon as you know you won't be able to make it," he says.

"Sure."

"Actually, do you have my cell number?" He takes out a business card and writes something on the front. "I know I gave it to your mom, but you should have it too, in case you ever have an emergency and need to talk."

"Thanks." The card feels valuable.

"Just try not to have any emergencies after midnight on the weekends. My fiancée's kind of a light sleeper," he says, and chuckles.

"Oh, okay."

"I'm kidding. Obviously call me whenever you need to." Smiling, he points to the crabitat next to me on the couch. "So what's with your little friend?"

"This is Pickles." I hold up the container for Dr. B. to get a better look. "We are totally on the same wavelength; he's my spirit animal."

I kind of hoped Dr. B. would laugh, but instead he shakes his head and lets out this sigh from his nose. "Because he can duck into his shell and hide at a moment's notice?"

Heat floods my cheeks. "I guess that *is* a painfully obvious metaphor. No wonder I got a C in English."

That does make Dr. B. chuckle a little, and I instantly feel better.

When I first started coming to Dr. B.'s, I figured he would be all about the Prozac. Half the kids in school are on Ritalin or Adderall or some other pharmaceutical (to be fair, a lot of those aren't doctor-prescribed meds but stuff bought from Sketchy Mike, this stoner senior who deals from the storage closet behind the gym), but Dr. Brooks explained that he's a psychologist, not a psychiatrist, and that just any prescriptions would have to come from a doctor. He looked over the stuff Dr. Calvin had me on and said that we should stick with that for a while.

But with what happened the night of Alex's show and missing my appointment last week, I keep wondering about the attractive lady with her attractive family and attractive dog in the antidepressant commercial. Like, maybe it's time for something new? At the very least it's got to be more medically viable than Mom's cake cure-all.

It feels kind of weird to bring it up though—like I'm not loving Dr. B.'s treatment or something—but all the commercials do say, *Talk to your doctor.*

"So, um, the other day I saw a commercial for some new wonder drug antidepressant . . . ," I start cautiously.

"Which one? The little sad-faced yellow blob, or the blue robe of sadness that the woman can't take off?" Dr. B. asks.

I laugh and tell him about the Attractives. "I don't know. Do you think maybe it's time to switch it up?"

"Well, there are a lot of things they don't recommend for people under twenty-five," he says. "Therapy is generally considered the best treatment for people your age."

"Oh, okay." All of a sudden I feel tears tickling my nose. I guess I didn't realize how much I just want some quick fix back to the original Molly Byrne, before the recast.

"Molly?" Dr. B. asks gently, but I don't want to look at him, because it's so stupid that I'm upset. Seriously, how hard is it to *not* cry in front of people?

"I get it. I just thought, well . . . There's been a few bad days lately."

Nodding, he says this is something I should definitely bring up with my doctor and offers to give me the name of a psychiatrist. "We can also try adding an extra session each week for a while. That might help too."

I start to tell him that would be great, but stop.

"Do you think my insurance will cover it?" Already our co-pay for the sessions is pretty hefty. Even with Mom's Coral Cove salon domination, the weekly cost has got to be eating up a chunk of her checks.

"Let's not make money the deciding factor in your treatment. I have a sliding scale for these things, so we can just say that your current co-pay covers whatever your insurance company won't."

"Seriously, Dr. B.? That's, like, beyond nice."

All at once I sort of pink up and actually get a little excited about Dr. B. getting me back on track.

"Now tell me about these bad days," he says.

"The other night I was supposed to go see my friend's band, and I just couldn't do it."

"You couldn't drag yourself out of bed for Burning Dante?"

"*Flaming* Dantes. But they're called Headless Naked Ken now." I regret this the minute I say it. Dr. B.'s face remains neutral, but something flickers across his eyes, and I just know he's thinking that this is more immature high school stuff.

He's probably regretting that he offered me extra sessions.

"We've talked about this before, Molly." Leaning forward, he nods. "Being depressed means sometimes you're not going to feel like doing things—that's okay. But sometimes you need to push yourself to get out there."

"Fake it till you make it?"

"In some ways." He crosses his hands in his lap. I notice for the first time that they are really big hands, a little like my dad's, except the fingers are more delicate, like maybe he plays piano or something.

"Given your history with Alex, the show might not have been the best thing for you to attend anyway, if you don't want to send him mixed messages. But you should try to get out and do things with your friends. You know, see a movie on a Friday night."

I think of my sister in her barely there bathing suit heading to Chris Partridge's house, and Elle's story about Meredith Hoffman falling all over Alex. "You're kind of dating yourself there, Dr. B. Kids these days really aren't headed to the drive-in anymore."

"Your generation. First no mix tapes, now no movies." He smiles and shakes his head. "You guys are missing out. The first time I got to second base was with Lizzie Mapleton at the mall movie theater."

"Okay, so what exactly is second base? Does the bra have to come off?"

Dr. B. laughs. "That's a question for your regular doctor."

"What did you see? At the movies with Lizzie Mapleton?" I ask.

"*Say Anything . . .* "

"Never heard of it."

"Really? John Cusack? Ione Skye?" He seems incredulous. "'In Your Eyes'?"

"Nope."

"It's only the single greatest romantic comedy of all time—in my humble opinion. I'm bringing in a copy for your next session. It should be required homework for every patient."

We talk some more about the bad days and about maybe adding some sort of exercise now that I've quit the swim team. Endorphins are good for the brain and all that.

In his crabitat on the desk, Pickles taps the wall.

Narrowing his eyes, Dr. B. looks into the cage. "Does he have a little couch in there?"

"Yeah, it's actually from the dollhouse I had when I was a kid," I say. "My mom always tells the story of how my dad stayed up all night Christmas eve putting it together so it would be ready for me in the morning."

Dr. B. nods. "Yeah," I add. "My dad did a lot of stuff like that."

DAY 25

⁘

Green Tea Cheesecake

Mom is worried about today's cake.

We're supposed to have dinner at my grandma's house tonight, and because of all her crazy cake making, Mom volunteered to bring dessert. She has the day off and spends most of the afternoon tinkering in the kitchen before summoning V and I to take a look. It does not look good.

"Is it supposed to be grayish like that?" V asks.

Not if it's supposed to look like the picture in *A Baker's Journey*, which is open on the counter. That cheesecake is a pretty pastel green.

V and I taste a bit of the filling; it does not taste good either.

In fact it's probably Mom's worst cake effort to date, but that might be a flaw in the recipe. Why would anyone think green tea would go well in a cheesecake?

I glance over at V; she raises eyebrows back at me. We *cannot* take this to Gram's.

Here's the thing about my grandma. She is the polar opposite of Mom. Only twenty years older, she's always been this gray-haired granny type—even when we were little kids and she was barely in her forties. Since the beginning of time, she's worn housecoats, had plastic covers on her furniture, and talked about "nice young people." I actually don't think she's ever said an unkind word about anyone . . . except my parents.

I guess my mom and dad weren't the best financial planners, and apparently Gram had never been crazy about my father to begin with, but I still remember hearing Mom and Gram arguing when we were staying with her after Dad died. My grandma went on and on about how Dad left us "high and dry." But then, she wasn't particularly supportive when Mom opened Dye Another Day either. She kept proclaiming that no one in town would ever pay more than twenty-five bucks for a haircut. And when we moved into the model home? Sheesh, was Gram huffy puffy. Each accent pillow she touched, every walk-in closet she walked into, my grandma asked my mom if she could afford it. "Yes, Ma," Mom would say, with growing annoyance.

"Well," Gram fired back, "aren't you fancy." If anyone in town ever heard the way sweet Amelia Vance talked to her daughter, they'd probably keel over from shock.

Mom goes out of her way to be extra perfect around Gram, and that just escalates everything. Like, Mom is usually so effortlessly stylish, but today she's wearing an unflattering pencil skirt with this overly fussy shirt. And she spent ten minutes going through her stash of shoes in the laundry room.

Short story long: this cake has got to go.

"So, what do you think?" Mom asks with the odd panic she reserves for her mother and talk of me being depressed. "When I tried it, I couldn't really tell if it was right."

"It's different." V raises eyebrows at me again.

"Are those the heels Gram called the 'street walker special'?" I ask, changing the subject.

"Crap, you're right."

Mom goes back to the laundry room in search of a more perfect shoe solution.

"We cannot let her take this mess," V whispers to me.

"I know. Maybe it could have an accident?" I whisper back, and V nods emphatically. Mentally, I scroll through a list of sitcom plot points. "Fake sneeze?" I suggest.

"Great," V says. "You are such a disgusting sneezer."

I stash my annoyance away; we have limited time.

While Mom is still buried in the laundry room, I make this incredibly loud *ahhh-choo* noise, and V and I hurl the cake onto the floor. It lands with a gross squishing sound.

V's dramatic "Oh shit" is so much more believable than mine.

"What happened?" Mom is back, with two different sandals in hand. Her eyes widen as she looks from V and me to the dead corpse-gray cake on the floor.

I apologize and explain how I accidentally pitched forward.

"You know how Molly always has those gross whole-body sneezes," V adds.

"I'm really sorry," I say again.

"It's not your fault," Mom says, but she's got that level-red panicky look in her eyes.

"That bakery by Jaclyn's is still open, and it's on the way," V offers. "We can just pick something up there."

"We could even take it out of the box and pretend we made it," I add.

Mom laughs a little. "She'd know. My mother always knows everything."

Gram's house is in the older part of town, and we pass our old house on the way. That rickety swing is still in the backyard; it's just not ours anymore.

In one of her baggy shift dresses, Gram meets us at the door. "Well, don't you girls look pretty?" She hugs V and me. Taking in Mom's overly complicated dress shirt, she adds, "You must be burning up in that in this weather."

"Good to see you," Mom says without skipping a beat, and hands Gram the cherry pie from Coral Cove Bake Shop. "Unfortunately, we had a little bit of a spill with the cake I made."

"Probably best this way. Lisa, you're a pretty girl, but you've never been much of a cook." Gram laughs warmly, like this is a funny shared joke.

V and I exchange a look.

"Well, I've been trying," Mom mumbles.

Nothing in Gram's house has been redone in my entire life. Same paisley couches, same olive-colored kitchen appliances, and a shag carpet that has managed to survive three decades relatively unscathed. There is something really nice about the fact that her house is always a constant. The only "new additions" to the place are a couple of these Georgia O'Keeffe–like flower paintings I made in junior high art class that Mom and I had framed for one of Gram's birthdays. Seeing them I have a momentary flicker of sadness. Art is the one extracurricular I kind of miss, even if I did drop out because I didn't have any "themes or underlying messages" in my work and felt like a giant fraud.

"Are you working on any new pictures, Molly?" Gram asks when she notices me looking.

"Not right now," I say, not adding anything about the fraud stuff.

I brought Pickles in his crabitat, and Gram takes a

genuine interest in him, letting Pickles crawl across her arm and getting him some veggie treats from the kitchen.

Gram is actually a pretty good cook, and when we were really little, V and I used to get out all her pots and pans and pretend to help her. When V was maybe six, she told Gram how much she loved this sausage-and-pepper dish that Gram had made. V had kind of a lisp back then, so the way she said "delicious" was really cute, and Gram was tickled. So now we're pretty much stuck with that every time we come over for dinner, even though V would never normally eat sausage anymore. Who's gonna be the jerk to say something about it to an old lady?

Like clockwork, the second we're all sitting down to eat, Gram turns to V. "Well, how is it?" she asks.

"Still de-liss-ous," V assures.

"I would have made those brownies you girls like, but your mom said she was handling dessert."

"I'm sure the pie will be great," I say. And it *is* tasty when we try some twenty minutes later, but I feel like a traitor eating it. Maybe we should have let my mom bring the horrible cheesecake?

On the ride home Mom is quiet and visibly bummed.

"You know," I say, "everyone loooved my hair when you braided it the other night. Maybe you could do it again tonight?"

I glance at V in the backseat. She rolls her eyes and shakes her head, but then joins in. "Maybe you could do mine, too? I have to open Jaclyn's tomorrow, and it might save me a ton of time if I didn't have to do my hair in the morning."

"Okay." Mom pinks up a little. "That might be fun."

And it actually is.

DAY 26

Crazy Coffee Crumb Cake

Want to go to the mall?" Elle asks.

"For serious?" I say.

"Yeah."

"Are you suffering from heatstroke?" I'm only half joking. For the past few years, every time I've so much as used the word "mall" in a sentence, I've gotten a lecture about what awful corporate citizens the big stores are and about all the pollution generated by the industrial-strength chemicals they use to clean.

We're sitting in Elle's living room, divvying up the summer reading list for AP English (the one advanced class I didn't get kicked out of), and sweating. Elle could give you a whole presentation about how AC is destroying the world.

"I need a new bathing suit," she says. "You probably do too."

"For the ten millionth time, I'm not coming back to the team. I still can't even look at Coach Hartley."

"I'm not talking about a practice suit but, you know, a fun suit."

"What's a 'fun suit'?"

She shrugs and tries to look nonchalant. "In case we want to go to the Y or something."

"You want to go to the Y?"

This does not sound like Elle at all.

"Maybe," she says. "It's been so hot out."

I just arch an eyebrow.

"I'll drive." Wasting fossil fuels for a trip that is completely within biking distance? This sounds even less like Elle.

"Who are you, and what have you done with my best friend?" I make an exaggeratedly confused face.

"Oh, come on." She throws her copy of *The Catcher in the Rye* at me. "It will be fun."

"Fine, the mall is air-conditioned."

Ninety minutes later my butt is numb from sitting on a white plastic bench in the Fins and Grins Swimwear dressing area, watching Elle try on and dismiss nearly every two-piece bathing suit in the store. She keeps freaking out that all the tops make her look "flatter than a run-over rabbit." She hasn't even mentioned that the swimsuit makers might use animal by-products or employ sweatshop labor.

"And this one gives me less than no butt." She tugs at the high-cut brief of a blue-and-red tankini.

"It looks good." I try to sound convincing and supportive. Elle has adorable freckles and beautiful wide-set eyes, but the truth is that she doesn't really have enough in the boobs or the booty department to fill out the suits she keeps choosing. It's not the kind of thing that's ever bothered her before, and I wonder why she's obsessing about it now. "They have some really cute tops with a little ruffle on the front. Those might make you look a little boob-ier."

Elle looks even more dejected.

When the buxom saleslady comes back and sees virtually every suit in stock on the floor of Elle's dressing room, she timidly suggests we try the juniors or girls department at Sears. Elle gives her the glare she usually reserves for people wearing fur or throwing cigarette butts into water sources. Violently Elle stabs her arms and legs back into her shorts and T-shirt. She looks like she might cry, and I remember that even though I'm the big blue bummer in therapy, it doesn't mean I've cornered the market on irrational teen angst.

"Umm, are you okay?" I ask.

"I'm fine. It's just, you know, not everyone in the world is a D-cup, and it would be nice if they could design a few suits for the rest of us that don't make us look like twelve-year-old boys!"

"Yeah. It's like, who makes these things, right?" I offer.

"Some sexist douche who completely objectifies women, that's who."

"Definitely." I have no idea what I'm talking about, so I change tactics. "Do you maybe want to get french fries or something? My treat?"

"Can the calories go straight to my tits?" she asks.

Laughing, I help put the suits back onto the hangers, and we head to the food court.

Elle is staring at the posted menus, debating which of the chain kiosks—Chick-fil-A, Sbarro, Arthur Treacher's—is the least environmentally damaging, when I catch a flash of familiar mahogany hair at the tables by the fountain.

My sister . . . in a little sundress that shows off all those curves Elle doesn't have.

She's with Chris Partridge and a couple of his friends from my grade—including Meredith "Hooters girl" Hoffman.

Of course. Chris's pool party two weeks ago is the reason why Elle and I are really at the mall looking at bikinis.

With her swimsuit-shopping PTSD, Elle definitely should not see this. Stealthily as I can manage, I try to shift her direction.

"You know, the crumb cake my mom is making tonight actually sounds pretty tight." I steer Elle toward the door. "Maybe we should skip this and head home?"

"Don't worry. I'll still eat the cake for you," Elle says absently. "That's the one good thing about having the metabolism of a rabbit on Adderall—"

That's when she notices Veronica. Elle's jaw drops pretty much to the floor like she's a Looney Tunes character.

"God, what is she wearing?" Elle says, equal parts disgust and envy. "I know that she's your sister, and women have the right to dress however they want, but she is seriously everything that's wrong with America."

V's dress has a sweetheart neckline and spaghetti straps and looks like something Jennifer Lopez or Rachel McAdams might be wearing on the poster for a new romantic comedy. In her wedge sandals she's almost as tall as the boys. Gloss on her lips, a hint of mascara, and all that mink hair. She's radiant, throwing her head back, laughing at something Chris is saying. You can almost hear the peppy rom-com soundtrack playing behind her.

"I can't believe Chris would be interested in someone like Veronica," Elle is saying, but I'm not really sure she's talking to me anymore.

The better question is, what guy *wouldn't* be interested in my sister? She's so amazingly luminous. And she's happy. Not force-yourself-to-get-back-out-there-every-now-and-then and fake-it-till-you-make-it happy, but really genuinely joyful.

Why isn't that me?

We have the same parents, the same DNA. We were

raised by the same gregarious go-get-'em mother. V and I are totally the nature *and the nurture* we learned about in freshman bio (back when I was an A student and paid attention to all of that crap). So why is V the way that she is and I'm the way that I am? How is that fair? How does that even happen?

All at once I want to talk to Dr. B. so bad that my hands are shaking. If he were here, he'd make a joke or say something to make me feel like I'm worth something, too. His cell phone number is tucked in my wallet. He did say anytime. . . .

But . . . Elle would give me crap about it crossing a line, and I'm so not having *that* fight with her again.

"I think I'm officially done with the mall forever," Elle announces. Setting her hemp-weave satchel on a chair, she starts rummaging around for her keys.

While she's got her head buried—"How do I lose them every freaking time?"—a really bizarre thing happens.

Alex walks in. He's by himself and kind of glances around like he's supposed to meet someone. Not gonna lie, he looks really sexy in jeans and a vintage Nirvana T-shirt. Just seeing him calms me down a little, and I feel myself smile. How did he know Elle and I were going to be at the mall?

I'm about to jog over and invite him back to the model home for crumb cake, but then he gives a wave and a nod to someone else entirely.

Looking over, I see that it's Chris and V's group, which

I guess makes sense. He starts toward them and exchanges hellos with some of the guys and gives Meredith a quick hug that makes me a little crazy even if it doesn't look particularly romantic. But the strange thing is that he gives V a hug too, like they know each other in some capacity other than me just talking about him and FishTopia all the time. I mean, I guess they could have met at Chris's party after Elle and I left, but how weird is it that neither one of them said *anything* about it to me?

Then the whole group disappears into the Ruby Tuesday restaurant.

When they're gone, I almost can't believe it happened. I'm just staring off into the restaurant entrance, wondering if maybe I'm the one whose brain has finally melted from the heat.

I turn to ask Elle if she saw them too, but she's stopped searching for her keys and is by the garbage bins, yelling at some junior high boys in Air Jordans for not putting their plastic utensils in the right recycling bin.

DAY 27

Lemon Dream Cake

You know how in those old Charlie Brown holiday specials, when the adults are talking, it just sounds like "Waa wa wa wa waa" to the kids? That's pretty much exactly what Mrs. Peck—this string-bean-thin college counselor who comes all the way from Orlando to get highlights done at Mom's salon—sounds like to me. We're at the dining room table (under the family portrait with Dad and his hands), and she's yammering on and on. I can tell that she's using words, some of which even seem vaguely familiar—"good," "school," "life," and "plan"—but they don't go together in any way that makes sense to me. It's all just muffled trombone.

"Waa wa wa wa wa, SATs in September," she's saying. "Waa wa wa wa, last chance."

Next to me on the table in his plastic crabitat, Pickles is

lounging on the dollhouse couch. He pops out of his shell and gives Mrs. Peck a sideways glance (to be fair, his eyestalks kind of make all his glances seem sideways), and I'm convinced he's sizing up this big gap between her front teeth, wondering if he could slip right through.

"Waa wa wa probably state schools at this point, at least for now."

Does Pickles have any aspirations toward higher education? What would his dream college be? He'd probably avoid any schools where the team is named after predatory birds, because getting eaten by the mascot would suck. Would he major in something practical like engineering—learn to design a better shell? Or perhaps he'd be frivolous and study theater or philosophy. I could see him digging into the whole "free will versus determinism" debate. (We had a unit on philosophy in European history last spring, and I thought it was pretty cool, even if I did get an F on the test because I spent the entire period drawing a king who looked like T.J. being hauled off to the guillotine.) Maybe Pickles would take some time off first, backpack around Europe for a few months, pick up bad accents from every country where he traveled, and grow some horrible facial hair somewhere between a goatee and beard, like Alex tried to do a few months ago.

Honestly, Pickles is probably too much of a homebody for any of it. "Why do I need to go anywhere?" he'd say.

"I've got everything I need right here in my shell." Gotta love him.

"Since you seem to have quit all your extracurriculars"— Mrs. Peck is apparently still talking—"the SAT might just be your saving grace. It looks as though you were in the ninety-second percentile when you took the PSAT sophomore year."

I want to tell her that sophomore year and anything BDF (before divisionals freak-out) might as well have been the 1400s. The time of the first Molly. Back before I even knew Alex. (For the five-hundredth time since yesterday, I wonder about him at the mall with my sister and her friends.)

". . . So if you can pull your GPA up the first half of the year and score in the top tenth percentile on the SATs, you might be able to salvage something. Does that sound doable? Otherwise we should really start to recalibrate our expectations for the more selective state schools."

Mrs. Peck is just staring at me, and I realize she wants an answer.

"SATs to the rescue. Got it."

Before Mrs. Peck can say anything else, my mom, wearing an apron over her skintight tank dress like a porny Mrs. Fields, comes in from the kitchen with a tray boasting today's misadventure in batter.

"I thought maybe you two ladies could use a little break," she says, and presents us with a lemon cake topped with a sticky yellow drizzle that looks exactly like raw egg yolk. My teeth hurt just from looking at it.

"When life gives you lemons, make lemon cake," I mumble.

"What's that, sweetie?" Mom asks, and I tell her it's nothing as I dutifully take a piece and smush the corner with my fork so she won't realize I'm not actually eating it.

Mrs. Peck, meanwhile, thinks this cake might be almost as magnificent as the SATs. After initially waving a slice away, saying how she "shouldn't" because she tries to stay away from sweets and is watching her (Elle-level skinny) figure, Mrs. Peck devours the whole thing and even gives a longing look toward mine.

"Really, this is just lovely, Lisa," Mrs. Peck says to my mom. "You simply must give me the recipe."

Of course Mom is only too happy to start talking about the 100 Days of Cake challenge, and how she just thought she would "give it a whirl" because she'd never tried anything like it before and she wants to show her girls how important it is to finish things, and more wa wa waa. Mrs. Peck nods enthusiastically, and Mom is beaming. At least one of us is benefiting from the $150 an hour Mrs. Peck is charging.

Then Mom turns her focus on me and asks how it's going. She's using the singsong, Molly-might-shatter voice again.

"Well, I think we've made some tremendous progress today. Right, Molly?" Mrs. Peck says, and looks at me. I'm not sure if she's trying to get me to go along with her lie so Mom doesn't question her employment, or if she is genuinely deluded enough to think that this afternoon was remotely productive.

"Sure." I nod. "SATs are the great white hope."

Mom cocks her head in a question, and then I feel awful again.

"Yeah, no, this has been really . . . informative," I say.

That must be good enough, because Mom nods and goes back to the kitchen, and Mrs. Peck starts waa wa waaing about how I'll definitely need to add a "community service component" to my applications. She gives me some pamphlets of places that have student volunteer programs but suggests that it would look more impressive if I could show initiative and organize a project on my own.

"Last year I had a young man put together a complete fund-raiser for the family of a friend who broke his back in a zip-line accident," she says. "He got into Brown, Northwestern, *and* was wait-listed at Yale."

I consider asking if I should encourage my friends to take up dangerous new hobbies to increase my chances of getting into Florida Atlantic, but think better of it. "I'll keep my eyes peeled."

"Good. Just make sure you act soon. A lot of places will be overwhelmed by volunteers once admissions season starts in the fall."

fore she leaves, Mrs. Peck reaches into her Day-Glo messenger bag and pulls out a yellow Hacky Sack iley face sewn on above her company name— A Ace!

s ball." Offering a huge gap-toothed grin, she tells m hopes it can help me work through some of my issu Senior year can be a very challenging time, but I think we're definitely on the right track with you now."

More than anything, I want to hurl the ball at the space between her teeth.

DAY 28

Blueberry Crumble Delight

The next day at FishTopia, I'm throwing the stress ball at the wall while Alex fills Charlie's water bottle up with these teeny nano fish. This is the first day we've worked together since I saw him with V and Meredith Hoffman at the mall, and even though I've been dying to ask about it, I'm too freaked out to say anything now. For some reason I'm scared of what he might say—that hanging out with V is more fun than being with me or something. (Hello, no shocker there.) So instead I tell him about my ridiculous experience with Admissions Ace!

"Even the woman's name is annoying. Mrs. Peck. She makes me want to peck, peck, peck my eyes out because she peck, peck, pecks on my last nerve."

I start talking in this extremely nasally voice that doesn't actually sound much like Mrs. Peck but is kind of funny, or at least I hope Alex thinks it's kind of funny. "Mawww-lee, you're never going to get into community college with those grades, so it's really now about whether you want to work at McDonald's or Walmart—although, Walmart is going to be tough this year. Come on, Mawwww-lee. You have to decide everything about your life right now, this very minute. Mawwww-lee, the clock is ticking!"

Alex chuckles. From his crabitat on the counter, Pickles gives me an encouraging look, so I continue.

"Then she's going on and on about the SATs, as if they're the cure for cancer. Aren't they, like, totally biased?" I'm not entirely sure what I'm talking about, but before Elle started on her save-the-planet kick, she was all about social inequality and spent a lot of time raging against things like "institutionalized racism" and "cyclical poverty." I'm pretty sure standardized tests came up a lot.

"Maybe," Alex says, and I can see that he's just humoring me, which is completely frustrating.

"And she said I need to start volunteering." I throw this out as definitive proof that my hour with Mrs. Peck was on par with stepping in dog crap and dropping your ice cream cone. "Don't you think it would look awfully suspicious if all of a sudden I started working at a soup kitchen or something? College admissions people probably gag when they see a billion seventeen-year-olds who just happen to suddenly hear the call of duty right before sending out their application packets. It's sooo hypocritical."

"I don't know, Mol." He's stopped fiddling with the fish and the water bottle. "What's so wrong about a little motivation?"

"Et tu, Alex?" I try to sound light, but I can feel that swirling, icky feeling in my gut, and all at once my heart is beating faster.

"Like, not to rip on JoJo or anything, but do you really want to end up like her? Working here for ten bucks an hour forever?"

"Well, I definitely don't want to find stray teeth at my boyfriend's place."

"Seriously, though."

"Of course not. I . . . I just don't see why we have to decide everything for all of eternity right this second." I swear my heart is beating directly in my eardrums. "I can't even decide when I want to sign up for driver's ed."

"So you really haven't thought about where you're going to college at all?"

Alex is looking at me as if he's uncovered something earth-shattering and majorly disturbing. Looking at me like T.J. did when he broke up with me because I wasn't the sunny dream girl that he'd thought I'd be.

For once this doesn't make me sad, but furious. Alex is the one who shoved me up onto some stupid pedestal and decided I was this "really cool girl." Dr. B. is right; this is Alex's issue, not mine. I'm fuming, but Alex just goes right on talking about his grand plans.

"I know I'm gonna have to get my grades up this fall," he says. "And I've been taking that prep class—"

"Shut up." I cut him off with a lot more force than is probably necessary. "Seriously, if one more person says one more flipping word about the SAT or service components or how I've already messed up my life beyond repair, I'm going to scream so loud that every last tank in here shatters into a zillion pieces. So can you please, please, please, please, please just stop talking about this?"

Alex is genuinely startled, like I legit slapped him. For what feels like two hours but is probably really only twenty seconds, we just stand there and listen to the hum of all the aquarium pumps.

"I'm sorry," he says, all ginormous golden retriever eyes, and instantly I feel a thousand times worse.

"No, I'm sorry. I didn't mean to jump down your throat," I say. "It's just, we're at FishTopia, we've got Pickles and Wang's Palace. Can't we watch *Golden Girls* and not talk about this stuff for a while?"

"Sure," he says, but he still seems really hurt.

We climb onto our counter, and he clicks the set on, both of us moving as if we're robots. It's the episode where Dorothy, Blanche, and Rose all have the flu but insist on going to the big Volunteer of the Year gala anyway. My heart is still sprinting in my chest, and it's hard to concentrate, which is fine, since Alex and I must have seen this one about five times. Still we diligently stare at the screen until everything is tied up with its perfect sitcom bow. The gals are the best of friends again, and they'll stay that way until the next installment, when some new situation will briefly test their bond for thirty minutes (actually twenty-two minutes, with all the commercials they run in syndication).

Pickles is peaking out of his shell and seems very satisfied with the conclusion. Lifting him out of the crabitat, I set him in my palm and stroke his shell.

"You see, it all works out okay," I assure him.

"Why do you like that little guy so much?" Alex asks hesitantly, like he thinks I might blow up at him again.

Shrugging, I tell him I don't know.

"He's not like a dog or a cat that can actually love you back or anything," he says.

"That's kind of the reason." As I'm saying this, I realize it's true. "Like, the world is so big, but to Pickles it's just a plastic critter box with sand on the bottom, and he is totally cool with that. He can munch on a carrot, drink his water, climb onto the couch if he really wants to mix it up. And when he doesn't feel like doing any of that, he can crawl back into his shell and shut out the rest of the world."

Alex looks at Pickles, as if he's expecting the crab to

confirm or deny this. Pickles does nothing but move one of his legs. Then Alex is looking at me like I've morphed into a wolf like in the stupid Twilight books. It's such a good thing I never agreed to go out with him; that would have made his disappointment in me so much worse.

On TV the *Golden Girls* theme begins. *Thank you for being a friend/traveled down the road and back again.*

Another episode is starting, so we sit back and watch.

DAY 31

Mango Explosion Cake

This has got to be Mother Nature's idea of a cruel joke," I say. It's been ten minutes since I got to Dr. B.'s, but I'm still sweating from the bike ride over. I had to put Pickles's crabitat by the window air-conditioning unit so he wouldn't overheat. "Seriously, a hundred and eight degrees is just mean."

Dr. B. laughs. Since I was too busy panting and sweating to talk when I first showed up, we're just listening to some of the music he had on when I came in. He's been trying to convince me that Pearl Jam's *Ten* is the greatest debut album in the history of the world or something.

I've heard some of the songs before on the nineties radio station my mom loooves. (She and my dad actually met at a club in Miami the night Kurt Cobain died. Grunge was a very big thing for them, and I'm not even making that up.) And

Alex played part of "Alive" on his guitar one day when we were hanging out on the FishTopia roof, but it's kind of cool to hear the whole album.

This one song, "Black," is so sad and beautiful that I get a little choked up listening to it. Eddie Vedder warbles in this deep back-of-the-throat way about how he has all these spinning thoughts in his head and all his pictures have been washed in black. Then there's this part about how he goes for a walk and hears the kids laughing, but it just sears him. I know that he's probably talking about some ex-girlfriend or something, but it's like the song was written for me.

When it ends, I have Dr. B. play it again.

Oh, and twisted thoughts that spin round my head
I'm spinning, oh, I'm spinning

"Good stuff, huh?" Dr. B. asks when it's done. I hadn't realized I'd closed my eyes, and now I'm all embarrassed.

"It's okay, I guess," I say, and then smile, because we both know I'm in love with it.

"Maybe it's just that they were big when I was so young and impressionable." Dr. B. winks at me. "But early Pearl Jam gets me every time. To this day, when I hear 'Daughter,' I can still smell the ramen my roommate was always cooking freshman year."

"Oh." The glow from the music immediately ends, and

I'm back in this world where everyone is obsessed with college.

Deep down I guess I knew that Dr. B. *had* to have gone to school somewhere to be a psychologist. But Dr. B. is, like, the only person in all of Coral Cove who isn't constantly nagging me about this stuff, so I never really think about it much.

"Where did you go?" I ask, because it's polite, not because I want to talk about college anymore with anyone ever.

He points to the two diplomas framed and mounted on the wall behind the desk. Clearly I'm not the most observant girl in the world, because I've been coming here for a year, and this is the first time I've ever noticed them. Squinting, I can just make out the regal font and the years. University of Pennsylvania.

An anvil drops in the pit of my stomach. So Dr. B. has an ivy-coated education. He's not just *one* of all those people fixated on college; he's kind of the king of college. And it makes me wonder about all our sessions, if he's been humoring me when he makes me feel smart or special. Maybe it's just some shrink tactic to keep me from getting hysterical?

Also noted: unless Dr. B. is some Doogie Howser prodigy who graduated at twelve, he's only, like, three years younger than my mom. When I'm twenty-five, he'll be forty-seven.

"So Penn for both undergrad and grad school?" I ask.

"Yup."

"So you're, like, super-smart?"

"Eh." He shrugs. "I was good at taking standardized tests, and my parents both went there, so I was a legacy. They give you points for that."

"My mom went to some cosmetology school in Boca," I say flatly.

"And your dad?"

"He went to Miami University." This is true; I wasn't lying to Gina and Tina. But I'm not even sure if he actually graduated or if he liked it or what his major had been. Mom talks about Dad in these safe, sweet little sound bites—how he ran to three different stores to get her the specific variety of mac and cheese she wanted when she was pregnant with V, how he once spent hours trying to solder the leg back onto my plastic horse figure after he accidentally stepped on it—but she rarely talks about who he was or what he did. For the nine millionth time, I consider how different my life might be if Dad were around.

"Where you go to college isn't the be-all and end-all," Dr. B. is saying. "If I had to do it all over again, I would probably take some time off, travel or do something daring you can only do when you're young. At the very least I would have gotten out of Philly."

"Is that where you're from? Philadelphia?"

"Born and raised."

"So how did you end up here? You don't moonlight at

J&J, do you?" I ask, happy that college isn't the be-all and end-all.

"Love, of course." He puts his hands over his heart in this mock romantic gesture. "My fiancée got a gig hosting *Coral Cove Today*, and the next thing you know, everything we own is in a U-Haul and we're driving down South."

"Oh, I've seen that show a few times. Local cable, right?" It's this grainy series on Channel 1 where they mainly just talk about the guy from the *Murder Island* movie and interview the J&J brothers. I've never seen the woman from the photo on Dr. B.'s desk on it.

"Yeah, but Whitney was only there a few months before she got hired by Fox 9 in Miami."

"You didn't want to go with her?"

"I did. I do, but her gig was only temporary at first, and I'd already started a practice here, yada, yada, yada."

"Bummer."

"Well, we'll work it out once we finally get married." He seems to remember that I'm there. "It's all for the best, though. If I had gone right to Miami, I might never have met you, Molly Byrne."

Feeling myself blush, I look down. "Thanks," I mumble.

"So tell me about how your week is going."

We talk about why I find Mrs. Peck so frustrating. And he seems to understand, even if he did go to Penn.

When I'm getting ready to leave, he reaches into the

black messenger bag by the side of his desk and pulls out a DVD. "I almost forgot your homework."

On the front of the box there's a picture of a dark-haired woman and the guy from *Hot Tub Time Machine* looking about a million years younger.

"Maybe we should watch it together," I suggest. "You know, so you can make sure I get all the cultural references."

"Oh, I think you'll be able to figure it out on your own."

"I don't know. Will there be mix tapes? Come on."

"Well." Flipping up his wrist, he checks his watch. "My next appointment isn't for forty-five minutes, if you want to start it."

I nod, and Dr. Brooks turns the oversize computer monitor on his desk around so that the screen is facing the little couch where I'm sitting, and he slides in the DVD. I'm wondering if he's going to try to turn his chair around so we're both facing the screen, but he just plunks down on the couch, Pickles's crabitat and three feet of space between us. I say a silent prayer that I don't smell putrid from biking.

Am I crab-blocking you? Pickles seems to be asking. I'd tell Pickles to stop being ridiculous, that Dr. B. is engaged and my doctor and Mom's age, but Pickles is a crab and all.

The movie is okay. *Of course* it's about high school graduation, which flips on my panic button. And *of course* the girl in the film is the ridiculously beautiful valedictorian—because that's *so* relatable. But the *Hot Tub Time Machine* guy's character doesn't really have much of a life plan, which is cool. Every time someone gives him shit about his future, I fall in love with him a little.

Still it's kinda hard to concentrate. He might be Mom's age, but Dr. B. smells sooo amazing—like the woods with a dash of cucumber.

When he notices me peeking over at him, he smiles, all excited in a way that makes him seem much, much younger than my mom. "It's good, right?" he asks.

I nod, a little dizzy from his smell. Life is so unfair.

A knock.

Initially I think it's part of the film, but then I realize it's coming from outside the office. Hesitantly the door opens a crack, and a young woman, maybe early twenties, pokes her head in.

"I'm sorry, Dr. Brooks," she says, looking from him to me, to the screen where the gorgeous valedictorian is trying to break up with the *Hot Tub Time Machine* guy by giving him a pen. "I was just wondering if we're still on for our appointment?"

I jump off the couch as if this girl knows exactly what I was thinking.

"Oh, of course, Jenny." Dr. B. is on his feet, turning off the movie. "I'm so sorry; time just got away from us."

DAY 32

Mocha Madness Cake

A few days after Alex joined the mile-long parade of
people telling me that my lack of ambition is an affront
to all humanity, we're back at FishTopia. Pickles watches
from his crabitat as Alex and I toss the smiley face stress
ball back and forth and discuss which type of fish each of
the Golden Girls characters would be.

It feels sort of normal, but Alex is bending over backward to avoid mentioning any subjects with even the most
tangential connection to the future.

"Blanche would be one of the idol fish," Alex says. "Flashy
and just a little high-maintenance."

"Yeah, and it's already wearing mascara."

"Exactly. Dorothy would be . . ." Alex pauses for dramatic
effect. "A brown clown goby."

This makes me laugh. "Why?"

"Because it's a good, reliable fish and gets along well with everyone." He nods with authority. "It's the first fish you get for the tank, the one you know you can always count on."

It's dumb, but something about this makes me giddy happy.

We're both standing there, still grinning these goofy grins, when there's a pounding at the window. On the other side of the glass, Elle is flailing her arms wildly and shouting something.

Alex curls his hand in a *Come on in* gesture, but Elle shakes her head.

"She, um, can't come in; Elle believes FishTopia is a jail for fish." Damn, it sounds even dumber when I have to say it out loud. "It's some kind of animal-rights thing."

Alex rolls his eyes. "I have a friend like that."

Still practically vibrating with excitement, Elle presses a blue brochure for something up to the window. Since there's no one in the store (as always), Alex and I head out to get the 411. The second we're through the door, Elle grabs my arm and starts pulling me toward the side of the strip mall.

"Sorry, Alex, but I have to borrow your princess for a few minutes," she says, giving him a wave.

"Whatever's clever," he says, but it seems like he's a little miffed. I guess the two of us were having an honest-to-goodness moment and it wasn't all in my head.

"Elle, we were in the middle of some—" I start, but she swats my objections away with her palm.

"I know. I'm sorry and all of that, but look!" She holds up the blue brochure, which it turns out is from Columbia University.

For pretty much ever Elle has been talking about how she wants to go there, but even if she got in, there's no way her mom could afford to send her anywhere out of state, and her dad can be a jerk about paying for stuff. So unless Columbia is having a clearance sale, I'm not entirely sure what all the commotion is about.

"Guess what!" Elle is literally bouncing up and down.

"You got a new brochure?"

"My mom and dad had an actual conversation—like, without almost strangling each other—and they figured out that if they each pay half the tuition and I get a job to cover books and living expenses, it's doable for me to go to Columbia!"

"That's great," I say, but I feel kind of like this time in seventh-grade gym class when Elle and I weren't paying attention during a dodgeball game and I got socked right in the gut with a red kickball.

"I know, right?" Elle is still gushing. "My mom is even setting up a trip to New York so we can check out the school in the fall. College tour, interview, the whole works."

I'm telling her that I'm happy for her, and I am. This is

what she's wanted for so, so long, and it's amazeballs that her parents—who haven't agreed on a single thing since the first *Jurassic Park* movie—were able to work together on it. But even as I'm congratulating her, I realize I'm crying. Pretty soon it's so bad that, even though Elle and I have been best friends since kindergarten, she can't understand any of what I'm saying.

"Oh, Mollybean." It's been centuries since she's called me that. "I'm sorry. I'm so sorry."

"Why are you apologizing?"

"I don't know. You're sad." Folding me into her arms, she smells like sweat and organic lotion and excitement. "Please don't be sad."

"No, I'm totally psyched for you." Garbled by sobs, it doesn't sound all that convincing. "On BFF law, I swear. I'll just miss you."

"You'll come with me," Elle says with sudden decisiveness— trying to fix another problem for me like she's always done, since sharing her crayons back in kindergarten. "There'll be so many cute boys in New York, and they all recycle and eat locally sourced food. . . ."

I'm nodding and telling her that it will be epic, because this is a big deal for her and she's so happy.

". . . And we can go on double dates, and it will be just like *Sex and the City* and *Girls* only more eco-conscious and with fewer gender stereotypes."

"Yeah, that would be completely off the hook."

I need to get away from Elle and her plans and her optimism and her amazing life that is all shiny and full of potential and nothing at all like mine. Because I ruin everything for everyone.

"I'm so happy for you," I say, "but I should probably get back to the store, before Charlie fires me."

"Yeah, you need to save up for New York!"

"Right."

Elle tells me to call her when I get off work. "Maybe we can 'grab a slice' to celebrate!"

Before going back into FishTopia, I try to pull myself together, but it's completely obvious that Alex has seen everything. To his credit, he doesn't say anything about how I look red and runny-nosed and ridiculous. He doesn't ask why Elle was flipping out, doesn't ask if I'm all right or if I want to talk about things. He just picks up the television remote.

"*Golden Girls* is starting in a few minutes," he says.

Climbing onto our counter, I bob my head in agreement, because actual words seem like way, way too much to attempt at the moment. And even though the temperature is still roughly the surface of the sun, I grab the hoodie from my backpack and zip it up to my chin. Without another word Alex climbs up next to me.

It's the episode where Sophia convinces Dorothy and

her ex-husband, Stan, to pretend they're still married so they won't offend Sophia's priest brother when he visits from Italy.

We've seen it at least three times, but Alex ardently laughs along with the laugh track, like he's trying to prove that he really, *really* wants to be here sitting next to me watching sitcoms. To show that he isn't exactly like Elle— just counting the days until he can start a shimmering new life of college campuses and frat parties and other magical things away from Coral Cove and FishTopia and me. That he would rather be here than at a Ruby Tuesdays with pretty girls like my sister and Meredith Hoffman.

"I'm thinking Rose might be a dottyback," Alex says when a Tampax commercial comes on. "You know, with that big eye, it always looks sorta baffled by stuff."

"Yeah, that's a really good one." I force myself to chuckle.

Inside his crabitat Pickles scurries over his favorite rock, completely oblivious.

DAY 33

Baked Alaska

Because Alex has his SAT prep class (vomit!), he and JoJo switch shifts on Wednesday, so she ends up shutting things down with Pickles and me. For the evening shifts, she's a game show girl. *Family Feud*, *Jeopardy!*, and *Wheel of Fortune*. It's not the *Golden Girls*, but it's a marked improvement over *Maury*. We lean on the counter and let Pickles crawl along the register.

Vanna White has only turned around the *N*s and the *S*s, and JoJo calls out "Baby needs a new pair of shoes." It takes six more spins of the wheel before anyone on the show can solve it.

I just look at her. "Seriously, how?"

She raises her shoulders. "I'm good with that stuff."

"Have you ever thought about trying out for the show?" I ask.

"Really, CCH?" She gives this dismissive laugh, and I feel bad for putting stupid pressure on her the same way people are always doing to me.

As we're cashing out the register, her boyfriend comes to the store to pick her up. He's cute in this dumpy sort of way, and he holds her hand and seems excited to see her—not the type to leave another woman's teeth sitting around at all.

When I'm opening the model-home garage door to park Old Montee, the same Mini Cooper that picked V up last week pulls into the driveway to drop her off. The same troop of slightly older girls are inside, their perfectly applied eyeliner somehow still intact, despite the heat.

Veronica, on the other hand, doesn't look like the girl on a poster for a rom-com anymore. More like a made-for-TV movie about troubled teens or a sitcom's "very special episode" where someone tries drugs for the first time and usually dies. Unlike her friends, V's lipstick is smudged around her mouth, and on her tight white top there's a stain that looks like soda or beer. She smells vaguely of alcohol and reeks of cigarette smoke. I have to fight back a cough, just being near her.

"Hey, sis-tah, whaz up?" she slurs, and her eyes have that sleepy boozy look to them. Noticing Pickles in his crabitat, she gives this goofy smile and taps the plastic. "Did you and your lobster buddy have a good day?"

"Dude, are you drunk? It's, like, eight o'clock."

"It's eight twenty-two." She taps the stylish silver watch she got with her Jaclyn's Attic employee discount. "No, maybe it's eight twenty-four."

"Are you?" I ask.

"What?"

"Drunk."

"What's it to you?" V's blue-green eyes (my eyes, Mom's eyes) narrow.

"Uh, you're my little sister."

"Really? When was the last time *that* mattered? To anyone? All everyone ever cares about are your problems. And YOUR problems are so big and bad that they're everyone else's problems now too." She's swaying more and getting louder.

"V, that's not—"

"God forbid anyone else in this house ever need anything."

"What is with you?" I have absolutely no idea why she's being so hateful. Even just a few years ago, we were thick as thieves. Before Mom hired the other stylists, she was always working until closing time, so V and I were on our own a lot, and V used to come to me for everything—help with her homework, questions about junior high friend drama, how to use tampons when she got her first period three years ago.

"V, I'm always around if you want to talk—"

"Yeah, right. Like you're ever there for anyone." She

shakes her head and rolls her eyes. "Like, did you even notice that Mom hasn't gone out with Toupee Thom for weeks?"

Thom Marin, the lawyer with the horrific hairpiece and an office above my mom's salon. For a while they were seeing each other several times a week, and for Valentine's Day, Mom let us stay at Gram's (something she hates to do) while Thom took her to Sanibel Island for a romantic weekend. But now that Veronica mentions it, I realize that he hasn't been around lately.

"They broke up?" Mom *was* weird when I asked her if they were going out a few weeks ago.

"With all her baking and worrying that you're gonna Robin Williams yourself, she doesn't really have a whole lot of free time anymore, does she?" V says.

"What are you talking about?" I've never said anything about making hokey family films or killing myself. "And I thought you didn't even like Thom?" The last time we talked about Thom, V claimed she would insist he ditch the rug if he and Mom got married. "All you ever did was make fun of him."

"What difference does it make what I think?" she says. "Mom liked him."

I open my mouth and then close it.

"Look," V continues, "if you really want to do the good sisterly thing, go eat your freaking cake and distract Mom while I take a shower. You know, have *my* back for once."

With that, V pushes past me into the house and jogs up the stairs.

After a few seconds of shock, I follow her in. The whole place smells like a bakery exploded, which is absolutely nauseating combined with the oppressive temperatures. More than anything, I want to flop onto my life raft bed, but of course Mom calls me into the kitchen, all excited. It's late enough that she's had time to clean up, so the kitchen is all sparkling model-home perfect again. On the cake plate in the middle of the marble-countered center island is a weird white dome.

"Voilà!" Mom says with a dramatic jazz hands–type gesture. "It's baked Alaska!"

"So that's why it looks like a little igloo. I get it."

Mom giggles nervously. "Oh, you know, I didn't even think about that, but it makes sense. You're so perceptive, Mol."

Guilt washes over me. *Yeah, so perceptive I don't even know when my mom loses her boyfriend,* I think.

She starts to cut me a huge chunk, explaining that she's impressed it turned out as well as it did, because there's ice cream inside, so you have to be careful how long you bake it, or else the entire inside will melt. "I have to admit, I'm a little proud of myself with this one."

Cutting herself a piece, she sits next to me and pours us both glasses of milk like we're five.

"Mmm," Mom is saying. "I think the meringue gives it a really unique flavor, right?"

"Definitely." For once I'm actually not lying. The baked Alaska tastes unique—not good, mind you, but most certainly bad in a way that's new and different from anything I've ever tasted. Even though the AC is cranked up, it's still sweltering in the house, which actually works to my advantage since the ice cream melts away.

"Actually it's pretty awful, isn't it?" Mom admits.

"It's okay," I say. "So whatever happened with you and Thom?"

"Thom Marin?" Mom asks, surprised, as if I'm referring to some other guy she dated for two years.

"Yeah. Did you guys break up or something?"

She shrugs and looks away from me, unconsciously smashing meringue with her fork. "It just kind of fizzled out; that happens."

The whole week before she and Thom went to Sanibel, Mom was so cute, debating what clothes she should bring. She must have packed and unpacked her overnight bag six times and even consulted V and me. *Is that little red dress too much? Do you think that I should bring jeans in case we're not going out fancy, fancy?*

"So it wasn't because you spend all your time worrying about me? Not because of *A Baker's Journey*?"

"Of course not. Why would you even suggest that?"

Obviously it's true. And somehow it's worse that she's lying to me about it. Worse that she feels like she has to walk on broken glass around me. Like I'm going to splinter into a million sad pieces if she tells me the truth.

"Besides," Mom adds, "other things are just more important at my age."

V is right; I am pathetic.

"Mom, you know I'm not asking you to bake these cakes, right?" I ask. "Like, you realize that this isn't some medically sanctioned treatment for depression?"

"I know that. I just want us to spend time—"

"This isn't going to make me better; nothing is going to make me better. So you should start going out with Toupee Thom again, and maybe every once in a while check in on what V is doing. She seemed pretty upset when she came home."

I want to think I'm saying this for good reasons—V is my sister; I'm worried about her; she *did* specifically say that no one is paying any attention to her—but it's maybe more because she was such a bitch tonight. Maybe I'm still annoyed that she hasn't even mentioned she hung out with *my Alex*.

"I didn't even know she was home yet." Mom frowns.

"Exactly. You have no idea what's going on with her." Grabbing Pickles's crabitat, I head out of the kitchen. "I've got homework."

"In July?"

"Summer reading. Why don't you worry about your other daughter for once."

I head upstairs to my bedroom and shut the door. I don't actually pick up *The Catcher in the Rye*, but I take Pickles out of his crabitat and let him crawl over the book.

"Is it as good as everyone always says?" I ask him.

I'm pretty sure he shrugs in his shell.

A few minutes later I hear Mom knocking on the door to the bathroom V and I share. Parts of their conversation float in through the upgraded six-panel door. Mom is pretty even keel, so it's mainly stuff when V's voice gets all high and angry.

"Just out with some friends . . . No, of course not. . . . I'm not. . . . Fine."

An upgraded six-panel door slams.

Pickles looks at me with his eyestalks.

"What? She said she wanted people to pay attention to her problems."

Pickles doesn't have to say that's not what V meant.

When I get up to pee for the third time that night—all that water we're drinking in the heat—there's a noise coming from behind the door to Mom's room. She must have the TV on. Just like me, she loves old sitcoms. (V gets our mom's looks, and I get her penchant for laugh tracks. How's that fair?) I remember the old house, watching reruns with Mom in her sagging-in-the-center bed, V complaining that the shows were so old and silly, but sometimes climbing into that center sag with us. All of us joking about how ridiculous it was that all six of the *Brady Bunch* children could be sooooo well adjusted, or admitting that we were totally crushing on Michael J. Fox's overachieving character on *Family Ties*. It felt safe. Like nothing bad could ever happen while we were in that bed.

I miss all that stuff. Even if I know I'm way too old for it now.

Still, I make my way right up to Mom's door, thinking I should apologize for earlier, maybe see if she wants company. But when I get closer, I realize it's not the TV at all. The sound isn't canned laughter but crying. My chirpy beautiful Mom crying; so much worse than her being annoyingly perfect.

And then I feel terrible for not eating the baked Alaska and for selling out my sister.

Back down the hall, I knock lightly on V's door. "It's me. Can I come in?"

"I think we've done more than enough bonding for one night, thanks," she hisses. "Go away."

So I do.

DAY 35

Key Lime Surprise Cake

FishTopia is closing.

Forty-five minutes ago Charlie came in while Alex and I were sitting on the counter watching *Golden Girls* and eating Wang's Palace lo mein instead of cleaning or checking the supplies or basically doing anything related to our actual jobs, but Charlie didn't say anything about that. He just called us into his office in the back room and told us that he's selling the store to a couple from Kansas who want to open a country diner.

"I'm sorry. I know this place means a lot to you guys," Charlie said. He's this huge Paul Bunyan kind of guy, who always seems to be staring off above your head when he's talking to you, but he seemed genuinely broken up. I still wanted to slap him silly, especially when he added, "We'll stay open for the next seven weeks, so the summer will be almost over by then, and I know you guys have to go back to school anyway."

He told us that we were both really good employees and he would be happy to give us references. "The new owners are probably going to need servers, and with tips, you'd make way more money than I can pay you anyway."

I was too numb and shocked to say anything before he went to go pick up Babe the Blue Ox, or whatever it is that Charlie does all day. But now it's just Alex and me, and I'm on a roll, all lathered up. The more I think about it, the angrier I become.

"What's going to happen to our regulars?" I demand, and Alex tilts his head.

We do have *some* frequent fliers. Not a lot, but there's Toupee Thom, who keeps a seventy-five-gallon tank in his office to calm his divorce clients. Then there's a sweet old couple who come in every six weeks to stock up on fish food and show off pictures of their grandkids in Baltimore. And one creepy dude, who looks like the mad scientist from an old black-and-white horror movie, is in here at least twice a month buying bulk quantities of firefish that he's probably using in some plot for world domination. Alex and I joke that he feeds the fish to the sharks that swim beneath his lair.

"All of their fish could starve without us," I say.

"I'm sure they'll just order stuff online or drive to Petco."

"And how is Creepy Dude going to take over the universe if he can't get fish here?"

"Molly—"

"Seriously, a country diner?" I say. "It's a hundred and five degrees. Who wants chicken and waffles? Like, if they wanted to open a sushi joint, maybe."

"That would certainly solve the problem of liquidating our inventory," Alex says, and I can't believe that he's making jokes about this. This is FishTopia!

"How are you not more upset about this?" I demand.

"I don't know, Mol." He shrugs. "This was a part-time gig to save up for school. I wasn't planning on making a career of it. Were you?"

What's wrong with wanting some stuff to stay the same? Why am I the only person in all of Coral Cove who isn't psyched to have everything be different?

"What about JoJo?" I ask.

"It sucks. But I'm sure she'll find something. Chuck is right; she'd make more money as a server."

"I just don't understand why—"

"Look, Charlie had to be losing money on this place forever. You can't really blame the guy. He's a businessman."

"But . . . but . . ." I'm so upset, I can't find the words. I'm furious that Charlie can shut us down, like the store doesn't matter, like we never mattered. He's never even here. What can he possibly know about it? I'm steamed at

Alex for being A-okay with it, because apparently this was just some stupid way for him to waste time until his real life begins after graduation. Even though she doesn't even work here, I'm mad at Elle for wanting to go to school in New York. It's like no one in the world cares about any of this stuff. Maybe most of all, I'm just angry with myself for being the way I am and not rolling along with changes the way everyone else does. Angry that I let my guard down and allowed myself to be a little bit happy here.

"But what, Mol?" Alex asks.

"This is, like, the only good, safe place, and now it's going away," I say, and then I'm even madder at myself for saying something so stupid. Alex must think I'm an idiot. Grabbing Pickles's crabitat, I race for the door.

Pickles crawls back into his shell in confirmation. *What's the point of all of this?* he seems to be saying.

"Molly, wai—" Alex reaches for my arm, but I storm past him and out the door. I jump on Old Montee and put Pickles in the basket.

No idea where I'm going, but I pedal so fast to get there that it hurts.

DAY 36 (TECHNICALLY EARLY MORNING ON DAY 37)

Banana Cream Coconut Cake

At three in the morning I have to pee (all that water), but on my way back I realize that Pickles isn't making all the usual noises he does at night, scratching the sides of his crabitat.

When I open up the tank, he's just lying there in the corner, kind of half in and half out of his shell. He's all curled up and dry, like the hands of an arthritic old man. Even before I reach in and put him into my palm, I know that he's dead.

Dead. Dead. Dead.

Little Pickles with the bright green shell and cute claws is dead. He led a modest life in his tiny tank, playing with his rocks and the dollhouse couch, crawling around in my hand, eating his pellet food and occasional fruit treats. He liked broccoli; he liked apples. He didn't have grand aspirations of leaving Coral Cove or going to the right college or getting on an upwardly mobile career track where he could "get serious about the biz." Once he spent an entire afternoon trying to flip over a pebble. His world was small, but he didn't realize it, he didn't know that he was utterly insignificant. None of that mattered; he died anyway.

Pickles clutched to my chest, I sink to the floor, boneless. I'm not sure when I start crying or how long that lasts. It feels like hours. Eventually I simply run out of tears, out of any emotion, really. I'm completely deflated, the defeated, shrunken skin of a popped balloon.

My whole universe becomes the cool hardwood of my bedroom floor, this dead hermit crab in my hand. Beyond my bedroom there are other alien worlds. Through the window it gets lighter and lighter, even with the blinds drawn. There are sounds in these worlds: V getting ready for a shift at Jaclyn's Attic. Shower running, doors opening and closing. Mom's voice and the cheery anchors from the *Today* show. "Good morning. I'm Matt Lauer, and this is *Today*!" Cars and birds and dogs whooshing and chirping and barking.

None of it affects me. All that stuff might as well be in a book or in some movie playing at the multiplex. It isn't a part of my world.

One of those otherworldly sounds—knocking. It takes a few seconds for me to realize it's someone at my bedroom door.

"Sweetie? Are you okay?" my mom asks. "I just wanted to make sure that you were ready for your appointment with Mrs. Peck at four."

And I remember that in one of those other, outside realms, I was supposed to have picked out my five dream colleges for my meeting with the counselor from Admissions Ace! today.

When I don't say anything, Mom hesitantly turns the knob and peeks in.

Seeing me on the floor, the *D*-word panic washes over her, and she rushes to my side, gets down on her hands and knees, and presses me against her amazing rack in a hug that is so tight, it's actually painful.

"Sweetie? What is it? What's wrong? Are you okay?"

"Pickles is dead." Even in my own ears, my voice sounds flat and detached and weird.

"Who?" Mom loosens her grip a little and holds my shoulders.

Opening my palm, I show her Pickles's shriveled little body.

"Oh no, your little pet lobster?" Relief practically floods her face, and that makes me angry. Pickles wasn't a person or even a dog or a cat who could love you back, but he was mine and he was important to me. Not just some lobster. He made me happy.

"He was a hermit crab."

"Oh, sweetie, I'm so sorry. What can I do?"

I shrug and say nothing, so my mom uses that smush-smush voice. "Let's get you a new crab. We can go today after work. Or maybe a gerbil like the ones you and Veronica used to have in grade school? That might be nice—"

"No, Mom, you can't just replace him with a freaking gerbil."

"You're right, sweetie." Mom is back to holding me too tightly. "He was very special."

I may be depressed, but I'm not an idiot. I know that to my mom (and, well, everyone), Pickles was a weird, creepy little thing she thought was a lobster. Mom didn't believe that Pickles was special, and she's only saying that to pacify me, and that's somehow worse than suggesting we get a gerbil. It's like she read all this in some "how to handle your depressed kid" book, which I'm sure she did. But it doesn't matter. Nothing matters.

"What's the point?" I say, but I'm not really talking to my mom. I'm not really sure who I'm talking to. "Everything good goes away, no matter what you do."

Mom is saying something about how that's not true, and her face is contorted with worry again like it was before she realized that Pickles was only a crab. But I can't really hear her. It's like she's back in that other world again—the one that's like a movie, or some book I read.

"I couldn't even keep a fucking hermit crab alive." I keep

right on talking to that unknown person. "V is right; all I do is make the people around me miserable."

"When did V say that?" Mom's jaw shifts, which is just great, because now she's going to yell at V and make things even worse.

"It doesn't matter."

"No, she should know better." She shakes her head. "That girl."

"Please don't say anything to V. I'm fine, I promise. You're right; he was just a crab."

"Honey."

"Really, I'm fine." I do my best to try to look fine. "Okay?"

"Okay." Mom dons this smile that is so big and forced, I wonder if her face will literally crack. Pushing herself up from her knees, she goes to the window and throws open the shade. The sun stings my vampire eyes.

"There, isn't that better?" she asks.

"It's great."

"Look how sunny it is out." She says this as if it's a good thing, as if it hasn't been suffocatingly hot for weeks and the light blazing through the window isn't already oppressive. "Why don't you get cleaned up and then come downstairs? Maybe tonight you can help me make peanut butter chocolate swirl cake? That's probably just what you need today!"

I can't look at her, and the sun hurts my eyes. I turn

back to Pickles still in my hand. This is hopelessness. Again I find myself wondering about my dad with his big hands. Maybe he would have understood how a hermit crab and a dumb fish store could mean a lot to me. Maybe his hands would have been big enough to hold me and keep me safe.

DAY 37 (THE REST OF IT)

Peanut Butter Chocolate Swirl Cake

S ince I was awake almost all night, I feel completely jus-tified staying in bed until I have to go to meet Mrs. Peck in the afternoon. But Mom has other plans. Around noon she knocks on my door.

"Sweetie, can you come to work with me today?" she says. "The receptionist called in sick, and we could use a little help."

"Do I have to?" I'm ninety-nine percent certain this is just Mom trying to keep an eye on me. "I'm pretty tired from last night."

"Just for a little while. I can give you a henna rinse or maybe braid your hair again—that looked so pretty the other night."

The thought of having to fake smile at Dye Another Day is absolutely nauseating, but maybe if I suffer through a few hours, she'll get off my back.

"Fine. For a little bit."

As I get up to get dressed, I see Pickles's crabitat and feel another gut punch. I couldn't bring myself to throw him away last night, so I ended up setting him back on the dollhouse couch and covering him with a blanket from the dollhouse bed. Pretty soon I'm going to have to throw him away before he starts to stink.

Dye Another Day is in the vaguely historic downtown part of Coral Cove. It's one of several brick shops and restaurants in this little roundabout by the movie theater. A few years ago Mom bought the vacant shoe store next door and expanded into the space—adding the spa area and creating a larger shampoo station.

V and I came for the grand reopening, and I'm sure I've come by a few times since, but it has been a while since I've actually looked around, and it's kind of shocking how nice the place is.

An inviting light blue awning hangs out front, and inside, the walls are a soft taupe. There are these big bold paintings of everyday objects—a blow-dryer, a stack of magazines, bottles of nail polish—I did a few years ago. I completely forgot that I told Mom she could use them. Maybe it's just the high-gloss frames, but they look better than I remember.

Also noteworthy, the place is packed.

There are five chairs, and all of them are constantly

filled with people getting color or cuts by Mom and her two other stylists—a twentysomething woman with a really intricate tattoo sleeve on her right arm, and then this incredibly dapper dude with highlights. Both of them look as though they belong in a much more exciting place than Coral Cove. Even with all the chopping going on, it's really clean; someone with a broom sweeps up the hair almost as soon as it hits the ground.

Everyone—the staff, the women Gram's age getting their rollers set, a young mom and her middle-school-age daughter, a business-suited guy on his lunch hour, some college girls home on break—is boisterous and optimistic and appears to be having a grand old time. And Mom is totally in her element. She knows everyone, and everyone knows her. They all share stories about their sig oths, their kids, their troubles with management at J&J. No one can get enough of Mom; she doesn't suggest that anyone replace their pet hermit crab with a gerbil. Even though I'm bummed and don't want to be here, I'm definitely impressed.

The receptionist actually is out, so I field a few calls, mostly just turning them over to whichever of the stylists is free to add the caller to the schedule. By the register, they're selling some flip-flops for people who come in for pedicures and don't bring their own sandals. Some pairs have little shells glued onto the strap for decoration. One is the exact green of Pickles's shell.

DAY 39

─ ∞ ─

Orange Pound Cake

The idea comes to me at four in the morning two days after Pickles dies.

I literally bolt upright in the sleigh bed.

I'm not supposed to go into FishTopia until the afternoon, but I have the keys, so it's not like I have to wait for anyone. I shower, get dressed, and then bike to the store as the sun is splintering the sky. Bonus: it's not even scorching this early in the morning, so I'm only moderately puddle-y.

By the time Alex comes in at ten, I've already done all the stuff we actually have to do—clean and check the tanks, open the register—but I've also swept and mopped the floors and washed what must have been a solid inch of dust off the front windows. (Alex was right the other day, you really could barely see inside.) Plus, in the back room supply closet, I found extra plastic letter and number stickers to fix the address on the door. And there are a couple cans of paint, so we can do something about the dingy walls. But now that I'm thinking about it, we should nix that and get something brighter, maybe a blue that will show off the fish tanks.

"Hey, Mol, I thought I was opening today," Alex says, reaching for the schedule behind the counter.

"You were; you are. I just wanted to get a head start."

Looking from me to the much cleaner store, to the cans of paint, Alex appears utterly baffled. "A head start on what exactly?"

"We're going to save FishTopia!" I announce.

"Save it from what? Chuck's selling the place," Alex says, and it's a little frustrating that he doesn't seem *at all* excited about my plans.

"Well, it's like you said the other day, Charlie is probably unloading the building because he's losing money here. So all we have to do is show him how much FishTopia can bring in, and then he'll see that he'd be crazy to let us—I mean it—go!"

"How do you plan on doing that? Creepy Dude and your mom's boyfriend can only buy so many fish."

Pinch of guilt again about ruining Mom's relationship with Toupee Thom, but I don't have time to dwell on that. I'll fix all that other stuff once I fix FishTopia.

I explain my idea to make a deal with Charlie. If we

can generate enough money in the next six weeks to cover mortgage payments and operating costs for the store, then he has to hold off on the sale. We can make flyers to try to get people in the doors, and we can start offering informational sessions where we teach people all about the joys of owning saltwater fish. Plus, the tanks and the fish really *are* beautiful, so if we rearrange the space, we could rent it for parties or events in the evening as another way to make money I tack on for good measure. Maybe there's no Mrs. Charlie . . . *yet*. "We could even have 'Under the Sea' themed dance nights!"

Alex looks really skeptical, and keeps repeating the phrase "I don't know, Mol" every time I slow down long enough for him to get a word in edgewise.

"We have to make it a place where people want to be— like my mom did with her salon."

"People need to get their hair cut. No one except Creepy Dude really needs fish."

"Don't you see? Yes, everyone needs a haircut, but no one *needs* to spend sixty bucks on it. No one *needs* a pedicure or massage or Mom's special shampoo, but my mom convinced people that they do. That's what we have to do."

"I don't know, Mol," he says again.

"That couple from Kansas isn't even coming back for another six weeks," I insist. "We can at least try."

"I guess."

"Great! I asked Charlie to come in, and he said he could stop by for a few minutes on the way to his kickboxing class."

"Charlie does kickboxing?" Alex smiles. This is what he took away from my whole spiel?

"Alex, focus. We have to get this place in order before one, so he can see the potential."

He picks up a roll of paper towels and the bottle of Formula 409. "Whatever's clever."

"Thanks." I'm touched. "It'll be great. You'll see."

"What happened to my store?" Charlie asks when he comes through the door two hours later, in boxing trunks and a stained wife-beater shirt.

"What do you mean?" I ask innocently. "We just cleaned it up a bit."

Cautiously he looks around like he's legitimately expecting a camera crew to jump out and announce he's been punked or something. "In the two years you guys have worked here, you've never done that."

"I know, I know, but that was before. Everything is going to be different now." Realizing I sound kind of manic, I slow down and tell him how we can turn it all around for FishTopia. I get to the part about having themed party nights to try to lure people in, when he cuts me off.

"Forget it, girl. I'm selling this joint."

Sensing that I'm losing him, I go in another direction.

"Charlie, you're a businessman, a great one—a visionary, almost." The flattery sounds ridiculously kooky, but Charlie stands a little straighter and he nods. Clearly I'm on to something. "You've always had a knack for finding diamonds in the rough and turning them around. You're like the next Jimmy Buffett."

"'Wasted away in Margaritaville'?"

"I think she means Warren Buffett," Alex offers.

"Him, too!" I agree enthusiastically.

"Well, that is true." Charlie nods again. Alex is fighting back a laugh, so he turns to finish cleaning the sea horse tank.

"Now, here's the thing: you were definitely on to something with FishTopia, but it just hasn't panned out yet. But it can. And it will, if you let us help you! This could end up being your biggest moneymaker yet!"

If Charlie were a cartoon character, his eyes would be replaced with throbbing dollar signs.

I explain my plan about him giving us six weeks to get things turned around. "Please, all I'm asking for is a chance to show you how lucrative this place can be. To prove how genius it was for you to go after the untapped saltwater fish market in central Florida."

Charlie presses his lips together and bunches his shoulders up to his neck. "I don't know—"

"You did say that the couple from Kansas wasn't coming back for six weeks, right?" Alex pipes in, and I feel my heart expand in my chest. "So really you're not risking anything. Worst-case scenario, we don't make the money and nothing changes for you. You sell to them, and we're all eating home-style meatloaf in the fall. No skin off your back at all."

"So what's in it for you two? Why do you care so much?"

"It's just a really great place!" I say. "And we all really like working here together."

Charlie wrinkles his nose, scoffs, "I must be paying too much."

"Anyway." I cut off that line of thought. "Like Alex said, there's really nothing for you to lose."

"I guess that's true," Charlie says.

I'm so excited, I give Charlie this really awkward hug, while he just kind of stands there and doesn't bend his giant lumberjack body into it. Eventually I feel his arms pat my back.

"You're not going to be sorry," I gush. "We're gonna make this place a gold mine."

"All I said was that if you make enough money, I'll *think* about it. I'm not promising anything."

Then Charlie heads out to his kickboxing class, and I turn to Alex. I'm grinning so hard that my cheeks hurt.

Smiling back, he shakes his head. "I guess we've got our work cut out for us."

"You're the best." I literally have to bite my tongue so I don't gush even more.

Maybe I should have gone out with him? Maybe we *are* a good fit? Maybe he's not immature, or maybe I'm equally immature, so it would work out. I push the thought aside when I remember him at the mall with V and Meredith Hoffman. Anyway, we've got a fish store to save! Once we get things squared away here, everything else will fall into place.

I just know it.

DAY 41

S'mores Explosion Cake

Even though it still feels like a million degrees in the store and we're probably high off paint fumes, it's definitely the best day I've had in a while.

Alex and I are painting FishTopia. At a hardware store a few strip malls away, we picked out this gorgeous aquamarine color that kind of looks like the ocean, and we got all the supplies. Charlie even said we could use money from the petty cash drawer. (Alex and I had no idea that this drawer even existed, which is probably a good thing, since I'm sure we would both have tried to justify lo mein as a legitimate operating expense.) Now we're back at the store, and Alex is doing broad stokes with the roller, while I'm coming in behind him with the brush to touch up any missed spots.

He brought a speaker for his iPhone, and we've got his music on shuffle. It's mostly fun stuff, like the White

Stripes and Mumford and Sons, that you can sing along to.

We're joking around, and it feels like things used to.

"I've got to hand it to you, Mol. Changing the color makes this place look a million times better," Alex says. He's wearing ripped jeans and an old Killers T-shirt, everything now completely peppered with paint. It's even in his hair.

Shit, he does look good.

"Yeah, I think we're really gonna pull this off." I want to say more about how much it means to me that he's helping with everything, how I'm super-grateful, but I'm not so good with earnest stuff like that.

One of Alex's band's songs comes on, and I recognize his voice right away even though I've never heard the song before. It must not be one of the things that he's tinkered around with on the roof.

"Is this the new Justin Bieber?" I ask.

Face turning adorably crimson, Alex mumbles that he didn't realize this song was on the playlist.

"Oh, you knew what you were doing." I giggle and point my paintbrush at him. "I can see right through you, mister."

"Well, what was I supposed to do? You won't come to any of our shows."

"I guess I'm a captive audience now, so show me what you got. And there had better be booty shaking."

"Mol . . ."

"Come on, please."

157

Finally he starts singing along.

His voice is so good—rich and kind of rough in this soulful way, a little like Eddie Vedder but with less word-swallowing—and the song is really great too. It's about a guy who can't get this girl he knows out of his head, so he keeps doing all this weird stuff to distract himself. He joins a Skee-Ball league and goes on a safari—but of course none of it works, and he starts seeing the girl's face on all the Skee-Balls, or the lion's mane reminds him of her hair. For a brief second I wonder if the song might be about me, since Chris said I was "Alex's Molly," but then I remember Meredith Hoffman and all the Hot Topic girls, and I realize I'm probably being ridiculous.

The chorus is really dorky but super-catchy, and I start singing along into my paintbrush like it's a microphone.

"I know that you don't care, but I see you
    everywhere.
 In a boat or with a goat,
 Flying high while eating pie,
 On a train with my aunt Jane,
 Just no way to escape, the beauty of your face."

I'm shaking my hair like a girl in an eighties rock video and belting out the words into my brush. Taking my right hand in his, Alex puts his other arm around my waist, and we start this kind of silly two-step somewhere between a slow dance and a square dance, where he's jostling me up and down.

When he tries to twirl me, my stupid feet get caught up in the tarp we put down to protect the floors. I tumble over backward and manage to pull Alex down on top of me.

It hurts, but we're both laughing so hard that I hardly notice. For a couple of seconds we stay like that, him on top of me on the floor. The whole situation is ripped from the reels of a sitcom, but not an old rerun, more like it's a new show, our show in high def.

"You've got paint on your face." Alex touches this spot on my check with his thumb. "I love this color; it totally matches your eyes."

All of a sudden we're not laughing anymore. Everything is quiet and feels important. His stomach rises and falls against my ribs as he breathes, and his breath smells a little like today's house special lo mein—ginger, garlic, and snow peas. This is the moment where he's probably going to kiss me. It might be our sitcom, but there's still a formula to these things. And I want him to, want to know once and for all how our lips would fit together. I'm starting to close my eyes in anticipation.

An image of Dr. B. and me listening to Pearl Jam in his office pops into my mind. At once everything is on a spin cycle in my head, and I'm confused and embarrassed.

As quickly as possible, I slide myself out from under Alex and try to stand up. My feet are still tangled in the tarp, so it takes a few minutes. Still on the floor, perched on his elbow, Alex stares up at me, this half smile on his face like he's extremely entertained by the whole thing.

"Come on, get back to work," I say in this strangely croaked voice.

Alex doesn't seem to mind that I'm ordering him around. He just picks up his roller and starts on another wall, humming under his breath the whole time.

Still flushed and sweaty, I go to the restroom and wash the paint off my face.

Shake my head to clear it.

I remember Dr. Brooks's cell number in my wallet and think about giving him a call. Whatever, he's my therapist. It's only natural that I've come to rely on him. He's helping me, and that's his job. He's got a fiancée anyway.

Calming inhale.

Exhale.

Probably best not to call; I have an appointment tomorrow, anyway. I can't wait to tell him about my plan to save FishTopia. Thinking about how proud of me Dr. B. is going to be, I actually feel a little giddy.

When I come out, JoJo is there for the evening shift, a bent look on her face as she takes in all our hard work.

"Looks amazeballs, right?" I ask.

JoJo shakes her head at Alex and me. "Why are you two A-hats messing with a good thing? We'll make a shitload more in tips if this place becomes a diner."

DAY 45

Old-Fashioned Carnival Funnel Cake

Sometimes Elle can be a lot to take, with all the yelling at total strangers and making you feel horrifically guilty for taking a shower that lasts longer than ninety seconds, but when I ask her to help hand out FishTopia flyers, she agrees in a heartbeat, even though she does still consider the place a prison for marine life.

As sweet as that was, I'm really wishing that I hadn't asked. She and I have been outside the store for twenty minutes, and all she's done is complain about how many trees died to make the flyers and how most of them are going to end up being thrown away, probably in the wrong recycling bin.

"And you couldn't have used the white paper?" she laments. "You had to do the extra environmental damage by using colored? It has to be separated because of the inks they use . . ."

Also, her mom is at work, and Elle couldn't find a babysitter for her brother, so Jimmy is scaring away any potential customers by repeatedly riding his bike into the side of Wang's Palace. People walking by keep giving us these looks of either raised-eyebrow horror or curled-lip disgust; it seems only a matter of time before someone puts a call in to Child Protective Services and we're all carted off.

A middle-aged woman comes out of the dry cleaner next to Wang's with multiple plastic bags of clothes draped over her forearm, and Elle swoops in, trying to hand her a FishTopia flyer.

"Once you get past the fact that the fish are being held against their will, the store really does have a lovely selection," she says.

The woman looks terrified.

Spinning around, she hurriedly clicks her key fob, and then practically dives into a Toyota minivan. Without even bothering to hang her dry cleaning on the hooks in the back, she speeds away.

Alex was supposed to be here half an hour ago, but there's no sign of him. When I check my cell phone again, there aren't any messages. I thought he wanted to save FishTopia too, so it stings that he's apparently blowing us off. And I can feel the downward cycling starting. Maybe I should call Dr. B.

"What the—" Elle's mouth drops open, and Jimmy briefly stops ramming into brick walls.

I follow their stares to a guy in a full-body blue-and-silver fish costume with metallic scales that shimmer in the sun. Through the window in the fish's fat-lipped mouth, Alex is flashing this huge smile. I start laughing harder than I can ever remember, and when he sees me in hysterics, it makes his grin even bigger.

With one flippered arm he waves at me. In the other one he's got a hundred-piece box of deep-fried fish nuggets. He holds them out to me, and I take one, even though greasy breading is the last thing in the world that I want to eat in this heat.

Vegetarian Elle of course brushes away his offer, but even she's grinning. "Don't you think that kind of sends the wrong message to potential customers," she quips. "You don't want them eating all the merchandise."

"How did you . . . Where?" I ask.

"On my way over I drove by Captain Snack's on Sunflower, and there was this guy standing on the side of the road in this getup, offering samples of their new extra crunchy. I'm a sucker for anything fried, so I stop, and I see the poor dude is literally dripping with sweat."

"Yeah, I can smell," says Elle, and I shoot her a look.

"He looked so miserable that I jokingly offered to buy the suit from him for twenty bucks." Alex is having trouble keeping a straight face. "And he just starts stripping, right there in the middle of the parking lot. The only thing he had on underneath was a pair of tightie whities!"

"Gross," says Elle, but I can't stop laughing.

"Ohmygod, I love it so much."

"He even threw in the samples." Alex holds up the box, and Jimmy comes by and takes a fistful. "Not gonna lie, I kinda understand; this thing is a freaking sauna."

I want to throw my arms around him, but my nerves and the grimy costume help keep my composure. Patting his right flipper, I volunteer to get him a soda from Wang's.

The three of us spend all day in front of FishTopia trying to lure people into the store and making sure Jimmy doesn't kill himself or anybody else. By six o'clock we haven't sold a single fish.

"It's because Alex smells like ass." Elle swats Alex's dorsal fin out of her face. "Who in their right mind would come here when you reek of fried death?"

Alex gestures toward Jimmy, who's furiously riding his bike in a circle in front of the store. "Please. People aren't coming in because they're terrified of getting run down by Dale Earnhardt Jr. over there."

"Guys, guys, let's not start blaming each other." I try not to let my panic show; I have to keep it together. "Eyes on the prize, right?"

Everyone mumbles agreement and looks at their feet, even Jimmy. Alex suggests that since the day is almost over and he has band practice that we close up for the night and pick it up tomorrow. Elle agrees, saying she has to get home and feed Jimmy something that isn't "genetically modified fish product."

They both offer me rides, but I say I'll take my bike, so they pile into their cars and drive away.

When they've gone, I go back into the store. We got some extra fans, so it's actually pleasant. Really, it looks so good since we fixed it up. The hum of the pumps makes it feel like the aquamarine walls are moving, gentle waves. And with all the tanks and lights cleaned, you can really see the amazing beauty of the fish. Those brilliant yellows and oranges, electric blues and greens, colors you can't believe occur in nature. And the bizarre ways some of these creatures are put together—with eyes on the tops of their heads or on antenna. Tentacles drifting in the water, an iridescent glow from the eel tank.

"Don't worry, guys," I tell them. "I'll find some way to save you; I promise."

DAY 46

Rainbow Ribbon Cake

Sometimes on *Golden Girls* a guest star shows up, and the studio audience gasps and claps because it's some person everyone knew in the eighties—maybe another big actor, or a politician or singer who was huge back then. I never have any idea who the person is, so the whole thing is utterly lost on me, a joke I'm not in on.

Anyway, nine times out of ten, the guest star rings the doorbell, and Sophia (sometimes Dorothy or Blanche, but never Rose) answers, and then slams the door in the guest star's face as soon as he or she says "Hi," because it's someone she had a falling-out with in the old country or New York or wherever.

It's the one time I don't absolutely adore the show or feel safe watching it. When the audience reacts to the stranger, it's this creepy reminder that there is a whole universe outside of the loud floral prints and wicker furniture in the girls' Miami house.

This is exactly how it feels when I come home from another fruitless day of trying to save FishTopia with Alex and Elle, and find Dr. Brooks in the model-home living room, chatting with my apron-clad mother and sipping a glass of red wine.

Dr. B. on my couch . . . with my mom.

Seeing him completely out of context like this is so jarring that I don't even recognize him for a few seconds. My eyes just send a message to my brain that there is some good-looking, clean-shaven guy in jeans and a polo shirt. Even when the synapses start firing and I make the connection that this is *my Dr. B.*, I kind of want to pull a Sophia and slam the door in his face. He doesn't belong in the world on this set, where my mom is wearing a breezy summer dress under her apron, where the big family portrait of the four of us before Dad died haunts the dining room table.

No, this is all wrong. Dr. B. and I have a different show, and it has a specific set—his office.

When they see me, Mom and Dr. B. both stand up.

"Wha—" I say, instead of "hello" or any sentiment a normal person might express in this situation. Feeling that my jaw is actually hanging open, I shut my mouth.

"Oh, hi, sweetie. Guess who I ran into at the grocery store on my way home from the salon?"

Probably she means it as a rhetorical question, but I go ahead and answer: "Dr. Brooks?"

Dr. B. gives a strained chuckle and tells me, "Yep, you got it!" Which makes me feel even stupider.

He reaches out to give me this weird quick hug. And yeah, I might be pretty damn confused about what's going on, but I can't help but notice that Dr. B. feels super firm and kind of muscle-y under his shirt. And he smells really, really good again!

Then there's a splinter of a second when the three of us stand there, before my mom must realize that running into someone at Coral Cove Food Mart and that someone drinking pinot noir on your living room sofa requires a few more steps.

"Since you've been spending so much time with Dr. Brooks, I thought it might be nice if we got to know him a little better too, so I asked if he might want to join us for dinner."

I freeze. I never did tell my mom about my extra sessions with Dr. Brooks—the ones he said he'd wave the co-pay on—and I have this moment of panic, thinking that she found out somehow or he told her. Not that I'm doing anything wrong or anything, but Mom likes to stay on top of my appointments and stuff.

"Oh," I say. No one mentions the extra appointments.

"I'm never one to pass on a home-cooked meal." Dr. B. smiles, and it really does seem like the bad dialogue of a TV series. "With my fiancée in Miami during the week, I pretty much live on takeout."

Up until Mom started this cake craze, she used to take great pride in pointing to this lame refrigerator magnet that V and I once got her that reads: *The house specialty is reservations.* But now Mom is going on about some new Bolognese she wanted to try, and giving Dr. B. this doting smile as if she were Julia Child herself bringing five-star cuisine to the masses.

"Well," she says. "I'm just delighted you could make it, Glen."

Glen? Glen!

On Dr. B.'s office door, there *is* a sign with his full name, and of course it was on his diplomas, so somewhere in the back of my mind, I knew he had a first name. But hearing my mom use it is so messed up.

Mom excuses herself to check on the pasta, and I look at the spot on the couch next to Dr. B. where she was sitting. There's also a red tulip chair (one of the home stager's "dramatic accent pieces") off to the side, and I'm not really sure which place is the most appropriate to sit. Remembering how we sat next to each other when we watched *Say Anything . . .* in his office, I go with the couch.

"So it's okay that I'm here, right?" he asks. "You seem uncomfortable."

"Yeah, it's . . . surprising, I guess."

"Sorry about that." He shakes his head lightly. "Let's just say your mom can be pretty, um, persistent."

A kick in my chest. He's only here because Mom attacked him in the produce aisle; of course, that makes complete sense. Mom's whole "everyone can be a client" and "never take no for an answer" shtick. It must show on my face that I'm hurt or something, because Dr. B. lightly touches my forearm—and there's a weird nervous electricity.

"Not that it isn't lovely to see you, Molly," he says, and even though he's probably required to say it for his job, I instantly feel lighter. "And it is nice to see you in your natural setting—like field research."

"Well, anything in the name of science, *Glen*."

"Why, thank you, *Miss Byrne*." He smiles kind of slowly, and looks right into my eyes, and I actually feel that same jolt of something even without touching.

The front door swings open, and immediately I slide a few inches away from him and toward the arm of the couch as V clomps in. Even though she's been at work at Jaclyn's Attic all day, she's still effervescent in a long pastel maxi dress and chunky wood necklaces and bracelets.

Seeing us on the couch, she raises her perfectly shaped left eyebrow in a question.

"You must be Veronica." Dr. B. stands and extends his hand. "I'm Glen Brooks, Molly's therapist."

"So you do house calls now?" V raises her eyebrow even

higher, a nonverbal way of asking me what's going on.

"Mom bumped into him at the grocery store and brought him home for dinner, " I say.

"Like a stray dog?" V asks.

"I promise, I don't have fleas," Dr. B. says.

The three of us laugh a little, but it seems more out of nervousness than genuine amusement.

Twenty minutes later we're all eating pasta with a "robust" (Mom's word) meat sauce that would be delicious if it weren't seven thousand degrees outside. Mom went all out. There's garlic bread where you can see that she used actual chopped garlic—not just garlic salt—and a salad with peppery dressing and caramelized onions.

"Really just delicious," Dr. B. keeps saying.

"I'm so glad you like it." Mom is practically sparkling. "The recipe is from Tabitha Hitchens, the woman who wrote *A Baker's Journey* and started the 100 Days of Cake challenge—Molly probably told you about that. . . ."

"Oh yes, she's definitely mentioned it," Dr. B. says lightly, and I look away.

I did tell Dr. B. about Mom's cake making, but I was so frustrated by the whole thing, I *may* have used a lot of expletives and the phrase "How am I the crazy one?" more than once.

"We're having her Rainbow Ribbon Cake for dessert,"

Mom continues. "I'm not sure how it's going to taste, but it looks lovely."

"I can't wait to give it a try," says Dr. B.

My sister just shakes her head above her spaghetti. If we were seated closer to each other, I'd totally kick her under the table.

"Veronica." Dr. B. turns toward her. "I meant to say something about it when you came in, but your jewelry is really unique."

"Thanks." V looks up and smiles; flattery will get you everywhere with that girl. "I work at this boutique on Marigold Drive, and they have some cool stuff." She twists the wood bracelet around her wrist. "I was actually the one who ordered it for the store. Jaclyn—the owner—knows that I want to get in to fashion merchandising, so she's started letting me help with stuff like that."

"Really?" Mom asks. This is totally news to me, too. Since when does V want to go into fashion merchandising? What *is* fashion merchandising? And V is fifteen. Even Mrs. Peck would tell her that she doesn't have to worry about "extra-currics" until junior year.

"Yeah, Jaclyn says I have my finger on the pulse of today's youth or something."

"Well, that's just wonderful." Mom smiles. I don't think she and V have been on great terms since V got grounded. "Why didn't you say something earlier?"

V gives her famous eye roll and mumbles something about how she tried.

"I'll have to start coming by the store more often," Mom says.

"Actually, the anniversary of the day I met my fiancée is coming up," says Dr. B. "Maybe I can come by and have you help me pick out a present for her?"

I wonder if he's just being nice. Let me rephrase that. I sincerely hope he's just being nice. I know it's probably mean and petty and all, but it's still driving me nuts that V apparently hangs out with Alex; I'm not sure I could handle her being all buddy-buddy with Dr. B., too.

"Sure." V nods. "If you tell me what she likes and bring in a picture, I can totally help you find something."

"Perfect."

"How did you meet your fiancée?" Mom asks. "I always love to hear about that when the brides come into the salon to get their hair done."

"It's kind of a cute story, really. Whitney and I were in the same line at the DMV, and we just struck up a conversation." When Dr. B. talks about her, his face just kind of brightens, and it's almost like he's a whole different person.

"Oh, that is so sweet," Mom gushes.

"On our third date I finally admitted that the other line had been significantly shorter, but I was willing to spend extra time at the DMV if it meant I got to meet her."

"Aww." Now even V is charmed.

Their story is romance-novel perfect. None of this awkward high school stuff; no gal disappointing a guy by being different than he thought she would be.

Dr. B. talks a little about how it's hard with Whitney gone during the week but adds, "I'm really proud of her. She had her first big investigative report on this week, and it went really well. They're thinking of giving her a regular feature."

All at once I'm struck by the *need* to save FishTopia. Not just for Alex and the fish, but so Dr. B. can be proud of me, too.

The rest of dinner goes on, and I start to get that floating feeling that I'm not really there but hovering over everyone. What a nice group. The mom who's still hot enough to rock her kids' clothes, two teen girls (one of them a knockout, the other okay), their polite houseguest. Everyone following the correct table manners.

"You know, Mrs. Byrne, it is absolutely remarkable how much you look like your daughters in that picture." Dr. B. points to the portrait over the table, and Mom blushes and thanks him.

Turning to me, he asks, "Is that from the dollhouse your father made you?"

"Wha?"

"The doll in the picture." He nods up at the little figure

I'm holding, which had been just one of the photographer's props to get a little girl to smile.

Mom cocks her head, and V rolls her eyes so hard, it's got to hurt.

"Oh . . . I . . ." There's absolutely nowhere good for me to take this sentence.

"That so never happened," V says incredulously. "We have a whole room upstairs of all the toys our parents coulda/woulda/shoulda given us. Dad *never* gave us anything good."

"I . . ." Dr. B. looks at me.

"Whatever. Are we done playing family time? I've got stuff to do." V pushes back from the table and storms off.

"You're still grounded." Mom is on her feet, like she might go after her.

"Fine. I've got stuff to do in my room," V calls as she hurries up the stairs.

All perfect and calm, Mom turns to Dr. B. again. "I'm sorry about that. Teenagers can be . . . difficult."

"No, Mrs. Byrne, I'm the one who should be apologizing," says Dr. B. "Molly's sessions are confidential, so it was wrong of me to ask in the first place."

Neither one of them really has anything to apologize for. I'm probably the one who should say I'm sorry. But I can't even look at them.

Everyone is really quiet until Dr. B. finally invents

some early-morning appointment and thanks my mom for the delicious meal but says he should probably be going. Mom doesn't even try to make him take a piece of Rainbow Ribbon Cake.

Later that night, Mom knocks on the door when I'm drawing a picture of Pickles on my phone with some dumb painting app.

"Come in."

"Sweetie." Sitting on the edge of the sleigh bed, she takes the phone out of my hand so I have to look at her. "I'm sorry I blindsided you by inviting Dr. Brooks over," she says, brushing my mouse-poop hair off my forehead.

"It's fine."

"He's very nice." She hesitates briefly. "But do you honestly think that he's helping you?"

"*Yes*, Mom." Unbelievable. She's the one who insisted I go see Dr. Brooks in the first place! Now V makes one stupid comment, and Mom is convinced that he's the worst shrink since Hannibal Lecter. "Don't I seem, like, a million times better than before?"

"Well, you have seemed pretty happy this last week or so."

"See, there you go."

She looks like she wants to say a whole lot more, but eventually she just sighs and nods, then asks, "Want a piece of cake?"

DAY 48

〜

Italian Cream Cake with Mascarpone

I'm still so completely, utterly mortified by dinner the other night that I don't even want to go to my appointment. But since I gave Mom the bad baby routine about how much Dr. B. is helping me, attendance seems mandatory.

My stomach is all bunchy, and I'm crushing the Admissions Ace! stress ball in my hand when I hesitantly walk into his office.

From behind his desk Dr. B.'s lips are pressed into a closed-mouth expression somewhere between disappointed and doting—the kind of look you give a sweet puppy that took a dump on your ten-thousand-dollar imported rug.

"So it seems you might have been misleading me about a few things," he says as I take a seat on the couch.

"I'm so sorry." If the stress ball in my hand were a lump of coal, it would be a diamond by now.

"What's up with that?"

"I don't know," I say, but Dr. B. is looking at me for more of an answer.

"I want you to think about it, Molly." He's back to that serious shrink tone he had during our first few months, before the music and the movies. "Why do you think you would make up memories about your father?"

I shrug. There are spiderwebs in the air-conditioning vent in the floor; I'm staring it at intently enough to notice. "I guess I just don't remember much about him at all . . ."

"And you feel bad about that?"

"Yeah. It's like, just because I don't know that we always ate grilled cheese on Wednesdays or whatever doesn't mean I don't miss him."

"Of course not," Dr. B. says, and explains that a lot of times people miss an absent parent, even if they never met that person. "It can be a huge void that takes years to get over."

"I wonder how stuff might be different if he were still around. Like, maybe it would have helped balance things out at home with Mom."

"This is all very normal, Molly." Dr. B. nods. "And this is the kind of stuff that you can feel safe discussing here— without worrying about hurting your mom's feelings or anything like that. But I'm still not quite sure why you would make stuff up for me."

Another me apology.

"For therapy to be effective, you really have to be brutally honest with me and with yourself."

"I guess you just kept asking questions about my parents, and you seemed to really like it when I talked about my dad. And I wanted you to like me."

"So you were telling me things that you thought I wanted to hear?"

"Maybe."

"Well, you have to stop doing that, Molly Byrne." He smiles. "And don't worry. Nothing you can tell me will make me not like you."

"For serious?"

"Of course."

The muscles in my stomach loosen, and I stop my assault on the stress ball.

"So nothing but honesty from now on," he continues. "Deal?"

"Deal."

He asks about V and our relationship, saying that she seems to "have a lot of pent-up anger" directed at me.

"I got her grounded a few weeks ago, and she's mad about that," I say. "I think I did it sort of on purpose, too."

"Let's talk about that, shall we?" he asks.

And almost everything I tell him is true.

DAY 52

Canadian Maple Leaf Cake

We are getting completely desperate!

It's been two weeks since I vowed to save FishTopia, and we're nowhere near making enough money to show Charlie that this place is viable.

Alex and Elle and I are outside the store trying to flag down customers again, but by now people have lost all interest. They've all already seen Alex in his fish getup, and it's yesterday's news. In fact, I'm pretty sure people have started actively going out of their way to avoid us now.

A kind-faced elderly woman with a walker approaches the store, and Alex waves a friendly flipper toward her.

"Get a real job, you bum," she spits as she turns and roll/walks away.

Closing my eyes, I try one of Dr. B.'s calming exercises.

A flipper on my shoulder: Alex.

"Maybe it's time we grab some Wang's and regroup inside," he says, and I realize I haven't had anything to eat since left-over cake for breakfast.

Elle nods. "It's about time I try this legendary lo mein you two are always going on about."

"Yeah, we should check on Jimmy anyway," I say.

Elle's brother had been so complainy about the heat that we said he could go inside and luxuriate in all the fans. That was about an hour ago, plenty of time for him to have permanently traumatized the fish.

As I'm pulling open the door to Wang's, I notice a giant stash of about fifty of our flyers (on colored paper!) in the outside garbage can, just as Elle predicted. To her credit she says nothing about it and only gives me the slightest side-eye.

"What we need is something big," I say as I push myself up to sit on the counter back at FishTopia. Elle and Alex follow, and we hand out the noodles and chopsticks.

"People love free stuff," Elle offers. "Maybe you could do 'buy ten fish, the next one is free'?"

"We actually already have something like that," I say.

"We do?" Alex asks, mouth full of lo mein.

"Yeeessss." I swat his shoulder. "Haven't you ever given out one of our loyalty cards?"

Reaching over him, I pull out one of the little fish-shaped

punch cards from the register. I think they're actually from a fishing supplies shop Charlie used to own in Okeechobee, because the fish looks more like a freshwater bass than anything tropical, and it has a big hook in its mouth. Also you can pretty much make out the old address that's been crossed out with black Sharpie.

"What d'ya know?" Alex laughs. "Creepy Dude might have already taken over the world if he'd known about this promotion."

"That's the problem." I sigh. "We have too few loyal customers for anything like that to work."

We all chew in agreement.

Nothing is coming together at all; we are the opposite of a movie get-in-shape montage.

"What about an app?" Elle tries again. "You know 'FishTopia Yourself.'"

"What exactly would that entail?" asks Alex.

"Like, gills on your sides and turning your arms into flippers?" I suggest.

"Maybe?" Elle looks less sure of herself.

"It sounds naughty." Alex winks. "Maybe the three of us could have a little FishTopia together, like in Molly's dream?"

"For the last time, it wasn't *that* kind of dream." I laugh. "And besides, everyone knows you should never FishTopia on a full stomach."

Alex suggests that we start a blog with funny captions

under pictures of various fish. "Like LOL cats," he says, adding in a ridiculous voice that sounds more extraterrestrial than feline, "'I can haz cheezburger.'"

Elle's brow creases into her righteous-indignation face. "Those sites are so disrespectful to the animals."

"I was not aware of that." Alex flashes me his crooked smile, and I shove a bunch of lo mein into my mouth to stifle a laugh. "Please go on."

"It's about fur dignity. If dogs and cats could read and write English, why would we assume they'd have atrocious grammar and spelling? And don't even get me started on the Chick-fil-A cows. It just doesn't make any sense."

"So this has been an issue with you for some time?" Alex continues. "That these animals, after working so hard to become literate, are picked on for petty mistakes?"

"Exactly."

Alex looks at me.

"Hey," I say. "I'm just thrilled we finally got her to come into the store."

"Fine, fine," Elle says. "I'll look up LOL fish."

Whatever comes up on her iPhone makes Elle all squirmy and fire-engine red.

"It already exists?" Alex asks. "Of course. The idea's a freaking gold mine."

"Not exactly." Elle chokes.

"What?" I grab her phone and start cracking up.

Leaning over my shoulder, Alex takes in the crazy shots of naked men, pouting their lips like trout and holding various fish in front of them.

"How is this a thing?" I say between gasps of laughter.

"That, ladies and gentlemen, is what it means to Fish-Topia yourself!" says Alex.

"Yeah," Elle says. "This would definitely be *one* way to get people in the door."

"Or send them away screaming!" I add.

Our hysterics draw Jimmy from the bowels of the store, and he stares at the three of us as if we were FishTopia-ing ourselves right there in front of him. For once he's quiet and still and somewhat normal. "What's so funny?"

"Nothing." Elle shoves her phone back into the pocket of her shorts. "Go back to torturing the sea horses."

"You guys are weird." Jimmy gives a dramatic shrug, pulls up his sleeves Popeye style, and races with his head down toward the back of the store.

"On that note, is it okay if I hop out a little early?" Alex stands and starts gathering up the stray noodles from his carton of lo mein.

Since technically he's the only one of us who's supposed to be working this afternoon, it's bizarre. It's also the second time this week that he's asked if he could leave early without giving any actual explanation. In the entire two years we've worked here together, he's never done that before. Maybe he's the one sneaking out for therapy now?

"Band practice?" I ask.

"No." His eyes dart from me to the floor and then the wall. "Just meeting a friend for coffee."

One of the Hot Topic girls? Meredith Hoffman? Chris Partridge and my sister? I remember Dr. Brooks saying Alex was too immature for me to waste time on. Remember Dr. B. saying that nothing I could tell him would make him not like me.

"Sure," Elle says. "We can hold down the fort."

"Now, you ladies promise not to get your FishTopia on with any other guys while I'm gone, okay?"

"I don't know." Elle does this little shimmy with her shoulders that is probably supposed to be mock sexy. It's definitely mock something. "Sometimes a gal's gotta do what she's gotta do."

Chuckling and shaking his head, Alex gathers his backpack and gives us a warning to keep Jimmy away from the starfish tank. Last week he got one stuck on his face.

When Alex is gone, Elle turns to me with this look that's all conspiratorial, like we share some juicy secret. She just sits there waiting for me to say something.

"What are you all psycho killer about?" I finally ask.

"He's sooo nice, Mol. I mean, meat in his lo mein aside, he's such a great guy."

"Yeah, he has his moments," I say, but I'm still thinking

how weird it is that he took off. Even when it wasn't his turn to stay late at the store, he almost always used to help me close up.

"And he's sooooo completely in love with you, it isn't even funny."

Alex's Molly. I love this color; it totally matches your eyes.

"Maybe he was a little into me before." I shrug and try to act like this absolutely doesn't bother me at all. "I think he's seeing someone now. Did I tell you I saw him with Meredith Hoffman a few weeks ago?"

I want to add that V was there too, and that she gave him a hug, but it would require mentioning Chris Partridge and having to go through all that again.

"Meredith 'Hooters girl' Hoffman? Puh-leese." Elle seems legitimately outraged. "What is it with these great guys dating completely vapid girls? There's more to a woman than how she fills out a tank top."

Even as she's saying this, I realize that Elle, herself, is wearing something kind of tank-top-esque. She doesn't fill it out like V or Meredith Hoffman would, but it looks cute and less aggressively confrontational Earth Mother than her usual getup.

"I like the new look, BTW," I say.

Elle blushes and bows her head. "I was just trying some-thing different. You know, it's been so hot lately."

"Yeah."

"Anyway, even if Alex is hooking up with Meredith, it's only because you've been giving him the runaround forever. I'm sure if you curl your little finger, he'll come running back. He's a good guy; he deserves someone like you."

"Like what? Someone who can't decide if she's going to get dressed in the morning? Someone who has a panic attack every time she hears the word 'graduation.' Yeah, that'll make him happy for sure."

"Why do you do that?" Elle asks.

"Do what?"

"Always put yourself down. I think you're awesome, and I should know. Isn't therapy supposed to help you with stuff like that?"

Why the hell is everyone who was on my case to start seeing a psychologist in the first place now jumping down my throat about Dr. Brooks not doing what they think he should be doing?

"Whatever," I say, amazed how much I sound like V. "Dr. B. likes me no matter what I say to him, which is apparently way more than I can say for you or anyone else."

"I'm just sayi—"

"Look, you literally have no idea what you're talking about, so give it a rest."

Elle opens her mouth like she's going to say something, but I shake my head. A few seconds later she starts to say something else, and I shake my head again.

Somewhere in the store there's this wolf-man howl that would be really terrifying if we hadn't already heard it three times today and didn't know exactly what happened.

Elle still looks like she wants to say something, but settles on an exasperated sigh.

"Just go get your idiot brother out of the suckerfish tank," I say.

DAY 53

Fruit Compote Cake

Alex's band is no longer called the Flaming Dantes or Headless Naked Ken, or any of the various other names they've tried out in the eighteen months since they formed. Currently they have no name.

"So you're called 'No Name,' like some paintings are 'Untitled'?" I ask. We're back on Elle's front porch again, all worn out after another-less-than successful day at FishTopia.

"No, we decided we're just not going to have a name for a while," Alex says.

"How can you not have a name?" Elle asks.

"Our music is what's important, so we're going to let *it* name *us*." Alex sounds serious, almost reverent. "One day when we're jamming, the name will come to us and we'll know."

"Like how some Native American tribes renamed people

as adults, based on things they had done in their lives?" Elle asks.

Alex nods enthusiastically. "Yeah, I think so."

Do the Hot Topic girls find this deep? Does Meredith Hoffman? To me the whole thing sounds patently ridiculous and pretentious and reminds me of the reason I dropped out of advanced art. Maybe this is what Dr. B. means about Alex being immature. I'm kind of glad he's probably got a girlfriend and the unnamed band can be her problem.

"We're playing Scream House next month," he adds. "The name might come to us right then; you guys should totally come."

"Of course," Elle volunteers us.

I just nod, remembering how upset he was when I didn't make the last show. No doubt the new girl will be there front and center.

"Wait, I got it!" Alex shouts with so much excitement, I expect a cartoon lightbulb to turn on above his head. "We should have a benefit concert for FishTopia—a battle of the bands to save the fish!"

"Ohmygod!" Elle screeches. "That's brilliant!"

"We could have it right on the FishTopia roof and charge, like, ten or fifteen bucks admission. Maybe get a keg, have some food. We can make sooo much money!"

Seeing as there is a ginormous sign on the door to the roof proclaiming that no one is allowed up there, I can't imagine

Charlie will be thrilled by the idea. And while Elle's mom might be too busy doing whatever it is she does to care, my mom certainly isn't going to go for the whole beer thing—oh, and by the way, I have no idea how Alex plans to get a keg. Visions of me fleeing Chris Partridge's party spring into my brain. "I don't know . . ."

"Oh, come on, Mol. This could be the service component for your college applications!" Elle gushes. "Like that kid who raised money for his friend who had the zip-line wipeout. This could be your zip-line kid!"

"What—"

"Think about it: 'Girl saves thousands of evicted fish'!" Elle continues. "That would at least get you into FIU!"

"I'm not trying to save FishTopia so I can get into college," I scoff.

"Fine," Elle says. "But you know it's a good idea."

"Well, it's definitely the best idea we've had so far," I conceed.

"It's pure genius, if I do say so myself," Alex jokes, and then starts explaining how he's gotten to know the guys from Sinking Canoe pretty well, and if they've all recovered from mono, they'll probably play. "And I think we could get Terminal Bitch and maybe even McLovin, although they're completely blowing up right now, so you never know."

Elle runs inside to get a notebook, and we start jotting down things we'll need and potential costs.

"What if we had a tarot card reader?"

"Someone doing henna tattoos?"

"A cotton candy machine?"

"We can use blue Christmas lights to set the mood," says Alex.

"And Molly can come up with an image for the event," says Elle. "Like you did for our swim team shirts a few years ago."

Alex cocks his head at me.

"Yeah, Molly's a really talented artist," Elle explains.

Shrugging, I say that I like to draw and paint, which used to be true. Back in junior high, art was always my favorite class. But then in high school the only kids taking advanced art were the kind of Hot Topic girls who used to come in and flirt with Alex. They were always explaining the deeper meaning of their projects—how the burning magazine represented the objectification of women, or a giant creepy rabbit was somehow about apartheid in South Africa. I started to feel really stupid, because my stuff was just what it was—a flower was a flower, not female sexual liberation. So I dropped it like I dropped everything else.

"That's awesome." Alex nods. "That can really tie everything else together."

Our to-do list gets longer and longer, and we divide up the tasks.

It's really hard not to get caught up in the excitement.

DAY 57

∞

Wakey-Wakey Eggs and Bac-y Cake

Over the last few nights, I stayed late at the store for hours sketching a logo for the event.

It was hard to decide what to draw, but in the end I went with the fish that Alex and I had compared to the Golden Girls a few weeks before—idol fish for Blanche, brown clown goby for Dorothy, Rose as a dottyback, and Sophia as a black bar soldierfish (we thought the massive eyeballs sort of looked like her glasses)—as sort of an inside joke.

Above the logo I wrote "Rock the Tanks" in chunky block letters and then filled those in with little fish.

I think it came out really well, but when the little bell on the door chimes and Alex comes in to take over for JoJo, I'm all nervous to show him.

He gets this weird look on his face and doesn't say anything at first.

"You got talent, CCH!" JoJo proclaims, turning away from Jerry Springer interviewing a man who wants to marry his dog.

"Thanks," I say.

"Cromwell still the art teacher?" she asks.

"Yeah." Ms. Cromwell, with her paint-spattered smocks and crazy hoop earrings. When I told her I was dropping art last year, she gave me this really sad once-over and asked, "Is there anything I can do to change your mind?" I told her there wasn't, and she promised she would always keep a space open for me.

"Cromwell was cool," says JoJo.

"Yeah, she really is."

"This is amazing, Mol." Alex finally says something. "I had no idea you could do stuff like that."

Feeling myself blush, I turn away and mumble, "I'm just full of surprises."

DAY 61

Raspberry Chocolate Swirl Cake

Elle, Alex, and I spend the whole day plastering flyers all over town (and at least a half hour pulling staples out of Jimmy's fingers; the kid really is a little masochist). When I get home, I practically devour the cake Mom has made, even though I suspect the recipe called for unsweetened chocolate but she improvised with Hershey's.

For once, I feel good.

DAY 63

Enchanted Black Forest Cake

Elle wants to go to the theater tonight to see a new documentary all about the evils of commercial farming. Remembering Dr. Brooks joking that I needed to get out and see a movie with friends, I actually laugh.

"What's so funny?" Elle asks, but I just shrug. We are *not* going to get into the whole Dr. B. thing again.

I try to convince her that we should see this new cheesy rom-com with one of the women from *Scandal* instead. It wouldn't normally be my thing, but the *Hot Tub Time Machine* guy from *Say Anything...* is the male lead, and it would be fun to tell Dr. B. about it at our next session.

Finally we decide to see both movies and make a night of it.

"We can sneak into the second movie after the first, like we used to," Elle offers.

"Definitely." When we were in junior high, we used to do that all the time, and it feels good to think of doing it again, like the old Molly is back in business.

Elle drives (with AC!). At the theater we get cherry Slurpees and a giant tub of popcorn that probably has a week's worth of calories, then we pump the weird liquid butter on top of that.

We buy tickets to the seven forty-five *A Bridesmaid, Always* and plan to sneak into the ten p.m. showing of *E-I-E-I No*, but Elle is trying to convince me that it might be better to see the depressing doc first. "That way we can totally veg out with the rom-com afterward."

"I don't know," I counter. "The times work out much better if we see the farming thing second." This is true; also, we might be tired and just bail on the documentary entirely, but I keep that part to myself.

As we're debating this, one of the theaters lets out, and a wave of people, all squinting in the light and excitedly talking about some action flick, swell toward us.

Smack in the middle of the group is Alex . . . and my sister.

They're not with Chris or Meredith Hoffman or any of the other people they were with the last time I saw them together. It's very clearly only the two of them . . . at the movies . . . on a Friday night . . . standing so close, their arms are almost touching. Alex leans down so she can tell him something in his ear over the noise of the crowd, and he smiles and nods.

My brain starts doing these rationalization gymnastics. Maybe they came separately and ran into each other? Maybe he's trying to recruit her to do something for his band? Maybe he's . . . Maybe she's . . .

No, maybe nothing.

They are on a date. The datiest date that ever was. The kind of date Dr. Brooks went on in high school when he got to second base during *Say Anything* . . . .

My sister and Alex are on a date.

Elle sees it too and gives me this super-pained look. I pull her arm, and we duck behind the condiments cart so Alex and V won't see us as they walk past.

"So it's V he's been sneaking off with!" Elle announces like some sort of Captain Obvious. "Wow."

I want to shrug it off, like I did when I thought he might be seeing Meredith, but I can't—I can hardly move. It's like someone scooped out my chest with a melon baller, just this horrible empty ache.

"That's sooo not right." Elle is getting all riled up like she usually does when someone with an SUV throws a plastic water bottle out the car window. "I'm going to give them a piece of my mind."

She's about to charge over, but I hold her hand and shake my head. What good would it do? What could it possibly change? I'll just be that pathetic little depressed girl crying in front of everyone again.

"But how could they do that to you?" she asks.

I shrug. I don't want to open my mouth, because if I do, I will just scream and I might not be able to stop.

"Should we get out of here?" Elle asks, and I nod.

We don't say a word the entire ride home. Some dumb Taylor Swift song comes on the radio, but we don't bother to change it.

Fuck, I am a Taylor Swift song!

There's a guy who loves hanging out with me, and I love hanging out with him. I was too stupid and scared to take it to the next level. And now he's dating the head cheerleader. (V's not on the cheerleading squad per se, but she did mention something about wanting to audition for the dance team next year.)

She's the pretty, fun girl he deserves; she even has my eyes.

"Do you want me to come in?" Elle asks when she pulls in front of the model home with its completely non-model family. "I could eat whatever cake your mom made today?"

I shake my head. Elle clearly wants to say something, maybe how she knew I liked Alex all along and should have said yes when he asked me out, even if he was kind of kidding. Maybe how my sister is a horrible vapid boyfriend snatcher and everything that is wrong with America.

Maybe just that she really wants to try Mom's Enchanted Black Forest Cake.

But she really is a good friend, so she doesn't say any of that, just squeezes my shoulder and tells me to call her later if I need to talk.

DAY 65

⁂

Honey Honeydew Cake (with Optional Walnuts)

There's this episode of *Golden Girls* where Dorothy is so annoyed with her ex-husband that she begs Blanche to go out with him, which Blanche reluctantly agrees to do. But then Blanche and Stan have this amazing time and want to see each other again, and Dorothy is hurt and furious and betrayed.

Not completely the same as what's going on with me and V and Alex (okay, it's actually not the same at *all*), but when I'm slumped on the family room couch watching a *Golden Girls* marathon and the episode comes on, I find myself really identifying with Dorothy and wanting to smack Blanche in her flirty little face. How could she do that to someone who is supposed to be like a sister to her?

It's been two days since Elle and I saw V and Alex at the movies, and I've successfully avoided my sister entirely. To be fair, it's not all that unusual, and if I weren't so stomach-churningly angry at her, I'd probably feel really crappy about the fact that apparently it's completely normal for us not to interact for whole days now. She's been out doing something all morning—maybe a coffee date with Alex?

In my pocket my cell phone dings that I've got a new text message—Alex asking where I am and if I'm okay, and I realize that I was supposed to be at FishTopia a half hour ago.

Instead of writing back that he is a jackass or that maybe he should ask Veronica if she wants to work there instead, I shoot Elle a note asking her to text Alex that I have the flu and he has to handle FishTopia on his own today. *Don't say anything about Friday!!* I add.

A few seconds later another message from Alex: *Elle says u r sick. Anything I can do?*

The rage bubbles back up in my throat. He doesn't get to do this—act all sweet and normal and into me when he's sneaking off with my sister.

NO, I write back.

Want me to come by l8r, I can bring lo mein?

I start to type out a message saying I doubt his girl-friend would like that, but think better of it and just write *NO* again.

OK, feel better. :)

Seriously, how can he pull this aw-shucks-nice-guy shit

when he failed to mention that he's dating my sister? MY FREAKING SISTER!

The emoji pushes me over the edge, and I hurl the phone across the room. It hits one of the decorative "accent pillows" on the other side of the sectional, which isn't particularly satisfying.

I can't wait to tell Dr. Brooks that he was right, that Alex is completely immature and I shouldn't have wasted a single thought on him.

But as much as I want to hate Alex, V is the one I'm furious at. I'll admit that maybe, *maybe* I did a subpar job of conveying my feelings to Alex—like, I can't even really understand them myself—so I almost understand him.

But WTF, V? Even if she's got her Jaclyn's Attic friends and we don't watch sitcoms in bed with Mom anymore, she still had to know how important Alex is (was) to me. I talk about him constantly. Even Mom keeps asking when she's going to meet him. The last time I checked, V isn't deaf; she had to know. So why? Why *my Alex*? Veronica is the girl that everyone wants, the breathtaking breezy girl who could have anyone in the world. Why did she have to take the one guy who was important to me? Because I didn't lie to Mom about her being drunk? That's some pretty serious payback.

And then she lies to me about it. (Okay, a lie of omission, but still.) Instead of doing the mature thing and letting me know, she says nothing. Nada. Zilch. Zero. Nope, she sat through family meals and car rides and shared mornings getting ready with me in the bathroom and kept mum. She let me go on and on about Alex and FishTopia without saying a single thing.

I squeeze the Admissions Ace! stress ball so tight that something pops, and sand spills out down my arm.

Seven episodes later the front door swings open and I hear V go into the kitchen. She comes into the living room with today's cake—something made in a Bundt pan—napkins, and a knife.

"Mom must be getting better; this one looks pretty good." She puts it on the coffee table and glances at the TV. "*Golden Girls*. Cool."

In my throat, that cold rage bubbles, and I'm on my feet snapping off the TV before she can even sit down. I start out of the room, but she blocks my path with this wide-legged stance, hands on her hips like Wonder Woman.

"Is there a reason you're not speaking to me, or is this just more of the big bad depression bullshit that we're all supposed to give you a pass on?"

Narrowing my eyes, I give her the most disgusted look I can muster.

"Really? You're not gonna say anything?" Her infamous ultra-hard eye roll. "No wonder you don't have a boyfriend."

"Well, that's certainly not your problem, is it?" The level

of venom in my voice is impressive. "You've got plenty of boyfriends, don't you?"

"What are you even talking about?" V looks genuinely confused. "I'm dating one guy, not that you EVER bother to ask me about anything in my life."

"I saw you at the movie theater with Alex on Friday night!"

A flicker of surprise dances across her face, like I've caught her and she feels bad, but then she just shrugs. "So what's the BFD? I'm allowed to hang out with people."

"The BFD is . . ."

I want to scream that Alex is *my* friend, that kidding around with him at FishTopia is *our* thing. That I know I'm a moron and my reasons for not going out with him may not have made sense to her, but as my sister she should have at least tried to understand that. That's what sisters do. I used to know when she was upset about screwing up on a math test or not getting picked for a solo in modern dance class, and she should know things like that about me. At the very least she shouldn't have started seeing Alex behind my back. But it's all mixed up in my head. And I have this nagging realization that if I really wanted Alex to be happy with a pretty, great girl who could make him laugh, then shouldn't I be happy that he's with V?

"Alex is too old for you!" I finally manage, but it sounds really dumb even in my own head.

"Really, Molly? You dated T.J. when he was a senior and you were a sophomore—not that it matters." V seems like the older sister, a million years older than me, certainly old enough to date a boy a few grades ahead of her.

"And we all know how well THAT worked out!" I say.

"Just admit it. You blew Alex off a million times, and now you only care because you THINK I'm dating him—"

"That's not true."

"Then, what? You were just playing hard-to-get for two years? Word of advice, Mol, guys hate a cock tease—"

"Well, that must be why you're so well loooved. You only cock please, don't you . . . you . . . you selfish little slut."

Okay, a low blow.

"I'm the selfish one?"

"*Selfish*" is what she's upset about?

"Are you even listening to yourself . . ." V's voice trails off into a squeak; her cheeks scrunch into her eyes and she gets all purple. She goes from seeming like the older sister to looking super-young, like when she was a little kid and used to follow me and Elle around. Sometimes she couldn't do some of the stuff we did—keep the Hula-Hoop spinning, balance on the handrail of Elle's deck—and she'd get so frustrated, just like she looks now. "Everyone in your entire freaking orbit has to tiptoe around you so you don't break. No one can talk about anything going on in their lives—good or bad—because it might upset Molly. Mom's baking a fucking cake every day for Molly. But I'm the selfish one? Why don't you do us all a favor and just off yourself right now so we can get on with our lives!"

The phrase somehow echoes throughout our sunken model-home family room, reverberating from upgraded plush carpeting to the upgraded recessed lighting domes in the ceiling.

Yep, my own little sister advised me to kill myself.

V seems to realize the weight of that too, and something in her face changes.

"Molly, wait. I'm—"

No way am I going to stand here and listen to her apologize. Because no way am I going to forgive her. Not for any of it.

Swooping down, I grab the cake from the table and bolt past V up the stairs. She follows, calling my name, but I've always been faster than her, even if I haven't exercised since quitting the swim team. She's just making it to the landing by the time I slam and lock my bedroom door.

"Molly." Out-of-breath V pounds on the door. "I didn't mean it."

"Go away!"

"I'm not even da—"

Still shaking, I slide earbuds in and crank up the music on my phone, and V and all her apologies go away.

Playing the songs that Dr. B. told me about, I take a few deep breathes and try to calm down.

After the entire four minutes and three seconds of "Hunger Strike," my bedroom door is still shifting slightly. V must be talking and knocking.

"Go away," I say again, my words all weird in my head over the music.

In all the time I've been the big blue bummer, I've never once thought about killing myself. Not in any real way, at least. Sometimes, when I'm really low, I kind of wonder what it would be like to not be here anymore. To sort of melt into the bed and blend with the Egyptian cotton of the sheets. Or maybe to become a permanent member of the studio audience of an old sitcom—just watch and laugh and be amused by a life I'm not a part of, a life that is always neatly wrapped up in half-hour increments.

But I've never wanted to actively end things—never considered shoveling down a handful of the painkillers I have left from getting my wisdom teeth removed freshman year, or slicing a zigzag into my wrists in the bathtub. I know that Mom keeps a handgun locked in a metal box in her closet, but I've never thought about going to get it.

In junior high, there was a kid on the Maxwell swim team who did that. "Blew his brains out" was how we all described it, and some of the boys talked about all the blood and gray matter and what it must have looked like when his dad found him. I think it was a way to deal with how freaked out we all were.

Does V really think I would do something like that? Does that worry her? I've never considered how much all this might have sucked for her, too.

It still doesn't give her the right to date *my Alex* or tell me to kill myself.

The cake is actually really good, by far Mom's best concoction. Not too sweet, with a pinch of salt, and the melon is almost refreshing.

An envelope from V's fancy stationary set pokes under the upgraded door, but I don't even bother picking it up.

Even after I'm disgustingly full, I finish off the cake, not leaving even the smallest piece for my sister.

DAY 67

※

Razzle-Dazzle Cake with Funfetti Frosting

As much as I've been dreading going back to the store and seeing Alex, I have to admit that FishTopia is looking awesome. He finished the cleaning and painting, and he swapped out the horrible fluorescent lighting with much softer bulbs.

Plus, he redid the labels on all of the fish tanks! Charlie never really had a system for that. Some tanks had half-peeled-off stickers from a million years ago—so you ended up with things like *antic Blue Ta* and *Candy C e Cor*, kind of like a fish *Wheel of Fortune* puzzle. Others had names written in black Sharpie (most of it smeared) on pieces of masking tape, and then there were the tanks of "mystery fish" that weren't labeled at all. We always had to invent prices on the rare occasions when anybody bought some of those. But now every tank has a typed label with the specimen's name and price, plus basic information or some trivia—*The humpback grouper is an ambush predator feeding mostly on small fishes and crustaceans. Blackcap basslets are territorial and don't accept other members of the same species, so keep only one in a single aquarium.* It's really cool, like something that you might see at an honest-to-goodness aquarium. It must have taken Alex forever to do all of those. It's almost enough to make me forget that he's been stepping out with my sister behind my back.

I'm so enthralled with everything, I don't even notice when Alex and JoJo come up behind me until Alex nudges me with his shoulder and asks what I think.

"Wow, this is amazeballs!" I say, and really mean it.

"Thanks." Alex smiles.

"Your boy has been a machine." JoJo seems genuinely proud, even if she does think that we'll all make more money if this place goes diner. "He even conned me into helping."

"Yeah, Jo knows a ton of random fish trivia."

JoJo looks slightly embarrassed about something for the first time since I met her. "You know, all the *Jeopardy!* with that A-hat Alex Trebek." Grabbing her purse, she announces she's "audi," and leaves me and Alex alone.

"So, um," he says. "V mentioned that you saw us at the movies the other night—"

Yeah, his FishTopia work is *almost* enough to make me forget about Friday, but almost isn't cutting it. Just hearing him say "us" in the context of him and Veronica makes me want to throw up in my mouth.

"I so don't want to talk about this . . . ever." I cut him off before he can say any more. I'm psyched that he's so committed to FishTopia, but that doesn't mean I'm cool with the rest of it. He's lucky I'm even talking to him. I still haven't opened V's note.

"I don't want you to think that we were talking about you behind your—" Alex tries to say something else, but I shake my head and reach for the remote to turn on *Golden Girls*.

"Can we just focus on the fund-raiser?"

"Mol, I know the whole thing is kind of weird—which I told V when she asked me—"

"I get it. You didn't do anything wrong. I still don't want to have a heart-to-heart about it."

"If you'd just let me explain what actually happ—"

"Seriously, Alex, if you say one more word about it, I swear I'm going to hurl. Can we just get things ready for Friday?"

"Sure." He definitely looks like he wants to say about ten thousand more words about it.

Most of the basic tank maintenance and stuff that we actually have to do each day is complete, but we still have to clean the roof deck and get it ready. Plus, we should probably clean the stairs in the back that lead up to the deck. I wouldn't be surprised if those haven't been touched since the place was built in the seventies or whenever. Since one of us has to keep an eye on the store, we take turns, which is good because it means that Alex doesn't have an opportunity to say any of those ten thousand words to me.

Every time I hear his phone buzz with a new text message, I automatically assume it's from V and feel this cramp of anger/sadness/general suck in my rib cage. Maybe she's asking if I jumped down his throat too? Maybe they're cracking each other up over what a whack job I am? Or maybe they're not even talking about me at all. I know it's probably messed up, but that would somehow hurt more. If they're going to have this dreamy Barbie and Ken romance, they *should* feel guilty, damn it!

Thinking about them together makes me want to curl up like a cashew and lie down in one of the piles of mouse droppings in the super-disgusting stairway. I try to channel all the emotion into sweeping away the dust bunnies and spider carcasses.

All the improvements and marketing efforts might finally be paying off. When I come down to tell Alex I'm done and he can start caulking the cracks in the roof's concrete, there are actual living, breathing customers—the most rare and exotic species in all of FishTopia.

A woman about my mom's age and two tweens—all with bright red hair—are examining these cylinder nano tanks. Alex explains that while those look cool, for salt-water fish to really thrive, you need a tank that's at least ten gallons. He shows them a couple of different models and demonstrates how the pump works, and then he acts all animated helping them pick out the fish. It's adorbs. The kids are super into it, and so is Alex (he clearly learned whole volumes of fish-ipedia by making the labels), and the mom is eating it up.

"You're so knowledgeable!" She beams. "Is your major marine biology?"

Chuckling, Alex says he's still in high school but that he has always had a passion for the beauty of sea creatures and wanted to work here from the moment it opened. (He says absolutely nothing about Charlie's minimum wage mix-up.)

"It really shows," says the mom. "You know, we must have driven past this place a hundred times, but we had no idea what it was all about. I'm so glad we found it."

"Well, unfortunately, we might not be here much longer." Alex gives her the whole spiel about Charlie thinking about selling and the fund-raiser on Friday.

Taking one of the flyers with my logo on it, she says that the event is past the kids' bedtime but maybe she and her husband will get a sitter and come by.

"Oh, you guys would have a blast." Alex nods. "There'll be music and drinks; it would make a really nice date night."

By the time they leave, she and the kids have gotten a dozen fish and a twenty-gallon tank with every possible accessory, and she's promised to try to convince some other couples she knows to come with her and her husband on Friday.

If everything weren't screwy because of the V thing, I would run over and give Alex the biggest, longest hug.

An hour later I'm watching *Golden Girls* and keeping an eye on the store, when a thirtysomething guy in a suit comes in. Channeling Alex's turbo upselling with the redheaded family, I ask if I can help him find anything.

"Naw, I just need gravel for my tank," says Suit Guy. "That still in aisle three?"

"You know it!" God, I sound like a dork; maybe retail isn't for me.

Bag of aquarium gravel in hand, he's at the register a few minutes later.

"Oh, I remember this one." He points to the TV. It's the episode where Blanche's brother is scared to tell her that he's gay. "It's pretty funny."

"Yeah, I love this one."

"It's so sad," he sighs. "Except for Betty White, every one of them is dead now."

I just stare at him. What?

"Get out!" I say, even before I realize what I'm doing. Why

would anyone ruin the nice happy bubble where everything is solved in a half hour? Who does that?

Suit Guy holds up his bag of rocks. "But I haven't paid yet."

"Just get out. We're closing early."

"But the sign says you're open till—"

"Doesn't matter. We can't sell you anything." I usher him to the door.

"Fine, I'm going, I'm going." He pulls open the door. "But just so you know, I intend to write this all up on Yelp!"

"Go right ahead."

"What's your name, so I can make sure to mention how unhelpful you were?"

"Veronica!" It was the first thing I could think of.

As suit guy mumbles to himself and leaves, I turn around and notice that Alex is standing there staring at me with this look that's somewhere between horrified and amused. "You realize we're trying to keep the store in business, right?"

"Trust me, he's not the kind of customer we want." I sound like an idiot.

Alex shrugs. "That guy's been in a few times; always seemed nice enough to me."

"Are you finished with the roof?" I ask, and Alex shakes his head. "Well, then you should probably get back to that. We need to have everything ready to go by Friday."

DAY 69

Down-Home Fudge Core Cake

It feels really good to be in Dr. B.'s office listening to nineties music and complaining about Alex and Veronica. I really haven't talked to anyone about it—Elle can be so judgey; Mom is, well, Mom; and obviously V and Alex are no-go's—and it's great just to get it all out. I'm not even sure what I'm saying anymore. It just keeps coming out like diarrhea of the mouth.

"I don't mind so much that he's seeing her." (Completely not true.) "But why would he lie about it?" (Technically omit.) "She's my sister, we live in the same house. Did she think I *wouldn't* find out? It's all the sneaking around, you know?"

"I've said before that your sister seems to have a lot of anger toward you," Dr. B. says. "This might be a manifestation of that."

"Exactly!"

"And we've discussed that Alex has some maturity issues," Dr. B. says.

"Ohmygod, I didn't even tell you. His stupid band doesn't have a name anymore; they decided they're going to let the music speak to them in a trance or some shit."

At that, Dr. B. outright laughs and shakes his head, but it's less warm than usual—more like the Joker.

"Seriously, Molly, why are you wasting time worrying about this stunted wannabe? The guy is a douche bag," he says, like he's the one who's pissed at Alex, or like he's actually talking about something else entirely.

It's weird already that I stop complaining long enough to look at him.

He's still dreamy Dr. B., but to be honest, he looks kind of rough—puffy purple pockets under his eyes, and he didn't do the best job of shaving this morning. There are little patches of dark stubble all over his face. Plus, his clothes are kind of wrinkly, like he may have slept in them.

"I'm sorry, that was unprofessional. I shouldn't have said that." Dr. B. shakes his head. "In fact, I probably should have canceled our session today. I'm sorry."

"Why?" Suddenly I'm panicked; maybe there *are* things I can say that will make him not like me. "Have I been too ranty. I'm so—"

"No, of course not." He waves away my concerns.

"You're always a pleasure. I'm just dealing with a personal issue and not in the best head space right now."

"Oh." So shrinks have personal problems too. Who knew?

"Obviously, no charge for this session."

"What happened?" I ask.

"Discussing that with you would probably be inappropriate."

His eyes droop, and he rubs his forehead and looks so freaking vulnerable. It just, I don't know, *does* something to me, and suddenly I couldn't care less about Alex and V or pretty much anyone else. More than anything else, I want to lean down and kiss him, but that would *definitely* be inappropriate.

"You listen to my problems all the time," I say.

"That's my job—"

"Well, you said we're off the clock." I try to sound reassuring like he does when he wants me to open up more. "So you can talk to me now, right?"

He sighs. "Let's just say my fiancée might not be my fiancée anymore."

My heart is beating really loudly all of a sudden. "Oh no. What happened with you guys?"

He shakes his head again. "She was supposed to come up this weekend, but she said she couldn't get away, so I volunteered to go down there, and then she dropped the 'I need some time alone to think' bomb."

"Ouch."

"That's your professional opinion, Dr. Byrne?" Dr. B. smirks.

"I mean, it just sounds harsh. Is that where you left it?"

"She's calling me back when she's done thinking."

"So you're supposed to wait around for her to decide if she wants to be with you?"

"I guess," he says.

"That seems pretty unfair."

"I don't think it's most people's idea of fun, no." He looks at his big hands, then up at me. "I'm sorry. I shouldn't be telling you any of this."

Then it hits me! "You should come to the FishTopia event tomorrow night!"

Sure, it might take away some of the sting of having Alex there with V if I have a sexy, older *man* man by my side, but honestly I ask because Dr. B. just looks so sad.

I reach into my backpack, pull out one of the flyers, and hand it to him. "It's a little cornball, but it should be fun."

Dr. B. looks at the paper.

"Cute fish," he says.

"There'll be beer and wine and stuff," I add quickly. "I could make sure that we get that pinot noir you liked at dinner."

"I don't know." Something between a laugh and a sigh comes out of Dr. B.'s nose. "Don't you think I'm a little old for a battle of the bands?"

Frustrating much? We listen to music here all the time, and Dr. B. is always stoked to share some bootleg or live recording he thinks I'll like. Why would it be strange for him to come see a show?

"What? You'd rather sit around waiting for her to call? You're the one always telling me to get out there."

"Molly, there are lines between patients and—"

"Don't be that way." On *Golden Girls*, Blanche knows how to work personal space and charm any man in the greater Miami area. Hoping all those reruns have taught me something, I try to channel her energy and use my best Southern belle voice. For good measure I pat his arm lightly like Blanche would.

That is probably *very* inappropriate, but I don't care. The thought of Dr. B. wallowing around his apartment waiting for the strawberry-blond news lady to call is too much. The thought of having to watch V and Alex make out at the fund-raiser is equally appalling. Dr. B. coming is a complete win-win.

"We'll have a great time. I promise."

Dr. B. looks at my hand on his arm and then up at me, baffled. If we were on a sitcom, this would be the moment when I'd ask "Too much?" and everyone in the studio audience would laugh. I put my hand back in my lap.

"You really want me to go to this thing?" he asks.

"It would mean an awful lot to me."

"Okay." He folds the flyer and tucks it into his pocket. "I'll try."

DAY 70

Almond Raspberry Wheel of Joy Cake

Tonight is the night!

The night when all of our hard work pays off and we prove to Charlie that FishTopia is worth it, or the night that we find out that we're big fat failures. Never mind that fiancée-free Dr. B. might show. All day I've felt like I might puke. I wonder if Alex was this excited about his show—the one I blew off. Well, this time I'll be there even if it's just to support FishTopia; cheering him on is V's job now.

I'm a few minutes late because it was hard to pedal over on Old Montee in a dress. The occasion seemed momentous enough to warrant a change from my summer uniform, so I'm wearing this silky, flowing tank dress I borrowed from Mom. Of course it's a little big in the boobs, but the print is this wavy blue-and-green pattern that reminds me of how we painted the walls of FishTopia so it looks like an ocean. And I swung by the salon and let Mom braid my hair again. I even put on some lip gloss and mascara, but I probably sweated all of that off on the ride over.

Chaining Old Montee to a signpost, I decide that if we do save FishTopia, I'll sign up for driver's ed. This night could be the start of the rest of my life.

"Wow. You look, wow," Alex says as he comes over from the parking lot, guitar in one hand, amp in the other.

"Thanks." Despite everything going on with him and my sister, I'm still happy he noticed.

"You look really good too." It's not a lie. His jeans fit really well (V's doing?), and he's done something different with his hair so that it's a little more tousled.

"Who knew we cleaned up so nice?" He smiles.

I pull open the door for him. "Should we go save some fish?"

Inside, the store looks amazing. All the tanks with their neat Alex-made labels, everything clean and relaxing, the fan keeping everything cool; it really wouldn't be a bad place to spend the afternoon. Maybe we could even add a small café? Some partnership with Wang's? The world tonight feels full of possibilities.

Elle is behind the counter selling tickets, and she practically tackles me the minute Alex goes upstairs to finish setting up the equipment.

"Have you met his band yet?" Elle demands, and grabs my hand.

"No, I just got here—"

"The keyboardist—he goes to Maxwell—has the same hemp-weave bag I do, and it turns out that he is huge into Greenpeace. We talked about sustainability for twenty minutes!"

"That's sooo cool!"

"Also, he's smoking hot."

I laugh. "Why was Alex holding out on you?"

"I know, right!" Elle is practically giddy. I think she's in love. "Anyway, he's got these amazing dimples, and black glasses, and his thumbs—"

"His thumbs?"

"He did this thing where he sort of cracked them. It was flat-out sexy."

"Wow."

"And." Elle lowers her voice as though FishTopia were teeming with spies. "Alex said he asked if I was single."

"Ohmygod!" I'm so stoked for her. Flickering thought of Dr. B.; he has to come, right?

"You have to meet him!"

Elle is going on and on about her knight in a shining Prius, when headlights from a Mini Cooper temporarily blind us through the glass windows of the store. Veronica hops out of the car, achingly beautiful in a short, strapless romper and gladiator sandals. I haven't spoken a word to her since the night she told me to kill myself.

"What is *she* doing here?" Elle's eyes narrow, and she looks cartoonishly angry, like steam puffs might come out of her ears.

"Coming to see her boyfriend's band play, I guess." From my stomach the cold murder-rage bubbles into my esophagus.

Stabilizing breath. This is the night we save FishTopia; no time to waste on my backstabbing baby sister.

"Do you need me to punch her in the tit for you?" Elle asks, and I tell her that won't be necessary.

Opening the door, V gives Elle a wave and a "Hey, Elle."

Elle crosses her arms and refuses to acknowledge V. She might actually make a "humph" sound.

V shrugs and turns to me. "Hi, Molly." Offering a sheepish smile, she jams her hands into her pockets.

"Thanks for coming," I say, stiff and formal, the president of the United States greeting a head of state from an uneasy ally.

"Of course. I know how important this is to you, so I tried to get people from Jaclyn's to come, but Nina's parents are out of town, so she's having a big party." V looks inordinately sad about this. "Chris and a couple of those guys promised to stop by in a little while, though. Hope that helps."

I tell her that's really nice, because it is. Thawing ever so slightly, I wonder what she wrote in that note I didn't read.

But I don't have time to deal with any of this, not tonight. If we can save FishTopia, everything else will sort itself out.

"Alex is upstairs setting up," I tell her, and she looks wounded.

"Okay, um, I guess I'll go say hi."

Elle gives me a confused look once Veronica is in the stairwell, and I flip up my palms.

"Well," she says, "if you change your mind, I can still tit-punch her."

Upstairs it really does look like an enchanted under-the-sea dance.

Before we went home to change a few hours ago, Elle, Alex, and I spent all day setting up the roof—stringing up these fish-shaped Christmas lights that Elle found at a secondhand store, and creating a makeshift stage for the bands. We constructed a "bar" with a soda station and little snack bowls filled with Pepperidge Farm Goldfish (get it?) and a bunch of cupcakes Mom and I made last night. Unfortunately (though, not at all surprisingly), we weren't able to get a keg, but JoJo got us a couple of six-packs and some cheap wine.

The roof is hardly packed, but it's still early, and people are slowly trickling in. That redheaded mom that Alex helped shows up with her non-ginger husband; a few people Elle still hangs out with from the swim team; Gina and Tina from AP English, who immediately ask me how far I've gotten on the summer reading list; a few of the Hot Topic girls with black nail polish (oh, well; they're V's problem now).

For once Elle's mom shows up, with Jimmy—who's wearing his stuffed-animal pelt from the playroom massacre—by her side. Giving me a kiss, she asks about my summer.

My own mom arrives with Gram, and already the two of them are arguing about something ("I know, Ma!"), but they stop long enough to tell me how great the place looks.

JoJo and her boyfriend with the stash of teeth are holding hands and look like they're getting along. "I have to admit, you did a great job, CCH," she says, and I'm kind of touched.

Toupee Thom comes up from the steps and looks a little lost, still in his lawyer suit.

"Molly." He gives me a quick hug, and I remember how attentive he was to my mom. Fresh splash of guilt that I'm the reason they broke up. "I saw one of the flyers, so I figured I'd stop by."

"Thanks," I say. "It's really nice to see you."

"Well, clients always really love the tank in the lobby. The fish have a very calming effect." My mom used to talk about how sometimes she could hear the dueling exes through the floors, so anything that helps is probably huge.

After a few minutes more of small talk, I notice he's looking around.

"Mom and my grandma are over by the food," I say. "I'm sure they'd love to say hi."

His face brightens, and he goes off to find them.

On the makeshift stage, Alex and the guys from his band call me and Elle over.

"I'm afraid it's not going to be much of a battle." Alex shakes his head. "I'm so sorry."

Apparently the bassist and drummer from Sinking Canoe haven't recovered from mono, which we had sort of expected. That would still have left us with three bands . . . except Sinking Canoe's drummer was hooking up with the singer from Terminal Bitch, and now all the TB members are sick too. And McLovin—the band that was totally blowing up when we planned this—literally blew up and parted ways over creative differences this morning. (They plan to re-form soon, but that's no help for us tonight.) So we've got Alex's nameless band, which, by definition, doesn't have a huge following.

"We're happy to play extra sets or whatever you guys need," Mark—the eco-friendly keyboardist—offers, looking directly at Elle. He is kind of cute, but his thumbs don't do a thing for me. Batting her eyelashes with her own dash of Blanche Devereaux's magic, Elle pronounces him a "lifesaver."

"Since we were advertising four bands and now it's only one, maybe we should charge five bucks instead of ten?" Alex suggests, and everyone agrees that seems fair.

Elle starts handing out five-dollar refunds to poeple already there.

Still, when I do the math, I'm not sure it will be enough to save the store, especially since we already lowered the price when we couldn't get the keg. The numbers start the spiral thinking in my head. But I push it back. This will work; it has to.

Alex and his nameless quartet take the stage and announce that they're ready to get the party started, and the thirty or so people cheer.

They start with a song I heard Alex tinkering around with once, and I can't believe how awesome they sound. No joke, they could be on the radio. They are kind of like those alternative bands that my mom and Dr. B. love so much, but more fun, with so much energy. Their drummer—this big teddy bear of a dude with great hair—flips a drumstick into the air and actually catches it, and when Alex plays a guitar solo, he closes his eyes and throws his whole body into it.

The keyboardist announces that one song is about global warming, and Elle literally swoons. That song is awesome too, and so rollicking that you don't even notice the preachy lyrics.

Before the next number, Alex takes the microphone. "This song goes out to a little guy we recently lost," he says. "Pickles, this one is for you, buddy."

It's so silly and sweet that I get a little misty. From the corner of my eye, I catch V talking to Toupee Thom and wonder if she's jealous that Alex mentioned Pickles. She looks unfazed, but she also thought Pickles was a lobster.

The band breaks into the song that Alex and I danced to while painting the store—the one about the guy who does all that crazy crap to forget the girl he's into. Bopping my head, I can't help but sing along to the chorus.

> "I know that you don't care, but I see you
>   everywhere.
> In a boat or with a goat,
> Flying high while eating pie,
> On a train with my aunt Jane,
> Just no way to escape, the beauty of your face."

And for the whole four minutes, I'm not worried about whether or not we'll save FishTopia or about Alex and V or about everyone racing off to start these bright shining lives. I'm not obsessing about whether Dr. B. will show up, or if he will still have a fiancée if does. I'm just having a good time.

Two hours later the energy had changed. Alex and the band are still playing, but they ran out of their own material a while ago and have resorted to cover songs. Now they're playing covers they don't even seem to know very well. I think they're in the middle of some Imagine Dragons hit, but it's hard to tell for sure. The only people still dancing are JoJo and her boyfriend and my mom and Toupee Thom, which actually is really sweet.

Maybe ten more people showed up. Most of them are friends of Alex's band members; none of them are Dr. Brooks. No messages on my cell phone from him or anyone else.

I barely scraped by in trig with a C minus, but even I can tell that we've made nowhere near enough money to cover FishTopia's operating expenses. We probably didn't even make enough to replace the money we took from petty cash for the paint supplies and fans.

Looking around at the sparse crowd, there's no mistaking that I've failed. Charlie didn't even bother to show up. He was probably only humoring me the whole time anyway. It really didn't cost him anything to let us try to ramp up our revenue, and he always knew the Kansas couple would end up slinging hash here by fall. I can't even be mad at him; I wouldn't trust me either.

A hand on my back. I turn around, and there's my grandma. "You did a real good job, sweetie," she says, and I know I'm going to cry.

How could I have been so stupid? How could I have ever thought this was going to work? It's beyond embarrassing how I dragged my friends and family down with me—like running away from the starting block during divisionals all over again. And for what? None of it mattered.

"Thank you." I need to get away from here before I start

crying in front of everyone—again. "I've got to check on something downstairs. Be right back."

Tears locked and loaded, I head through the door to the stairs.

I manage to make it to the landing before losing it completely. Stumbling down the lower flight, I smack headfirst into Dr. Brooks's chest. He catches me on the upper arms and holds on.

"Hey," he says. "Sorry I'm late. I got caught up in the off—"

I try to duck my head, but he has already seen that I'm crying.

"Molly, what's wrong?" he asks.

"The whole thing is a flop; we failed. I failed." I'm full-on sobbing now. "I can't do anything right."

Pulling me closer, Dr. B. says soothing things into my hair. "Shhh, sweetheart, it's okay." I'm probably getting snot and mascara all over his shirt.

"The world would be a better place if I just disappeared."

"Don't say that." His voice is so forceful that I can't not look at him anymore, so forceful that I manage to stop crying. This close, I can smell the wine on his breath. "A lot of people would be devastated if you disappeared."

"Would you be?" I can't believe I said it out loud.

He nods slowly, and everything is suddenly important and underwater, like we've fallen through the floor into one of the tanks in the store.

"Really?"

"Yes, Molly." His voice is deeper than normal, and kind of gravelly. "I would miss you very much."

The space between us seems to be eclipsing; his breath is my breath. He's still holding me at the elbows, but somehow my arms are around him, too, his body sweat-dampened and solid. Not a boy but a man. As still as possible, I wait for him to kiss me.

"Molly we can't—" he starts.

But I cut him off with a kiss.

He doesn't throw me down on the steps and ravish me, but he doesn't *not* kiss back either. His lips are soft and firm and skilled. Lips that know what they're doing.

Nothing at all like making out with T.J.

It is hands down the most erotic moment of my life. Almost without thinking about it, I start to press into him more.

"You promised to co—" V, screaming into her cell phone, thrusts open the door to the stairwell.

Immediately Dr. B. and I become marble.

Stopping midsentence, Veronica looks from me to Dr. B. Her blue-green eyes (my eyes, Mom's eyes) expand to Frisbees, and one delicate hand floats up to cover her mouth. On the phone in her other hand, some guy is still talking. "Ronnie? You there? I said I'm on my way."

Without saying a word, V hurries past us down the stairs.

Clenching his eyes, Dr. B. massages his forehead and swears under his breath.

"Should I go after her?" I ask, dizzy from the whiplash of being suddenly ripped from one intense situation to a completely different one.

Dr. B. exhales a chuckle-sigh. "I honestly don't know." More of the pinched-with-pain expression, more face rubbing. "Maybe?"

I jog down the steps after my sister. I make it out the door in time to see her climbing into the passenger seat of a green Honda with an FSU bumper sticker.

I'm staring after the taillights when Dr. B. appears at my side, all restraightened and tucked and collected.

"You missed her?" he asks. I nod, and he chuckle-sighs again. "I guess that's the kind of night we're having."

He asks if he can give me a ride anywhere, but I tell him I have to clean up our fund-raising failure.

"Can I do anything to help?" he asks, which is totally sweet, but I think of my mom and Elle and everyone up there and realize what an epically bad idea it would be for him to make a special guest appearance right now. One more thing I've screwed up.

"No, I can handle it," I say. "So I guess I'll see you Monday?"

"I don't know if that's the best idea, Molly. We should probably talk about setting you up with another therapist—"

"NO!"

"Molly, this really complicates things."

"I know, but I'm already losing FishTopia and Elle and everyone. I can't lose you, too. Please?"

"Okay, okay. We'll talk Monday." He sighs. "And, Molly, please don't disappear."

I want him to kiss me again, but all the underwater tension is gone.

Pulling myself together, I go back upstairs and manage to say good-bye and thank everyone without coming off like a total freak, but they probably all know what an epic waste of space I am.

Soon it's only Elle, Mark, Alex, and me. Mark asks Elle if she wants to go grab soy lattes at a vegan coffeehouse he knows that's still open. She looks at me.

"Yeah, have eco-friendly fun," I say. "Thank you so much for helping out with everything."

Hugging me, she says that she's sorry we didn't make enough money, but it really was great, regardless.

Trying not to ruin her high, I just agree.

Alex and me alone at FishTopia is fitting, I guess. Although, all the joy that this place brought me seems swept away with the crushed Goldfish crackers and plastic cups. Barely speaking, we wind the fish lights, break down the folding chairs and tables.

I wonder if he knows V left and who she was with.

Wonder if Alex is hurt that she didn't stay till the end of the show. (Those self-absorbed Byrne girls, never supporting his band!) Wonder what, if anything, V will tell him about what she saw between Dr. B. and me. Hopefully nothing.

We pick up crushed cans and sweep. But we got here at six this morning, and I'm pretty much a walking corpse at this point. Alex must feel the same.

He plants the broom down, staking a claim on the moon. "Let's get out of here. This mess will be here for us tomorrow."

Mom hates it when I ride Old Montee after dark, so I don't even protest when he insists on loading my bike into his trunk and driving me home.

We don't say much on the ride. OneRepublic and Coldplay fill the vacuum of the car.

Pulling into the upgraded driveway, Alex kills the engine like T.J. used to do after our dates, when he'd shove his tongue down my throat and feel me up while I floated above, completely disconnected from my body. *You're just kind of different from what I thought before I got to know you.*

"So this is my stop," I say. "Thanks for the lift."

"Anytime."

Gathering my backpack to leave, I feel I should say more. Even if he is banging my sister, he still went above and beyond with my stupid plan. He's still a really good friend.

"Um, I wanted to thank you for dedicating that song to Pickles. That was really . . . It meant a lot to me."

"I'm glad you liked it. I know he was your spirit animal and all."

"And thank you for helping me try to save FishTopia."

"Molly," he says, more serious than I've ever heard him in the two years we've been hanging out. "That place meant the world to me, too. You know that, don't you?"

He takes my hand; that lightning strike. On the pads of his fingers, those calluses are harder than I imagined they would be. Alex gives my fingers a gentle squeeze, and I want to squeeze back to see if maybe we *would* be good together. But, as absolutely ridiculous as it sounds, considering how I've been carrying on, I actually feel like I'm betraying V. After all, she did show up tonight, and tried to bring people. And maybe I'm betraying Dr. Brooks, too? It wasn't like he *didn't* kiss back tonight. Even if he did try to shrink break up with me after.

Feeling tears of confusion and frustration and exhaustion, I pop the door and jump out.

"See you tomorrow," I call, and hurry toward the front door.

"Molly, wait." He's out of the car now too. "Your bike."

"Oh yeah."

He gets it out of the trunk, and looks at me for direction.

"You can just leave it there," I call, and hurry inside before he can say anything else.

DAY 71

———⊶⊶———

Blue Velvet Inside-Out Cake

We're at the Miami Seaquarium. Dad and V and I, just like I told Dr. B. But while V and I are the ages we are now, Dad hasn't changed a day from the giant portrait above the dining room. With his big, big hands and his canyon of a voice, he's pointing out facts about the various exhibits. All those beautiful jellyfish that look like ballerinas dancing through the water, and the penguins waddling up to the edge of the enclosure to entertain us.

"Molly." Dad gestures to the giant Pacific octopus, its thick red arms full of suction cups. "Did you know that he's actually a mollusk, just like Pickles?"

It warms my heart that Dad knows about Pickles and doesn't just think he's a little lobster. "And sea otters have the world's densest fur!" Dad says. "Up to one million hairs per square inch."

Who knew Dad was a regular Jacques Cousteau? Just like Alex knew all that stuff with the redheaded family the other day.

"Fish just run in our family," Dad is singing now. "Salt water instead of blood."

The dream song still tickling my brain, there's a moment before I remember. A few seconds when I'm content, even if I'm not sure what's real and what's not.

Then it all comes crashing back.

Spectacular failure.

FishTopia is going out of business because, despite all the hours and hard work that Alex and Elle and I put into saving it, we raised around three hundred dollars. The weird kiss with Dr. B.; Veronica catching us and running away; Alex taking my hand when he dropped me off. Me running away and almost leaving my bike like Cinderella's extra-heavy glass slipper.

Crap.

A thousand pounds of bricks on my chest, I wonder how I was ever able to fall sleep last night in the first place.

More than anything else, I want to go back into the dream where Dad is alive and a part of our family. Where he would have ideas about how to save FishTopia, where he would make sure that Veronica and I never fought over guys or groundings or anything.

But Alex and I left FishTopia such a mess that it's not

fair to him if I completely bail. So I pull myself out of the sleigh bed.

Even though I'm dreading talking to her, I stop by V's room. I have to tell her *something* about what she saw between Dr. B. and me last night. But the truth is, I have absolutely no idea what she saw, what we were doing, and if it's even going to happen again. So yeah, not entirely clear how to explain that one.

She's not home anyway. The stone shower (an upgrade, of course) in our model-home bathroom is still beaded with water and smells of her lilac perfume.

I say a silent prayer that she'll "do the good sisterly thing" and not tell Mom about what she saw—exactly the way I *didn't* do the good sisterly thing when she came home drunk a few weeks ago.

It's a little after eleven by the time I get to the store, but Alex has already finished almost all of the cleanup from the party. On the counter are two clamshells of the house special lo mein from Wang's Palace (the yummy trifecta: baby shrimp, green onions, and red cabbage), and an episode of *Golden Girls* is frozen on the ancient TV screen, even though the back-to-back block doesn't start until the afternoon.

Seeing my confusion, Alex smiles and points to the TV. "So it turns out the VCR on this thing actually still works, and I've been recording some of our favorite episodes for a while. I figured we could use some today."

He pushes himself up so he's seated on the counter and pats the spot next to him for me to join.

I do.

And for a little while I forget that we couldn't save this place, and that Alex is with my sister, even if he did take my hand last night. I forget about the kiss with Dr. B., and V running down the stairs. Forget that everyone is leaving, that everyone except for me has grand plans to take over the world.

We're watching the one where Dorothy, Blanche, and Rose are arrested for prostitution the night they're supposed to see Burt Reynolds's show, when Charlie jogs in, punching the air in his kickboxing clothes.

Both Alex and I hop off the counter, though at this point I don't think either one of us is remotely concerned about being caught doing anything. What's he going to do, fire us?

"You didn't come last night," Alex says, not even accusatory, a simple statement of fact.

Charlie offers a look as blank as grade-school paste, and then nods, seeming to remember. "Oh yeah, the big bash. Sorry about that; something came up."

He doesn't bother asking if we raised the money or how things went, which I suppose is fine, considering. Neither

Alex nor I offer up details of our groan-worthy gala.

"I've got some news for the two of you, and I think it's ultimately good." He makes this open-palmed gesture like someone in an old-timey movie trying to sell you something. "I know that I told you that we'd stay open for the rest of the summer, but the new owners want to get started on renovations as soon as possible. So your last day is going to be Wednesday."

"But that's . . . ," I start.

"Just four days away," Alex finishes.

"That's the good part for you guys! The new owners asked if they'd be displacing employees, yada, yada, yada, and I told them I'd promised everyone that we'd stay open through the summer. I really fought for you."

This seems extremely unlikely.

"So," he continues, "they offered to pay your wages for the next three weeks as a severance package."

Alex and I don't say anything. Canned laughter from the TV expands to fill the whole sales floor as Sophia refuses to bail the other girls out of jail unless one of them agrees to let Sophia go in her place to see Burt. I'm not even looking at the screen, but I've seen this episode so many times that I know exactly what's happening. Can even remember the purple-and-teal dress Blanche is wearing; it looks a little like some of the pastel butterflyfish we have.

Alex and I continue to stare at Charlie.

"Oh, come on." Charlie is annoyed we're not thrilled with this arrangement. "What kids in retail get a severance package? Isn't that the dream, getting paid for not working? You're welcome."

"That's very generous," Alex says flatly. "Thanks for looking out for us."

I don't say anything, because I'm floating above everything again.

Alex and I don't say much the rest of the day. We watch more of the taped episodes and then the ones that play on the Hallmark Channel in the afternoon. Ironically, one of the shows the network plays is the Burt Reynolds one, but we watch it anyway, despite having literally *just* seen it. We laugh even harder at the end when Burt himself makes a special guest appearance. The following episode is this weird sad one where Blanche's late husband comes back and explains that he had faked his death because he'd been framed by his business partner. Blanche is furious at him for leaving her, but eventually she comes around and forgives him, simply grateful that he's still alive and back in her life. Of course it turns out the whole thing is a dream.

I think about my own dream with Dad at the aquarium, wonder how my mom would react if he reappeared in our lives. I know I'd forgive Dad for sure.

I don't remember falling asleep on the counter, but I wake up forty minutes before we close, Alex nowhere in sight, his hoodie tucked under my head like a pillow.

Heart in my throat, I jump off the counter. FishTopia is ending, and I've missed nearly two of our last hours!

"Alex! Alex, where are you?" I race through the rows of displays, past the starfish and the yellow tangs, the sea horses with their curled tails and eyelashes.

Finally I find him in the back watching a tank of tropical fish. He's just studying them, his hand lightly on the glass like he's a little kid.

"You're awake." He smiles.

"Why'd you let me sleep so long?"

"You seemed tired." He shrugs.

We make our way back to the front of the store.

"Well, at least we've got time for one more episode," I say, but Alex shakes his head.

"If it's okay with you, I'm gonna cut out of here a little early. Don't worry. I already cleaned all the tanks and took out the garbage—"

"Oh." Seriously, he's leaving early during one of our last days ever at FishTopia? "Hot date?" I ask, trying to sound casual and not turned inside-out.

Alex looks at the linoleum flooring as if it might contain all the secrets of getting into a top tier college.

"Look." I sigh. "You've got to stop acting like such a total freak about it if you're gonna keep dating my sister, and you should prob—"

"What? I'm not—"

". . . ably not hold my hand like you did last—"

". . . dating Veronica," Alex finishes.

It takes a minute to sink in.

"Wait, you're not?"

"No." He shakes his head. "She's been going out with Chris since June. How do *you* not know that?"

All at once I've got this movie-flashback ability to perfectly recall the fight V and I had the night she told me to kill myself so everyone would be better off. *Now you only care because you think I'm dating him.* I guess she never technically said that they were dating, but it was pretty damn implied.

And what about Alex? He didn't exactly deny that they were hanging out either. *I don't want you to think that we were talking about you.* Okay, so maybe I could have let him explain things. Maybe I should have listened to what V was saying outside my door or read her note, but the whole thing is still really weird.

And how *could* I not know that my sister has had a boyfriend all this time? We used to know everything about each other. She used to come to me crying when someone hurt her feelings. How could Veronica hide her first real relationship from me? I'm the worst big sister in the history of time. . . .

No, no, I'm not.

"If you're not dating, then why were you at the movies with her that Friday night?" I'm all revved up again. Going to a movie together on a Friday night is the datiest thing of all time. The first time that Dr. B. got to second base was when he went to see *Say Anything . . .* at the theater with Lizzie Mapleton. "Just the two of you. Elle and I saw."

Letting out a long breath, Alex tilts his head. "First of all, it wasn't just the two of us. Chris works there and he kept sneaking down from the projection room. At one point the whole film stopped because it got stuck and he had to run back up and fix it."

Maybe what V and Alex were laughing about?

"Oh," I say.

"But I told you, we *have* been hanging out occasionally." Alex looks at the ground again. "Ronnie has been crazy worried about you and just wanted someone to talk to about it."

"Oh."

"And if you really want to know the truth, I *did* feel shitty about that at first, and I made it totally clear to her that I didn't want to talk about you behind your back. But then I realized she was really just looking for someone to tell her that you're gonna be okay."

"Oh." The SAT is going to be awesome, since this is now apparently the only word I know.

In my defense this is all a lot to take in. Alex and Veronica not dating. All this time V has just been worried about me? Then why is she always so yell-y and hostile? What's with all that pent-up anger Dr. B. keeps saying she has against me? There's definitely something huge that I'm missing. Again, I wish I'd read her note, but it was gone this morning. She must have gotten it last night after catching Dr. B. and me.

Alex presses his lips together in this frustrated smile. "So, what? For a week you've been pissed at me because you thought V and I were kicking it behind your back, and yet it never once occurred to you to just ask me about it? That's pretty screwed up, Molly."

It is.

I'm pretty screwed up, but that isn't exactly breaking news. I'm just the screwed-up girl who ran away from the divisionals meet and got the team disqualified. The screwed-up girl who couldn't even keep a hermit crab alive.

The floor is really interesting. One of the Goldfish crackers from the party must have made it downstairs and missed our broom efforts; there are orange crumbs on the floor under the counter. Also a few teeny tiny drips of the blue-green paint (the paint Alex said reminded him of my eyes), which must have landed outside the range of our tarp.

"Molly?"

When I finally look up, Alex is grinning at me as if I weren't the world's most stubborn idiot.

"I'm sorry," I say.

"Don't be. I'm pretty stoked you were so upset when you thought I was seeing someone. At least it means I haven't been that off base about us."

He puts his hand on top of mine on the counter, and I'm too confused to move it. The minute Alex explained he wasn't dating V, this almost ecstatic sense of relief flooded me. I used to get really bottled up before a race during swim meets, but then when I would hit the touch pad at the end and pull off my goggles, it was the most amazing release to look up at the board and see a time that didn't suck, and to know I'd survived. That's *exactly* how it feels to know that Alex and V aren't together, like all that worrying was for nothing.

But now we're right back where we were two months ago, when Alex asked me out and I blew him off. When I wasn't sure if I could live up to being *Alex's Molly*. Nothing has changed. The thought of him pulling a T. J. Cranston still wrecks me.

And I can say anything to Dr. B., and he'll still like me; he promised (and he didn't not kiss back!).

"Molly," Alex is saying. "You have to know how I feel about you, and I think that you feel the same way. So can we please stop pussyfooting around and give us a shot?"

My heart is racing; panic flooding my throat, making it difficult to breathe.

You're a great girl, Molly. You're just kind of different from what I thought before I got to know you.

"I don't—"

"If you're worried about blowing up our friendship, I hate to break it to you, but the fact that I'm in love with you has been blowing up our friendship for a long time now."

"What?"

He's in love with me? How is it possible to be so dizzyingly excited about something and still filled with enough dread to sink an ocean liner?

"Molly." He leans in, his hand still on mine. "Look me in the eye and tell me you didn't want to kiss me that day we were painting, or last night in the car."

"I . . ."

So close. The slight oily smell from the house special lo mein on his breath. There are these little tan freckles on his forehead that I never noticed before, the slightest fuzz on his cheeks.

No, no, no. This will ruin everything.

"I can't." I back away, and he lets go of my hand.

"Why?"

"I'm not good enough for you. You won't like me."

"What does that even mean? I'm telling you I like you." He sounds so frustrated. Already I am fucking up everything!

"I just . . . can't."

"So it's not okay for me to date someone else, but you don't want to date me."

"No. I mean . . . Alex . . . I just—" The words catch in my throat.

"Fine, if that's the way you want it, I'm done." Redder and angrier than I've ever seen him, Alex grabs his bag from behind the register, knocking over this old marga- rine container where Charlie keeps thumbtacks and spare pennies. Everything splashes onto the ground, creating a mildly dangerous obstacle course.

He starts for the door, but I reach for his arm.

"Alex, wait."

"Wait for what? Huh, Molly? Until you get jealous because you *think* I'm dating someone else again? Is that what I should wait for?"

"Alex, stop. . . . I . . ." I can hardly breathe, everything all circular and twisty in my head.

"Look, Molly, I know that you've got problems, and that has never once been an issue for me. I dig *all* of you. But that doesn't give you the green light to jerk me around like this, to give me *just* enough hope to keep me hanging around."

"I . . ."

"So you can go play mind games with some other guy, because I'm through letting my heart break."

"Stop," I beg.

"You know, I'm glad this place is closing, because it means I won't have to waste one more second of my life on you!"

Then he's gone, the bell on the door chiming behind him.

I want to run after him, but I can't move, the spilled thumbtacks somehow pinning me to the floor.

Gasping for breath, like I finished the two-hundred-meter butterfly and I can't get enough oxygen. Everything is a slurry of lights and sounds and suck. Alex's face bunched with anger. T.J. calmly telling me I wasn't like he thought I would be. My mom and her perfectly adorable baking skills. V telling me to make life easier for everyone else by pulling the plug on myself.

Dr. B.

He can make this better. He'll make this better.

This has to qualify as an emergency.

Hands shaking, I pull his card out of my wallet and punch his cell number into my phone.

He picks up on the third ring. "Molly, I'm so sorry. I meant to call you today."

I try to calm down as I explain that I need to see him, that there's no way I can wait until our Monday afternoon appointment.

With that same soothing voice from last night, he tries to talk me down, calls me "sweetheart" again. Almost immediately I feel a little better.

"Where are you now?" he asks. When I tell him FishTopia, he sighs. "I'd pick you up and take you to the office, but I've had a few drinks, and I probably shouldn't be driving anywhere. I'm sorry."

"Oh." My heart drops to my sneakers, and the panic starts again. My breathing kicks up like when characters on sitcoms start hyperventilating and have to breathe into a paper bag. I *need* to see him. "Maybe I could come to your place? I have my bike."

Even as I ask, I know that I'm being totally inappropriate. He's my doctor, not my boyfriend, not my dad. But I *have* to.

"I guess you could do that." He doesn't sound at all convinced that this is a good plan, but after a pause he warms up to the prospect. "Yeah, sure. I'm near the old downtown in that strip of condos on Otter Bay Drive. Pretty close to you."

I don't even bother locking up the store. I'm out the door and unlocking Old Montee before he even finishes giving me the address.

Knowing that I'm going to see him, I start to get excited in a good way, not the panicky can't-get-oxygen way. Dr. B. really is so much better than the Xanax from Dr. Calvin.

It's only a ten-minute bike ride down the road to a row of old attached brick buildings with new, cheery paint jobs. There aren't a lot of apartments or condos in Coral Cove—mostly single-family homes—so this is where everyone's dad temporarily moves after a divorce. Elle's father made a stop here before going to Jacksonville; so did Mom's dad before he went out West. If Dr. B.'s fiancée does decide she's done with him, he's all set.

Finding the right unit, I lock my bike to a NO PARKING sign.

I'm heading in, but then I realize I must look awful. Why didn't I take a second to do something with my hair or make sure that I wasn't all snotty before charging over? Fishing through my backpack, I find a hair thingie and twist my frizz up into a sloppy topknot; Mom says it "shows off my pretty face." I put on some tinted ChapStick and wish I'd thought to bring some of the makeup I wore last night.

Dr. B. opens the door, looking more casual than I've ever seen. He's wearing worn jeans and an old Penn T-shirt. It's clear he hasn't shaved since yesterday, and his red eyes make me wonder if he's slept at all. For added weirdness, he's got a wad of bloody gauze wrapped haphazardly around his right hand, and a tumbler of something amber and alcohol-y in the other.

"Welcome to my humble abode, Molly Byrne," he says, and lets me in.

The condo isn't at all what I was expecting. It looks like Shabby Chic threw up on a Pottery Barn. Pale blue slip-covered couch and wing chair with vintage floral throw pillows, antique-looking wicker tables, a fireplace with a lavender vase on the mantel . . . and a heap of broken ceramic-and-glass-type stuff on the white stones of the outer hearth and scattered on the surrounding floorboards.

"I'm sorry," he says when he notices me staring. "I was trying to straighten up. I didn't realize you'd get here so quickly. I . . . uh, had a little accident."

"Is that how you hurt your hand?"

"Something like that," he says, and I follow his eyes to a fist-size depression in the wall, chunks of plaster on the floor underneath it.

"Is everything okay?" I ask. "Did you talk with your fiancée again?"

"As a matter of fact I did." He smiles the world's saddest smile and shakes his head. "Just this morning she called, and I started to tell her about what happened last night—I didn't name you, obviously." Suddenly he looks at me, worried. "I'm sorry. I guess I should have asked for your permission first—"

"No, it's fine." If he's telling her about it, that has to mean that something *did* happen, right? That there *is* something to tell and I didn't just invent the whole thing.

"Anyway, she stopped me and said I didn't need to apologize. Would you like to know why?" He gives this big forced grin that doesn't really make me want to know why at all, but I nod. It appears he's really over that whole thing about not sharing personal stuff with me.

"She said she can't go on lying to me and giving me false hope. Because she's not really thinking things over; she's already thought and decided. We're done-zo because she's in love with this new Dolphins running back and they're moving in together."

"That sucks; I'm sorry." In my pocket my phone is vibrating with a new call, but it seems rude to look at it while Dr. Brooks is pouring his heart out.

"Apparently, she met him covering a charity event a few months ago." Dr. B. gulps the majority of his drink. "She doesn't even like football. In the entire six years we dated, she complained every fucking time I turned on a game."

Six years. Wow. No wonder he's taking it out on the wall. In the fireplace pile of broken things, there are a couple framed photos, and I can almost make out part of her strawberry-blond head.

"Seriously, that's not cool," I offer.

"What ya gonna do?" Dr. B. says to his empty glass, but after a minute he straightens up. "Enough about me. You sounded really upset on the phone. What's going on? Is this more of what you were saying last night, about how you felt you failed the store?"

"Sort of. I went back to clean up today, and Alex . . . Well, it turns out he isn't actually dating my sister after all. . . ."

Looking at the disaster in the fireplace and in the wall, where Dr. B. very obviously punched a hole, I feel heat on my cheeks. He must think I'm such a high school moron. Here I am having a panic attack because Alex *isn't* dating my sister, and Dr. B.'s girlfriend of six (SIX!) years—who he was planning to spend his life with—told him she's leaving him for some football star.

"Uh-huh." Dr. B. nods, but he looks like he's entire galaxies away.

"Yeah, they were only meeting to talk about me. I guess they were worried or something . . ." I peter out.

"And that makes you feel violated?" he asks absently.

Shrugging, I tell him I guess so. Saying anything more about Alex seems mean, considering what Dr. B. is going through. "I'm sorry. It . . . it seemed like a much bigger deal an hour ago. Maybe I should go."

Dr. B. shakes his head emphatically. "No, I'm glad you're here."

"You are?"

"Yes."

My heart swells.

"Can I get you something to drink?" he asks, looking at his own empty glass.

"I'll have whatever you're having."

"Somehow I don't see you as a straight Jack Daniel's kind of girl."

"Then how about a Jack and Coke?" I say, the teeniest bit proud that I know that is a drink.

He raises an eyebrow at me.

"What?" I try to sound casual. "I've had alcohol before; I'll be eighteen in a month."

"A fact that I am painfully aware of." He gives this small, knowing smile like we share a secret, but I feel like I've missed something.

Still, I grin back and follow him into a generic galley kitchen, where he refills his glass with straight whiskey and makes me one that's about two thirds soda. I'm not sure if it's a lot of Jack, but it tastes absolutely awful—worse than the sacred FSU punch at Chris's party. For the second sip, I hold the glass up to my mouth and don't actually swallow anything. Hopefully Dr. B. doesn't notice.

Back in the living room, he turns on the stereo and takes a CD from a rack in the corner.

He holds it up for me before sliding it into the tray on a bookshelf stereo. "Now, I know you may never have seen one of these before, but they are called 'compact discs,' and this is how we used to get our music back in the Stone Age."

"My mom *has* told tales about that ancient technology." I joke, but seriously, why does he always have to bring up our age difference?

The music starts, some mopey women singing about fading into someone that I think I once heard on a CW show. Dr. B. sits next to me on the frilly couch—not that close, but not that far away either.

"You might have the edge on music, but I'd bet you a very special episode that I've seen more eighties and nineties sitcoms than you have," I volunteer.

"Oh, I sincerely doubt that," he says.

But he appears genuinely impressed with my encyclopedic knowledge of nearly every episode of *Family Ties*, *The Cosby Show*, and especially *Who's the Boss?* Apparently he had a huge thing for Alyssa Milano as a kid.

"*Golden Girls*, though, that's my absolute jam."

"Get out." He laughs. "I used to watch that every Saturday night with my parents back in Philly."

The whole thing definitely feels different from our sessions, but I'm not sure I would call it date-like, just more comfortable.

Through the windows, I can see that it's getting dark; I guess I hadn't thought through how late it was when I came over. There's no way Dr. B. can give me a ride home—I can tell he's drunk—so I probably should get going before it's pitch black. But when I mention this, Dr. B.'s eyes droop, and he looks boyishly crestfallen, much closer in age to the guys I go to school with than to my mom.

"No, stay a little longer?" he says. "It's silly, but I don't want to be alone right now, and I like talking to you, Dr. Byrne."

As if I'm going to say no to that!

For once I'm the one who's helping someone sad—a bummer buster! But I am a tad worried when Dr. B. tops off our glasses, despite the fact that I haven't actually drunk any of it. My phone is going off again, but I click the ignore button without even taking it out of my pocket.

"I guess the doctor can stay in for a little while longer," I say.

"Good! Are you hungry? I don't think I've eaten anything for days."

"Me either!"

"You know, my years as a therapist have taught me there are two kinds of people in the world—stress eaters and stress starvers. We might have to look out for each other, Molly Byrne, make sure we don't waste away."

"Don't worry." I smirk. "I've got your back."

"Good to hear." He jokes that he hasn't been back to the grocery store since the time my mom accosted him, and we both kind of giggle, because it seems strange now that it was ever weird for us to hang out outside my appointments.

The only unexpired things we can find in the cabinets and fridge are a packet of Nestlé Toll House chocolate pieces and a box of Bisquick.

"Chocolate chip pancakes it is!" he announces, and we mix up the batter.

Stab of guilt thinking about Mom and the cakes and how she probably wouldn't be on board with this type of therapy.

When the food is done cooking, we take our plates and glasses (Dr. B.'s freshly topped off again; mine now full of plain Coke) into the dining area off the kitchen, where instead of a dining room table there is a giant wooden pool table and two worn recliners.

Just seeing it makes me laugh. "One of these rooms is not like the others." I wave my hand around to indicate the rest of the *Martha Stewart Living* condo.

Laughing, Dr. B. explains that when he and "Fox 9's own Whitney Lowe" moved here, he agreed to let her choose all the furniture—with his money, he might add—as long as he could have a pool table instead of a big formal dining room table that no one ever uses.

"And she still gave me crap about it." He shakes his head. "I let her decorate our whole place like we were ten-year-old girls having a tea party, and yet whenever anyone came over, she would go on and on about how she was marrying a child."

"That's a bitch move."

"You know the best part?" Dr. B. asks. "She told me today that I can keep it all. I'm now the only single straight man in the Western world who owns this many slipcovers."

"You should burn them," I say. "In a symbolic cleansing or something."

Pointing a finger at me, he nods. "You're the best."

"Thanks," I mumble. God, my face is on fire.

We sit in the recliners and eat the pancakes (well, I eat mine; Dr. B. mainly just picks out a few chocolate pieces), and talk more about *Golden Girls*.

"So, which one is your favorite?" he asks.

"How can you ask that question?" I'm actually a little serious. "They're all great in their own ways. It's like asking a mother to pick her favorite child."

"Molly." Dr. B. smiles. "You really are a thirty-seven-year-old trapped in a teenager's body—not that it's a bad body, mind you. It's truly a lovely body."

His comment is flattering but weird. Like, I'm glad that he knows I have a body (I definitely wanted him to notice my body last night), but there's something off about the way he says it.

"Um, thanks."

I really should get going. Dr. B. looks like he might fall asleep in his chair. When he actually starts snoring, I reach into my pocket to call Elle and see if she can come get me—even though I know she'll give me a the lecture to end all lectures.

"Do you play?" Awake again, Dr. B. points toward the pool table.

"A little." Back when I used to go to such things, I played a few games at swim team parties if someone's parents had a table in the basement, but we were mostly dicking around. I don't know any of the rules or anything.

"Show me what you've got!" With a sudden burst of energy, Dr. B. springs from his chair and reaches into the table pockets for the balls. When all the solids and stripes are ordered, he rolls the triangle up and down on the table a few times and tells me to pick out my cue while he refreshes our drinks.

Having no idea about the criteria, I grab the shortest pole from the rack. Dr. B. calls out that he's got to "drain the weasel"—an expression I never in a million years would have imagined him saying—and ducks into the bathroom. I take out my phone to see who called before. Five voice mail messages. The first one from Elle.

"Ohmygod, Molly. Mark is *amazing*! Call me ASAP. Also, V and Alex aren't dating; they're just friends or something! Call me back!"

Well, that information might have been helpful earlier in the day.

Then four messages from Alex. The first one from right when I got to Dr. B.'s

"Molly, I feel shitty about the way we left things. I shouldn't have put you in that position. . . . Call me back if you want."

This is good. Even if I am still confused about everything, I hate myself when I think of Alex hating me. Before I can listen to the other messages, Dr. B. reappears, sipping his drink to keep the whiskey from sloshing over the side.

"Why don't you get things started?" I suggest.

Dr. B. is really good. He ends up being stripes and manages to sink more than half the balls in his first turn, always announcing which one he's going to be sending into which pocket. He even does these trick shots where he puts the cue behind his back or tosses it from hand to hand.

"Dude, are you some sort of pool shark?" I ask.

"What can I say? I saw *The Color of Money* a lot when I was a kid," he says.

"Never seen it."

"Oh, it's a classic," he says. "That can be your next movie assignment."

I wonder if he means we can watch it together like we did with *Say Anything* . . . . Wonder if he means we'd watch it in the office or if I would come over here again. I think I'd like that, but maybe when he hasn't been drinking quite so much.

Clearly he's mega-sloshed. While his hands are pretty sure when he's shooting, he stumbles multiple times as he circles the table, and his eyelids are sagging. Plus, he's all sweaty, even though the air conditioner is jacked up so high that I'm freezing in my shorts and tank top. If I were a sitcom wife, I'd definitely have to say something about him slowing down. But I'm not, and saying something would make things weird.

Maybe this is just his thing? There have been more than a few nights when Elle and I have had to pour her mom into bed when she came home totally wasted. Maybe this is just what some single adults do? (Obviously not perfect ones like Mom.)

Finally Dr. B. misses a shot and announces it's my turn. "I'm really glad you came over." His words are running together. "I was having a crap-tastic day, and you've managed to cheer me up. Thank you."

"Anytime."

Leaning over the table, I position my index finger into a loop for the cue and do a couple of practice slides like I saw Dr. B. doing. When I actually try to take a shot, however, the cue slips and skids against the table without even hitting the white ball.

"Scratch that scratch." Dr. B. laughs and comes over. "Your stance is all wrong." Putting his hands on my hips, he guides my legs back from the table. My shorts are pretty short, and his ring fingers and pinkies graze my outer thighs. It would be kind of exciting, except alcohol is radiating off him and he's swaying and totally unsteady.

"Now let's do something about your arms." He could just as easily show me, but instead he stands behind me, kind of draping himself over me as he bends my arms into position. "There you go."

Moving to steady myself, my butt rubs against the bulge of his crotch. Instinctively I hop away, and he chuckles under his breath. Thrusting my arms into the shot, we tap the three ball into the right middle pocket.

"Thanks." Straightening up, I move away a few inches, but Dr. B. is still lightly holding my right wrist. "My mom's gonna be getting really worried. I should get going."

"Come on, Maw-leee." It's the same look that Alex had earlier when he almost kissed me. Dr. B. even stretches my name out the same way. But he smells of whiskey, and his eyes are glazed over. He's so unstable, he'd probably tumble over if he weren't holding on to me with one hand and leaning heavily on the table with the other.

Without warning his lips smash into mine, tongue trying to work its way into my mouth. Sloppy and hot. And *nothing* like last night.

Last night everything felt meaningful and romantic and slightly tortured in a *Twilight* kind of way. . . . Last night I wanted him to kiss me so bad, the ache became a solid, tangible thing. But this is just gross and awful and a little scary.

I push him away, and he would fall over backward if he weren't still holding my arm.

"I should go."

"So you're seriously going to leave?" His tone changes to a mix of incredulousness and anger, but it's still slurry, which makes it even more dangerous somehow. I have no idea who this person is. "I'm gonna lose my fucking license for *this*!"

"What are you—" I start, but stop. Of course. Even if

it's only for a few more weeks, I'm only seventeen; and he's my doctor. Even if I was the one who kissed him last night, he could get into a lot of trouble for what we're doing.

"Is this some sick game for you?" he drawls, and I freeze. Just four hours ago Alex was telling me to stop playing mind games.

"I . . ."

"You flirt with me for months, and I try to ignore it—try to be the good guy, try to help you, blah, blah, blah. But the minute Whitney is out of the picture, you bat your lashes and *insist* I come to your fucking fish fest. Then you invite yourself over and prance around and rub your ass against me. You win, Molly. You want me to say 'uncle'? Uncle, all right? I admit it, I want you. Whit's off screwing some NFL star, so why not? Let's do this."

"I didn't mea—"

But I did mean this. Some of this, at least. I did start acting more like Dr. B. was a guy I was crushing on than like he was my doctor. I did invent stuff so he would like me. And I did want him to come to the fund-raiser as more than just my shrink, definitely wanted him to kiss me on the stairwell. But . . . I didn't want this. At least not this way, with him drunk and mean and disgusting.

"No."

"So why are you here, then?"

"Because . . ." I can feel myself starting to slip. He's the one who makes me feel safe. But this is the opposite of safe. "You're my doctor . . ."

"Oh, so now you're just my patient again? The sad little girl with the hermit crab who makes up stories about her dead dad?" He pulls me closer to him. "Is this what you did to that douche in Barbie and the Rockers? No wonder you made him crazy."

Without thinking, I jerk my knee up into his junk, really, really hard. Letting go of me, he crumples over into a moaning heap on the ground. Not looking back, I run out the door and to my bike. In the dark I struggle with the lock, get it free just as Dr. B. makes it to the door.

"Wait, Molly. I . . ." Dr. B. is calling after me, but I'm pedaling as fast as possible down the road.

I can't stop thinking about Pickles and his simple little life on the dollhouse couch in the crabitat.

Somehow I make it home. From the kitchen Mom calls out something, but I hurry up the stairs with an excuse about needing the bathroom.

So hard to catch my breath.

On my bed, panting.

Finally I take out my phone to call Elle, and remember Alex's other messages.

Message 2: "Molly, I canceled on my friend and I'm

coming back to the store. I'm sorry. Obviously you don't have to go out with me if you don't want to."

Message 3: "Okay, back at FishTopia, but you're not here. It looks like you left in a hurry. Are you okay? Just give me a call when you can. I'm sorry."

The last one is from hours later, Alex's tone completely different:

"When I couldn't get in touch with you, I got worried, so I called V and explained what had happened. And you know what she said, Molly? She said I shouldn't feel bad about anything because you're fucking your shrink—that she saw you guys making out at the fund-raiser. So I guess you won't be calling me back."

Then I actually do need the bathroom, to throw up.

DAY 73

Roasted Apple-Butter Spice Cake

My old-fashioned alarm clock gongs, and I text JoJo to ask if she can cover for me at FishTopia. When she writes back that she can use the money, I tell her she can have all my remaining shifts. Then I go back to bed.

On her way to the salon, Mom knocks on my door and asks if I'm okay.

"I'm fine. I just . . . have really bad cramps."

When she knocks eight hours later, I pretend to be asleep. She leaves a bottle of Midol on my dresser, along with a piece of cake.

At some point in between Mom's two knocks, Dr. B. leaves a voice message on my phone. "Molly, I just woke up. I don't remember everything that happened last night, but I remember enough to know I was an ass. I'm so sorry.

Please call me. And if you're looking for your backpack, you left it here."

Deleting the message, I flip over onto my stomach and go back to sleep.

DAY 74

—∞∞∞—

Cherry Oatmeal Upside-Down Cake

Text from Dr. B.: *Molly, please. Can you just let me know that you're okay? As your therapist, if I don't hear from you, I should probably call your mom.*

I write back: *I'm fine; DON'T even think about calling my mother.*

Several times I start to text Alex a message, but I have no idea what to say.

When Mom knocks on the door, I tell her I still feel crappy, and she asks if I want her to make an appointment with her gynecologist. "You're almost eighteen," she says. "It's probably time you started seeing someone anyway."

What a weird idea. In a few weeks I'll magically be an adult. I wonder if Mom thinks I'm having sex with anyone, wonder if she knows about V and Chris. (Are they having sex? How can I not know that?) Wonder when Mom had sex for the first time and if it was with Dad—maybe the night they met when Kurt Cobain died.

If it were weeks from now, and I were eighteen, would that have changed what happened between me and Dr. B.? Would I have known what I was doing by going over to his house? Would it have changed what happened between me and Alex? Would I finally have had the instruction manuals for these games I didn't realize I was playing?

"Maybe," I tell Mom.

At some point I start reading *The Catcher in the Rye*. It's pretty good. The whole thing—according to SparkNotes—is a discussion with a therapist. I wonder if Holden Caulfield ever made out with his shrink or kneed him in the balls?

DAY 75

Triple Berry Summer Butter Bundt Cake

This is the last day of FishTopia. The last day to watch *Golden Girls* reruns with Alex on the antiquated TV. The last day for environmentally unsound clamshells of house special lo mein. The last day of all the brilliant fish swishing around in their tanks unaware of how small their lives are.

I spend it lying around in the sleigh bed and then lying around in the bonus room so Mom can't accuse me of not leaving my room.

My phone dings with two text messages. I assume—okay, hope—that they'll be from Alex, saying something about the end of our FishTopia era. They aren't. One is from Elle asking where I've been; the other is Dr. B. suggesting he put me in touch with another therapist.

At some point I hear Mom and V talking about me through the model-home walls.

Mom: "I don't know. Do you think I should call Glen Brooks?"

Veronica: "NO! I mean, I think she'd see that as a total invasion of her privacy."

And even though I'm still mad at her for suggesting I kill myself and for telling Alex about Dr. Brooks and me, I do appreciate that she's not blabbing to Mom about what she saw at FishTopia.

I miss my sister.

I miss everyone.

DAY 76

Red, White, and Blueberry Cake

I'm still in bed when Elle comes charging through my door with two fully loaded chili dogs from Haute Dogs. It used to be our favorite place before she became an animal advocate and decided we couldn't eat there ever again.

"I got a call from your mom asking me to check on you while she was at work. I figured the situation called for drastic measures," Elle offers as an explanation, and I feel bad for making my mom worry . . . again. The big blue bummer bringing her joy to the masses. "Just maybe don't mention the hot dogs to Mark; he's a pretty strict vegan."

I almost ask who Mark is, but then I remember—Alex's keyboardist from the no-name band. Flood of guilt that I've been too busy wallowing in my own stuff to realize that something important is going on with my friend. I never even asked her how their coffee date went after the fund-raiser, which now seems like a million years ago.

"So are you guys, like, an official thing?" I ask.

"I mean, it's been less than a week, but we've been out almost every night, and he usually texts me a couple of times during the day."

Even though I really want to scrunch down under the covers and go back to sleep, I take a bite of chili dog; it is frighteningly good. "So tell me everything!"

And she does.

How Mark is totally progressive politically but still kind of old-school when it comes to romance. "He always holds open doors, and he insisted on paying for dinner at that really pricey raw-food place in Maxwell!"

How when she couldn't get a babysitter for Jimmy one night, Mark took them both out for non-dairy ice cream at the hippie cart.

How when they kissed—second date, with tongue—it was amazing. "I know it's too early for this Nicholas Sparks destiny crap, but I think I could really fall for him," she gushes.

"That is so amazing." I *am* really happy for her, but I can't help but think of how tingly and important it felt to kiss Dr. B. at the fund-raiser, and how awful it was when he tried to kiss me the next day.

"You have to get to know him too!" Elle is saying. "Tonight we're seeing a lecture by this guy who wrote a book on sustainability in the entertainment industry; you should come with."

Depression or no depression, that lecture sounds physically painful. "I don't think I'm quite ready for the outside world yet."

"Oh God, Mol. I'm such a idiot." Elle changes tone. "What's going on? Your mom was pretty worried."

Where to even begin? With my botched seduction of my shrink? Alex telling me he was through with me and storming out? I go with the classic rom-com misdirection between Alex, Veronica, and me.

"So it turns out Alex and V weren't dating, like, at all."

"I know! Mark told me. Did you get my message about it?"

"Yeah, about two hours too late."

"Oh no! Did you sort things out? Are you together yet?"

"Um, nope, not so much." I tell her all about Alex saying he was in love with me ("I knew it!") and then storming out when I told him I couldn't go out with him. ("No!")

"But I don't understand." Elle looks legitimately confused. "I mean, it sounds like he was a total dick about it—no woman has to go out with anyone just because he wants her to—and I'm BFF law on your side no matter what, but didn't you want to go out with him? Like, isn't that the reason we were so mad at V when we thought she was dating him?"

"I guess. I just didn't want to ruin everything once he

realized I wasn't this amazing girl he thought I was."

"Why would he think that, Mol?"

"That's exactly what happened with T.J. He thought I was the coolest thing since FSU mystery punch, and then he decided I wasn't really all that."

"T. J. Cranston is a jerk-off who asked you out because he liked the way your ass looked in your team suit." Elle is all huffy puffy now. "Alex is someone you've talked to almost every day for two years. I'm sure he's already figured out that you don't shit rainbows."

I shrug again. When she says it like that, it does make me feel like a bottom-feeder.

"Mol, I know you hate it when I say this, but shouldn't your therapist be helping you with stuff like this?"

"Well, I might have been too busy trying to get into Dr. B.'s pants for that."

"What?" Elle's eyes narrow, and even though I'm still reeling and disgusted by what happened with Dr. B., I'm hesitant to say anything about it to her, or to anyone, really. 'Cause saying it aloud means it actually happened, that I probably can't just go back to our next session and pretend it's all good with us. And I kind of want to.

"Molly? What happened?"

Even though I know it will change stuff, I tell her everything, like everything-everything, from how I started lying to Dr. B. so he'd like me, right on up to him drunk and grabby. For once Elle doesn't interrupt, just listens, eyes growing wider with each new detail.

"You should call the police," she says when I finish. "He committed, like, fifteen crimes."

"But I was the one who kissed him the night before, and I was the one who insisted on going over there even after he told me he was hammered."

"It doesn't matter. What the dude did was wrong."

"But I'm pretty sure I went over there because I *did* want to sleep with him, just not like that."

"Whatever, Mollybean. You're allowed to change your mind—kisses aren't freaking sex contracts. You're always allowed to say no at any point. And he's the adult—he's your shrink, for God's sake."

"I know." As I say it, I realize it's true. But here's the thing: everyone we know besides me is counting the days until they can run away to college or to some real-world job on their own, all of them demanding to be treated like grown-ups. So how can we hide under the label of "still a child" when it's convenient?

"At the very least, this guy shouldn't be practicing. You need to report him to the medical board or somewhere." She takes out her cell phone and starts looking up how to get your shrink arrested or something. "Let's see where we go."

"Don't." I take the phone from her and set it on the bed.

I understand why she's saying what she's saying and

how I must sound, but as scary as he was that night, I still miss Dr. Brooks. That circular panic starts in my head every time I think about not going back for our appointments. And so much of our time was great. Does one stupid night when he was sauced negate all of that?

"Molly."

"No, E. Please don't make me the poster child for shrink sexual harassment or whatever your latest cause is, okay?"

"You can't just let him get away with this."

"I'm not some endangered rhino or whatever. You don't need to save me."

"But—"

"Seriously, just promise me you won't tell anyone until I figure it out."

"Molly—"

"I call BFF law."

Shaking her head, she mumbles, "Fine, I won't say anything yet."

"Thank you." I nod. "So tell me more about Mark."

DAY 77

—❦—

Flowerpot Cake with Fondant Flowers

When I get on my bike, I don't have a destination in mind. Maybe it's a muscle-memory thing that brings me to FishTopia.

Only, it's not FishTopia anymore. There's brown paper taped up on the windows, so you can't see inside, and a plastic tarp over the block letters of the old sign reads, COMING SOON: MRS. K'S COUNTRY DINER!

The exclamation point seems like overkill.

My keys still work, so I let myself in.

The walls are still the blue-green color that Alex said looked like my eyes, but all the tanks and fish are gone, returned to some fish factory far, far away. (Or maybe really close. I don't have any idea.) Mrs. K! and her country crew haven't really done much else, and the place is essentially empty. Maybe it's that I'm not used to seeing it like

281

this, but the space looks much smaller, somehow less important. And the laminate surface of the counter where Alex and I used to sit is way more chipped than I ever noticed.

"Hello. May I help you?" asks a man, maybe sixty-five, with a trim white beard and kind eyes.

"Oh, I, uh, used to work here, and I was . . ." What? Coming by to look for ghosts; coming by to re-create something long gone. "Um, just coming by to drop off my keys."

"Oh, yes. You must be Molly!" The man is all lit up with excitement. "Charlie Harrison spoke very highly of you! Said that you were quite the go-getter and we should snap you up before you got another job."

"That was really nice of him."

"You haven't gotten one, then?" he asks. "Another job?" Seriously, Charlie, what did you say to this dude—that I was a pro when it comes to watching TV and not cleaning? That I spearheaded an illegal rooftop fund-raiser and managed to raise enough money to cover the cost of one season of the *Golden Girls* on Blu-ray? "Let me go grab my wife—Mrs. K. She's handling the hiring."

"Oh, that's okay. I'm not really looking for anything right now. But I know the other girl who worked here—JoJo Banks—was really hoping you might be hiring waiters. She's really great too."

"Oh yes, we talked with her, but she turned us down."

"Really?" *Really?* "I guess she must have found something else."

"What about the other high school student Charlie mentioned? Alex, I think it was. Do you think he might be interested?"

"I'm sorry. We really haven't been in touch."

"Well, if you do see him, just let him know we'd love to talk to him."

I'm through wasting my time with this.

"Yeah, sure," I say. "And good luck with the new place."

"Thanks." He smiles. "You'll definitely have to come for the grand opening!"

Promising to try, I set my keys on the counter. It's sad and it's not. Alex and our time together is what I miss, not the building that housed us. How I didn't realize that before is one of life's great mysteries.

Unlocking my bike, I give the building one more once-over, amazed that I never noticed the cracks in the front window or how uneven the concrete of the sidewalk is.

Maybe Alex was right. My need for everything to stay exactly the same was what screwed things up. If things never change, they eventually decay.

I'd love to call him. I could even use the job offer as an excuse—tell him that I know he's avoiding me but people are looking for him.

But I don't.

DAY 79

Caramel Walnut Upside-Down Banana Cake

Based on where the light coming through the upgraded windows is hitting the upgraded hardwood floors, it's got to be after noon when I wake up. I actually feel pretty good. One perk about depression, you get your rest.

On the floor outside my bedroom door, Mom has laid out slices of the cakes from the last few days, like a dessert sampler from a high-end restaurant. The whole thing is so cute and bizarre; I start laughing, which feels really good. Mom is such an adorable kook sometimes.

Hot water from the upgraded rain showerhead is amazing, and by the time I'm clean and dressed, I'm famished. I gobble up the old cake to tide me over on my way downstairs.

It's Mom's day off from the salon, and she's in the kitchen sifting flour into a large mixing bowl. She really has gotten pretty good. There's hardly any mess, and she has this authority over the appliances—she's totally made them her bitches. Leave it to Mom to achieve anything she sets her mind to, even something totally random like baking a hundred different cakes.

Seeing me, this giant grin splits her whole face, and she looks positively radiant. I kind of expect she might break into "Be Our Guest" or something. Then she freezes and doesn't say anything, as if I'm some small woodland creature she's stumbled upon in the forest and doesn't want to scare away before she can snap an Instagram pic.

"Can I help?" I ask.

"You want to?" Mom asks, with the type of enthusiasm that would suggest I've been elected president of the United State or am going on a date with Prince Harry.

"Yeah. Gotta learn to cook for myself at some point, right?"

"Of course." She hands me a bowl and a wooden spoon and says I can combine the dry ingredients. "You know, one of the reasons I started this was that I thought it was something that you and me and V could do together."

"Really?" Yeah, nope, had no idea about that.

"When you were little, you girls would always get out Gram's bowls and pans and help her bake. But then you'd come home, and we didn't have half the equipment, and I was always working so much that we never really did any of that stuff. I figured maybe it wasn't too late to try it."

It sort of makes sense that she wanted us to spend time together, but maybe she could have just asked us to go on a walk or something.

"So what's on the menu today?" I ask, and she goes through all the ingredients and explains that she's trying to make sure that everything is organic for Elle.

I tell her that Elle is dating the environmental keyboard player.

"These two might be legit made for each other," I say. "It's crazy."

"Oh, good for her." Mom gets a little misty. "See, there really is someone out there for everyone if you just open your eyes."

I'm about to ask if that means she and Toupee Thom are back on after the fund-raiser, but V comes in from the garage.

"Mom, have you seen my—" She stops when she gets to the kitchen and sees me. Unabashed hatred floods her face. "What are YOU doing here?"

"I *do* live here."

"Yeah, you do, and for four freaking days Mom's been asking me whether or not we need to haul you to some *Girl, Interrupted* hospital, and now, just like that, poof, you're perfectly fine? You waltz down the stairs at your leisure and decide to play baker's helper, and you're suddenly the golden child again?"

As I'm turning to defend myself, my sister bats the bowl of dry ingredients out of my hands to the upgraded floors, sending up this giant cartoon cloud of flour and baking soda that whitens her dark eyebrows and the front of her hair.

"Veronica Caitlyn Byrne!" Mom shouts like V is six again.

"What's your damage?" I ask.

"My *damage* is that we all have to kowtow to you and your stupid moods, because Dad killed himself and Mom is so terrified you're gonna do the same that she lets you get away with anything!"

"Dad died in a car accident . . . ," I begin, but a bunch of things are starting to come together in a way that makes more sense than all the stories I've always been told.

"Yep, he did!" V is screaming, flour flecks falling off her face, which would be hysterically funny if everything she was saying wasn't so horrible and world-altering. "He hit a tree at ninety miles an hour because he was aiming for it. It was the middle of the day; it wasn't even raining out."

"Wha—"

"Guess the kicker!" V doesn't wait for an answer. "Dad was on his way to get YOUR birthday cake! So now Mom is making seven THOUSAND cakes because she's convinced the reason you're such a sad sack of seventeen-year-old is that you never got a cake for your third birthday or some ridiculous psychobabble. Because everything in the world is always about you. And it has ALWAYS been about you."

"Veronica!" Mom again.

"No, I'm sick of this shit," V yells. "It's time somebody finally said something."

V spins on a wedge heel and clomps out of the kitchen, flour hitting the floor in her wake.

"Come back here—" Mom gives up on the scream about halfway through. V's already gone.

When I was a kid, I found this cool book at Gram's about the solar system. I freaking loved the thing. Even before I could read, I'd study the glossy pictures of each planet. And in second-grade science class, I used the book as the model for this poster I made with construction-paper planets. (My teacher especially dug that I'd used aluminum foil to give the moons a shine.) But then one day some NASA scientist or whoever got information back from a satellite and decided Pluto wasn't a planet anymore, that my book and poster, and every poster made by every second grader since forever, was wrong.

My dad is Pluto.

Everything I've always thought about him is wrong.

"Is that true?" I turn to Mom. "About Dad?"

Mom opens her mouth, then closes it.

"Is it?"

Pressing her lips together into a thin line, she nods.

All this wasted time.

Time imagining how much better our lives would have

been with Dad. Time trying to explain how I could miss someone so much who I hardly knew. And all the while he had actively *chosen* not to be here with us.

All that time talking over crap with Dr. B. All that time meeting with the guidance counselor at school. And those humiliating appointments where Dr. Calvin wrote some scripts and offered me finger puppets. All that time worrying about why I am the way I am and how to fix me. All that time, and Mom could have simply told me the truth. It's no different from my mouse-poop frizz. I got Dad's crappy genes just like I got his crappy hair.

Why does V know this?

Who else knows this?

Gram?

My dad's parents in Missouri, who send us five-dollar checks for Christmas and our birthdays and see us once every few years if they happen to be in Florida?

Any of the friends that my parents had in Miami?

Who else?

"Molly, let me ex . . . ," Mom is saying, but she might as well be back in that Charlie Brown world where adult talk is nothing but sad trombone.

Without even acknowledging her, I step over the mess of spilled dry ingredients and charge back up the stairs to my bedroom. I pick up my phone and scroll through the call log to the most recent outgoing call.

Dr. B. picks up on the first ring. "Molly, I'm so glad you call—"

"Did you know about my father?" I demand. "Is that why you always wanted me to talk about him?"

"Know what? About you making up those stories?"

"Not that." I bat his response away as if he were in the room with me. "When my mom first talked to you last year, did she tell you that my dad killed himself?"

"Oh, wow." Across the line, Dr. B. inhales a deep breath like he's just a regular Joe Blow who doesn't know any more about human behavior business than the rest of us. "No, Molly, I had no idea."

"She didn't say anything about it at all?"

"No. I mean, I really wish she had. That could have been helpful in our treatment."

"It could have been helpful for ME." My voice cracks at the end, and I think I might cry . . . AGAIN, because that's what I do. Maybe because that's what my dad did—cry and slam into trees at ninety miles an hour on bright sunny days.

"Molly—"

"Might have been nice to know that I'm just made this way and no amount of stress balls or headshrinking can help that."

"It doesn't work that way," he says. "You're still your own person." He sounds like Dr. B. again, and I remember that before I invited him to the FishTopia event, before I kissed him, before I jammed my knee into his balls, I liked him because he seemed like a nice guy who genuinely wanted to help.

"Can we set up an appointment?" I ask. "Please? Maybe something today or our old time?"

"Molly, I want to put you in touch with a colleague. She's a psychiatrist, so she could help you with your meds, too. I think she'd be a great—"

"I don't want another shrink." I hate myself for whining, but how could he even think about leaving me NOW?

"I am so, so very sorry about what happened." He sighs the saddest of all sad sighs, and I can picture him rubbing his eyebrows. "You didn't do anything wrong—so don't blame yourself; it was my fault—but I can't be your therapist anymore."

"You were drunk. Just don't drink at our appointments, and we'll be fine." Even if he was a scary gropey jerk, I still *need* him.

"Molly, I should have set you up with a different therapist a long time before that night." A sigh that is somehow even sadder than the last one. "It's the first thing they tell you about in school—warning signs that you're developing feelings for a patient or she's developing them for you. They were all there, but I just kept thinking, *She's only seventeen. Don't worry about it.*"

There it is again, this limbo where I'm straddling two worlds and not fitting into either.

"You're dealing with some really big issues, especially with this new information about your father," he continues. "Please don't let what happened between us prevent you from getting treatment. Can I at least give you Dr. Frankel's contact info?"

He lists some information that I tune out. I'm back to floating above myself, watching everything from a nice place somewhere else.

DAY 80

Chocolate Chip Spice Cake

That is seriously effed up," Elle says when I tell her about my dad's non-accident accident.

We're on the model-home deck in my backyard, on the grass, Elle's brother is running in dizzying NASCAR ovals. The cake we're eating is from a few days ago. I guess Mom didn't really feel like finishing the one yesterday after V dropped the truth bomb and the corresponding flour bomb.

Suddenly Elle stops chewing, mid-forkful, and pushes her plate aside. "Oh God, we're eating a dead person's dessert."

For a few seconds I contemplate this. "No, it's not actually like that at all."

"It's still creepy, though," Elle says, but takes another bite; even I have to admit that Mom's getting really good at this. "It's like cake equals death, or maybe it's that the lack of cake is death. The whole thing feels like an English question about symbolism."

It *is* messed up. But the cake thing doesn't weird me out as much as it probably should. It just makes me sad that Mom was so desperate and clueless that the best way she could come up with to help me was to start some AP English bake-a-thon.

My memories of Dad's funeral are the vaguest of vague. Casseroles and trays of cookies that I kept thinking were for my birthday, stacked on the kitchen table. Hundreds of hands patting my head and saying gentle things; no one wanting to play My Little Pony with me. But the weird thing is, as little as I remember, I do have pretty distinct memories of blowing out candles while sitting on Mom's lap with Gram there. I guess my unconscious makes things up even when I'm not just saying stuff because it's easier or I want my shrink to like me.

"Did your mom explain why she told V and not you?" Elle asks.

The truth is, I really didn't give Mom much of an opportunity to explain anything. She came up to my room a few times and asked to talk, but I couldn't bring myself to look at her. She'd taken away Pluto.

It's bizzare, but I can't articulate why I'm mad at Mom. There's probably never really a great time to tell your kids, "Oh yeah, your dad actually meant to take a header into that tree—he couldn't be bothered to hit the brakes."

"No," I say. "I guess she was only trying to look out for us."
Elle scrunches her face when I say this. "You should tell
her that." Elle sighs. "Having a mother who looks out for
you actually sounds kind of great."

On cue Jimmy starts some new endeavor where he
picks up speed and hurls himself in a feetfirst slide into the
white picket fence. (It *is* the model home. Of course there's
a white picket fence.)

"At the very least you should hear what she has to say,"
Elle says, completely ignoring him. She asks if I've decided
to do anything about Dr. B., and I tell her that I'm still
thinking about it.

"Molly, what's there to think about? The guy is a jerk
and might be danger—"

Before she can finish, Mom bursts through the door to
the deck, even though it's barely eleven a.m. and she usually
works until at least six. The panicky depression/Gram look
is splashed across her face.

"Is V with you?" she demands, eyes flittering from me to
Elle to Jimmy.

"No," I say, even though that's obvious.

"Oh God." Her hand rises to her throat, and she fiddles
with this little gold scissors necklace V and I got her for
Mother's Day. "Have you seen her at all today?"

Even when I'm *trying* to avoid my sister, I usually bump
into her in the hall or in the Jack-and-Jill bathroom between

our bedrooms, but thinking back through the morning, I come up completely blank.

"What's wrong, Mrs. Byrne?" Elle asks.

"Jaclyn Noble called. Apparently V didn't come in this morning, and no one at the store can get in touch with her."

"She's got to be home," I offer. "Her phone's been ringing nonstop all morning, and you know she'd never leave the house without it."

Mom explains she thought that too, that she went in to talk to V last night, saw her phone on her nightstand, and figured she was in the bathroom.

"She was so mad, I just thought that I'd give her a little time." Mom is clutching the hell out of the necklace. "Then when she was gone this morning, I figured she had already left for the store. But I don't think she's here."

From the yard Jimmy shouts that V isn't in the house. "I always check to see if Veronica my love is home when we come over. The lump on her bed was just a pile of clothes."

"Oh God," Mom says. "Do you think she's been gone all night?"

"I'm sure she's fine," Elle says, eyes flicking toward me.

"Jaclyn said none of the girls had any idea where she might be." Mom is winding up. "Should we call the police?"

"No, no. She's probably just at her boyfriend's or something," I say.

Mom's a few words away from tears. "I didn't even know she had a boyfriend."

Welcome to the How Can You Not Know That about Veronica Byrne club. "We're friendly with him, and he lives pretty close by. Maybe Elle can take me over there and we can check?"

Elle nods and grabs her keys.

"Should I come too?" Mom asks, but as upset as she is, even she has to realize how much worse that would potentially make things. Bad enough having your sister show up.

"No," I say. "Why don't you stay here with Jimmy in case she calls the landline or comes back or something? We'll shoot you a text as soon as we find her."

Elle and I hurry outside and climb into her dad's old Jeep.

"It was off Stanhope Drive, right?" she asks, and I have a weird flash of the only other time we ever went to Chris Partridge's house, the night of his party when I ran into V on my way out and she said I should stay so we could bond or something.

"Yeah." I nod. "She's got to be there, right? Like, that's where she had to go?"

"I'm sure she's fine," Elle assures. "She was probably just terrified to face you and your mom after all that."

We turn down Stanhope, and I recognize Chris's house as the one with the bright blue door. The second Elle puts the car into park, we spring out, and we're breathing hard by the time Chris's brother Robbie comes to the door in swim trunks and an FSU T-shirt.

"Yo, Chris, some more of your *high school* friends are here," he calls through the house, and then disappears.

"Ronnie—" Chris jogs to the door, but his face falls when he sees it's the other Byrne girl. "Oh. Hi, Molly. Hi, Elle."

"Is my sister here?" I ask.

"Um, no." Chris nervously shifts from foot to foot and jams his hands into the pockets of his khaki shorts. He doesn't sound at all believable.

"I don't even need to talk to her or anything, but my mom has no idea where V is, and she's about to put her picture on a milk carton."

Seeming even less sure, Chris tells us he doesn't know where she is.

"Can you just let us know if she's all right, then?" Elle says.

"We're all getting kind of worried," I add, and it's true. If she's not here or at the store, where else could she be? How do I know so little about her these days? "Please."

"Okay." Chris sighs and nods and looks extremely relieved. "But I'm only telling you this because I don't know if she *is* all right. Yesterday she called me from the pay phone at the Shell station on Sunflower and asked me to come get her."

A pay phone?

"She was all upset, and she'd done this really weird white thing with her hair. But when I asked her what the deal was, she just kept saying that she'd screwed up . . . with you." He points his head toward me.

"She said that?" I ask.

"Yeah, but she didn't want to talk about it, and she was pretty, I don't know, snappy with me. I was supposed to work, but I told her I'd get someone to cover for me at the theater if she wanted to hang out or whatever—she just seemed so messed up. But instead she had me drop her off by the park in old town. She said she wanted to see her grandma."

"Really?" I ask.

"I felt douchey leaving her there, but she, like, insisted," he says. "Does your grandma even live there?"

"Down the street from the park, yeah."

"She was just so weird about the whole thing." Chris looks completely lost. Next to me Elle makes a sympathetic clicking noise with her tongue. "I tried her cell a bunch of times last night, but she never called back. And we usually talk every night. I reached out to a couple of her friends, but they didn't know anything either."

"I'm sure she's fine," Elle says, but she doesn't sound that convinced anymore.

From my phone I try my grandma's landline (Gram might be the only person in the twenty-first century who doesn't have a cell) but get the machine. I have some vague memories of her volunteering at the library some mornings.

"Maybe V is there and doesn't feel right answering the phone?" Elle suggests. "You know, it's not her house, why deal with someone else's telemarketers?"

"Maybe," I say.

Elle and I decide to drive over and check. Chris wants to come too, but with V not having her phone, we decide it's better if he stays here in case she comes back or tries to reach him here. We exchange numbers and agree to keep each other updated if either one of us finds something.

"Like, even if she doesn't want to talk to me," he says, all sincere and sweet, "can you just let me know if she's okay?"

I don't know a lot about Chris Partridge other than that he was shocked that I could be Alex's Molly, he's a fan of FSU frat punch, and he's unlikely to use natural enzymes instead of chlorine in his swimming pool. It is, however, crystal clear how much he cares about my sister, so I decide he's a good guy.

On the drive to the old part of town, Elle and I hardly say anything; both too nervous, I think.

Several texts come in from Mom asking if we've found V and if she was at her boyfriend's. *Almost*, I shoot back, which makes no sense, but anything else will only panic her more.

When we get to Gram's, Elle and I pound on the door, but no one answers. Then we simply try the knob, and, of course, it's unlocked. People in the old part of Coral Cove are forever leaving their doors unlocked. We let ourselves in, and Elle starts looking through the rooms at the front of the house, while I run to the three bedrooms in the back, where Mom grew up, and where V and Mom and I all stayed when we came back after my father died (I mean killed himself).

The little twin bed where I slept and listened to my grandma fight with my mom about my dad when they thought I was asleep. *He left you high and dry.*

"V!" I call. But the room is empty, as is Gram's bedroom with its neatly made bed, and Mom's old room too.

There's this episode of *Golden Girls* where Sophia accidentally donates Blanche's leather bomber jacket, not knowing that there's a winning lottery ticket inside the pocket. Once the ladies realize their mistake, they spend the rest of the show running around the city looking for the coat and the ticket, until they finally trace it to a homeless shelter and decide the people there need the prize more than they do. That feels nothing at all like Elle and my running around now. This is sheer terror.

"She's not here." Elle appears at my side. She doesn't even bother saying that she's sure my sister is fine. "What now?"

"Maybe we just drive around? Try the bus station? I don't know."

Though we don't have any clear plan established, Elle

and I sprint full-speed back to the car and start driving *somewhere*. The urgency makes us feel more productive and less helpless.

"Remember at the FishTopia event, she mentioned someone named Nell or Nina?" Elle is saying. "Maybe Chris knows her?"

"Good idea," I say, but I bet he's already tried her. "I'll shoot him a text."

We're turning down Sunflower Street by our old house, when I notice a flash of something shiny in the backyard swing—my sister's hair.

"Stop the car!" I scream, and Elle slams on the brakes. "There." I point to my sister sitting in the backyard swing a quarter of a football field away.

Elle pulls up to the curb, puts the Jeep in park.

"I'll go talk to her. Can you let Mom and Chris know?" I say, already unbuckled and halfway out the door.

Jogging through our old yard, I almost trip over an orange lawn sprinkler, and I'm struck by the sense that it doesn't belong here, that our sprinkler was silver. How weird to be back in this place that's no longer ours. I hope the nice family who bought it doesn't mind a few trespassers.

As I'm getting closer, I call out Veronica's name. She raises her head in acknowledgment but doesn't get off the swing.

"Hey," she says flatly when I'm finally next to her.

"You ran away from home to our old home?" I ask. Since she doesn't scream or throw anything at me—doesn't really say anything—I hesitantly sit down next to her on the swing where she and I must have sat thousands of times before.

She still has a few flecks of flour around her eyebrows and in the front of her hair, and she's wearing the same tank dress she was yesterday, only it's all bunched up. For once she doesn't look as though she walked off the pages of *Seventeen*. She looks more like she's the pretty but rumpled female lead at the end of an action film, having survived multiple chases/explosions and possibly even being shoved in a car trunk. Her skin is really cold and sort of clammy when I touch it.

"Did you go to Gram's? Have you been here all night?" I ask. Of course the heat wave finally broke yesterday. It's probably in the seventies now, but last night it got pretty chilly. Can you get hypothermia in Florida during the summer?

Shrugging, she tells me she walked around the park and the old neighborhood for a while before coming here. "I don't think the new people are home." She points to our old house. "I went up and looked in all the windows; they made it different."

From the outside, I can see little changes. The new owners have painted it a slightly orange neutral, the bushes are trimmed, and they've planted these little flowers around the side. Whoever has my old bedroom has hung up lacy pink curtains.

"Why didn't you tell anyone where you were? Everyone was worried, and Mom is freaking hysterical."

"Really?" V sounds almost hopeful.

"Yeah. Elle and I have been running around all over town looking for you. You can't pull shit like that."

"I'm sorry." She looks at me, then down again. "Thanks."

She just sounds so spacey and vague, I rub her cold arms. I'm really angry with her again. But not because she told Alex that I was sleeping with Dr. B., and not because she threw flour and insults at me in the kitchen. I'm angry because I was terrified that something might have happened to her.

"Mol," V says. "You know I didn't mean it when I told you to kill yourself, right?"

I *did* think she meant it, and I was really mad and hurt, but now it all seems really long ago. "It's okay."

"It was just pretty hard watching you sort of face-plant at life so much," V continues, like I didn't already forgive her. "And Mom had me believing if I didn't keep you in my sights at all times, you were going to jump off the roof of the J&J factory. It was a lot, and then when you started giving me shit for dating some guy I wasn't even dating, when you hadn't even bothered to ask me about the guy I was dating for weeks, I kind of lost it."

"I shouldn't have done that. I should have just listened to you," I say. "And I'm sorry I called you a slut. Chris seems like a really nice guy."

She nods. "And I shouldn't have told you all that stuff about Dad. I've wanted to tell you about it forever, and I kept telling Mom that we should, but you know, not like that."

"Why do you even *know* all that stuff? Why did Mom tell you?"

"I don't think she meant to tell me. When you got all screwy, I found her going over the accident report one night. At first she wouldn't say anything, but once she started talking, she just kept going and going. It was like she couldn't keep it a secret any longer without going crazy or something. So she passed the crazy on to me."

She seems so sad and out of it and cold.

"V, it's all good. Let's go home, okay?" I wrap my arm around her.

"Okay." She gets off the swing, and we start toward Elle, who's leaning against the side of the Jeep trying not to look like she's watching everything.

"Molly?" V asks.

"Yeah."

"Thanks for coming to get me."

"Well, let's see how thankful you are after Mom grounds you for the rest of your natural life."

DAY 82

〜〜

Huckleberry Heaven Cake

It's hot again.

So hot that Elle finally convinces me to go to the outdoor pool at the Y with her and Jimmy, even though I haven't been in a pool ADF.

The place is packed, but Gina and Tina from AP English are already set up at lounge chairs by the deep end, and they invite us to share.

Jimmy drops off his stuff and then charges forward and does a huge cannonball into the shallow end, soaking all the old ladies in bathing caps tiptoeing around waist deep. A million lifeguards blow their whistles.

Gina and Tina can't stop talking about starting school in a few weeks, and all the college visits they went on over the summer. Zoning out, I focus on how delicious the warm sun feels on my back. When I hear that they're talking about the summer reading and *The Catcher in the Rye*, which I finished last night, I perk back up.

"I don't know why everyone loves it so much," Tina is saying. "Holden is such a whiny little bitch."

"I know, right?" adds Gina.

"Eh, he's okay," I offer. "He's just depressed."

During adult swim (I'm finally old enough to go in!) I get into one of the lap lanes and swim the length of the pool a few times. ADF I forgot the feel of the water under my palms. The way your lungs tighten when you need to breathe, how you can be hot and sweaty but cold and wet at the same time.

"Looking good out there, Byrne." Elle hands me a towel when I get out. "You coming back to the Coral Cove Swordfish in the fall?"

"Not a chance." It occurs to me that at some point between signing up for the team because Elle was doing it, and hysterically fleeing the starting block during the divisionals meet, swimming became something I didn't really enjoy. It was something I was doing because I was good at it, and Coach Hartley kept telling me how important I was to the team. I was never doing it for me. But I do decide to call Ms. Cromwell and ask if I can still get into the advanced art class.

When Elle drops me off, there's a package for me. Inside is the backpack I left at Dr. B.'s, and a typed note.

Molly—

Once again, let me tell you how very, very
sorry I am for everything. Like I said, you did
nothing wrong. I was the one who let things
go too far. I was the adult, and you were my
patient.

I called my old adviser from Penn the day
after everything happened, and he helped
convince me to go back to Philly for a bit and
help him with his research, I think that it might
be good for me to reconnect with my family
and friends up north. I'm leaving at the end of
the week.

Please don't let your experience with
me prevent you from seeking treatment. I'm
enclosing the information for Charlotte
Frankel—the psychiatrist I told you about.
She's more traditional than I am, but she's a
good person, and I think that she'd be able to
help you. Therapy is personal, though, so if
she's not the right fit, please try to find someone
else to work with.

You really are a great girl. And there are a
lot of people who would be very, very sad if you
just disappeared, including me.

—Glen

He also enclosed Dr. Frankel's card and the DVD of *Say Anything* . . . with a Post-it note stuck on the front. *In case you want to watch the ending.*

So that's it, I guess. He's gone.

I remember the fluttery vagina butterflies I'd sometimes get when we made eye contact during a session. How soft his lips were during the good kiss.

Maybe it's the newness of this information, or maybe it's that it hasn't sunk in yet, but I actually don't burst into waterworks or fall through the floor. No, I just feel sort of numb.

I go downstairs and taste the day's cake.

DAY 84

Asian Bubble Tea Cake

'm on my way downstairs to watch the *Golden Girls* block, when I notice V sitting up on her big frilly canopy bed, surrounded by thick fashion magazines.

After running away from home to our old home, V wasn't grounded for the rest of her natural life, but pretty darn close—three weeks. While half the kids at school have their phones confiscated as a form of punishment, Mom required V to essentially safety pin hers to her sleeve at all times. Plus, V had to get one of those Find My Phone apps. The big shocker? Even though V hemmed and hawed, you could tell she was pretty darn pleased that Mom was so concerned about her. The two of them are actually getting along way better than at any time I can remember.

V's bedroom door is open (she's also not supposed to

shut doors if there is any question about whether or not she's home), but I knock anyway, and she waves me in.

"Do you maybe wanna go downstairs and, you know, bond?" I ask.

"I'm in the middle of something here. Maybe in a little?"

Telling her sure, I turn, but she stops me. "Do you wanna take a look? It kind of involves you."

For the first time I notice that she's not reading the articles about how to make your man crazy in bed or get killer abs in three minutes a day. Instead she's marking up the outfits in the fashion spreads, cutting images out, writing notes. Next to her is a chunky sketchpad where she's drawn her own designs in colored pencil. Slim skirts and long sleeveless tops, and these breezy but fitted dresses. Everything is classic and clean and perfect for Florida summers. The sketches themselves are really well done, and I wonder how I never realized we had that in common.

"Oh, they're so pretty," I say. "I didn't know you could draw like that."

"Well, I'm no Molly Byrne, but I get by."

I tell her that I'm going to take Ms. Cromwell's advanced art class and that she should take it too.

"Two Byrne girls in the same CCH classroom? That might be fun, or the start of the apocalypse. I'll definitely think about it."

Explaining that those weren't the sketches she wanted to show me, V flips back a few pages in her notebook, settles on some drawings of female figures in these fluffy-looking jackets with animal heads. Climbing onto the bed next to her, I get a better view.

"Ohmygod, are those . . ."

"They're the stuffed animal pelts that Jimmy made from the playroom tiger!"

"For serious?" They are honestly adorbs.

"Yeah, Jaclyn liked them so much, she said we could make prototypes to sell at the store."

"That's amazing."

"Here's the kicker. To help make them I was going to go to this dressmaker in Maxwell who sometimes does stuff for Jaclyn. But then Mom found out that the *Baker's Journey* woman has a sister who did *A Seamstress's Journey*."

"Get out!"

"So yeah, when Mom finishes with the cakes, she's going to start that and try to figure out all the stuff in the sewing room. I told Jaclyn we might not have the prototypes for a while."

Mom and V together, thick as thieves. After all my complaining about the cakes, there's a part of me that's a little jealous. Is that the problem with a group of three, that things almost always break down so there's an odd one out?

"Well," I say. "There'll probably be a good amount of fingers stitched together at first, but after a month on that thing, she'll be ready to set the fashion world on fire."

"Have you talked to her yet?" V's tone is weightier. "About all the Dad stuff?"

"Mom and I are fine." This is true-ish. The second everything started going down with V disappearing, any active anger I had toward Mom instantly evaporated. Nothing like the thought of a new potential tragedy to foist togetherness onto everyone and make an old tragedy less tragic. Since then I've been perfectly polite. I've eaten a piece of each day's cake (that hasn't entirely been a hardship; Mom has gone full-on Duff Goldman) and answered any surface question she asks about my day. Like I told Elle, I know that whatever she did, she did it to protect me. But I still can't shake the feeling that she unilaterally took away Pluto.

"Really?" V arches a perfect eyebrow.

"Yes, really."

As she is showing me more of her drawings, we talk about the looks she likes and how her dream is to design something for Jennifer Lawrence on Oscar night.

"Why haven't you ever stopped by Jaclyn's?" she asks. "Even after I told you they were selling my bracelets, you never came in."

"I guess I thought you wouldn't want me there." I shrug.

"That you'd be embarrassed to have the crazy girl who tanked the divisionals meet show up."

"Whatever, Mol. You're my big sister." V gives her signature eye roll. "And seriously, who besides Coach Hartley cares about some stupid swim meet from two years ago? You've got to get over that."

Maybe she's right; maybe the rest of the world really doesn't view the world as BDF and ADF.

"Fine. I guess I'll have to come, then."

Lowering her eyes, she says that Elle came into the store a while ago. "She told me that you weren't hooking up with your shrink . . . and then she gave me a forty-minute lecture about how my nail polish was going to render the planet uninhabitable in two years or something.

"That's Elle."

V shrugs. "So, um, what was going on with you and him the night of the fish thing?"

A part of me wants to just tell her the whole story—like I know she wouldn't go all *Law & Order* the way Elle did. "It was just a misunderstanding," I say.

She nods, even though her face is a portrait of utter disbelief. "Anyway, I told Alex you weren't sleeping with Dr. Brooks. I hope that's okay."

Alex knows Dr. B. and I were never together, but he still hasn't reached out? I guess that speaks volumes. Maybe it's better that way.

"Thanks. That means a lot to me." I know it's probably not fair to ask, but I do it anyway. "How is he? Alex. Do you see him much?"

"Chris said Alex went to one of his pool things last week—not that I was anywhere but here." She closes her magazine and flips over onto her back. "You really did a number on him, Mol."

"I know." I let my head fall back against one of the pillows. "What is wrong with me?"

"You're a cock tease?"

"Shut up!" I throw one of the model-home pillows at her.

"Too soon?" She smiles all innocent-like and bats her eyelashes.

"Yes, too soon! A hundred years from now will still be too soon."

"Sorry."

"So, what about you?" I ask.

"What about me, what?"

"Like, Chris seemed pretty freaking worried when his poor little Ronnie was out in the cold Florida night. . . ."

"It's really none of your business." She smiles again, devilish this time. "But if you're asking if V is still in the V club, yes, I am a card-carrying member. . . ."

This is sort of surprising, but it makes me happy. Not because V hasn't been getting her sexy on, but because she sounds more like my sister.

"But," she continues, "I'm definitely the girl to call if you need a hand . . . job." She throws the pillow back at me. "Or at least I used to be, before Mom put me on lockdown."

It's not quite how I imagined V and me sharing this stuff, but it's pretty darn close.

And it feels good.

DAY 87

Fun No-Fry Funnel Cake

D r. Frankel is a dead ringer for Dorothy from *Golden Girls*!

Unfortunately, we don't have the witty back-and-forth banter Dorothy has with Rose and Blanche. I'm ruler-rigid in one of the two chairs in her office. It was the only seating option; there aren't any couches or chaise longues like Dr. B. had. I remember my first sessions at Dr. B.'s, when I gave one-word answers and twisted up into myself, unclear on what I was supposed to say, until he finally got me talking about music. Probably not gonna happen that way here; there isn't a stereo or any DVDs. If it weren't for the diplomas on the wall (LSU, Tulane; and graduation dates showing she's old enough to be Mom's mom), it would pretty much be the police investigation room on any cop drama.

"So, how do you know Dr. B.—uh, Dr. Brooks?" I ask. Doesn't really seem like they'd be traveling in the same circles or, you know, on the same planet.

"Glen Brooks and I have worked together with several patients. As a psychiatrist, I can prescribe medication, so sometimes he'll send someone to me if he feels they could benefit from that."

"But you do this, the talking part, too?"

"Yes. I believe that is a crucial part of any therapy; I wouldn't prescribe a drug for a patient who wasn't in some type of psychotherapy too."

"Good to know."

"Should we start with that, then?" She smiles. It's a good smile, a million times warmer than anything else in the room, and I relax the tiniest bit. She asks who has been writing the scripts for my meds, and when I tell her it's my pediatrician and that he's had me on the same stuff I've been on since ADF, she smiles the warm smile again. "It might be time to review that, figure out what's working and what isn't."

"But . . ." I explain about Dr. B. telling me that meds weren't really recommended for people under twenty-one.

"The drugs are tools. They're helpful for some people; other people don't need them. And your needs can and do change. It's about finding the right balance for the individual. Some people find it useful to think of it like cooking. Have you ever made a cake, Molly?"

Is she shitting me? "Um, yeah."

"You know how some recipes call for a little more of one ingredient, some a little less? Sometimes you discover it's best to bake the cake on a lower temperature for longer; other times you'll want to use a higher temperature for less time. The basic ingredients might always be the same, but it's about tweaking until you find out what works."

I nod; I still can't believe she used a cake metaphor.

"With your permission, I'd like to have your pediatric records faxed over so I can take a look. If you'd like, you can also have Dr. Brooks's notes sent to me so we can try picking up where you left off with him."

What would be in Dr. B.'s notes? All the stuff about my dad I made up? That he suspected I had a thing for him? That he maybe had a thing for me, too?

"But sometimes," she continues, "I find it's best to begin anew with a different therapist, to make a fresh start."

"I think I'd like that," I tell her. "A fresh start."

The nuclear fusion smile again, and she asks me to explain what brought me to therapy in the first place. So I start with the end of sophomore year, how I stopped caring about everything and how Mom and I went to the counselor's office and Mom got so upset when the counselor suggested I was depressed . . . which all makes so much more sense now than it did at the time. Half the kids at school are on some type of meds, half of Mom's clients and *their* kids are depressed, so I couldn't figure out why Mom was code-red alert about it. But of course it was because of Dad. Dr. B. was right about one thing; therapy *is* easier when you have all the information.

"I actually recently found out that my father killed himself," I tell Dr. Frankel. "My mom had always told my sister and me that it was a car accident, but it turns out the car crash was intentional."

"That's a very big revelation. How did that make you feel?"

"A lot of stuff. Mad that no one had ever told me, kind of betrayed because I'd thought one thing forever and it wasn't true," I say, and then I admit the thing that I haven't been able to say since V hurled the truth at me in the kitchen. "And honestly kind of scared."

Dr. Frankel asks me to go on.

So I tell her how even when I've been at my worst, I've never thought about killing myself in any real way. "But knowing about Dad makes me wonder, like, is that the next phase of this? Is it that kind of progression? I graduate from running away from swim meets to running in front of trains?"

"No, Molly, it doesn't mean you're going to commit suicide too." She explains that while there are some genetic links to mental health conditions, Dad and I are two separate people. "If your father had been an Olympic sprinter, he might have passed on some natural talent, but obviously that wouldn't mean you'd have the same career, not even if you tried to do everything the exact way that he did."

Deep down I guess I knew this, but it's still a relief to hear it.

"And that's one of the reasons why you and I are working together," Dr. Frankel continues. "We want to make sure that nothing like that ever happens to you."

Maybe it's the authority in the way she says it, or maybe it's simply that she looks so much like Bea Arthur, and Dorothy rarely lies about anything important, but I believe her.

By the time I leave, I'm legit tired. I'm still not sure if I'll ever go back to Dr. Frankel, but I can tell that if I do it's going to be a shit-ton of work.

Of course I can't help but think about how different it is from when I used to leave Dr. B's office. Then I was practically giddy replaying over and over again each time he'd smiled or laughed at one of my jokes. It made feel so special . . . and wrong.

My stomach flops over at the word. Wrong.

Me crushing on Dr. B might have been what made it wrong at first, but at some point he started making it wrong too. And he had to know that—he went to freaking Penn! Suddenly I'm all rage-y thinking about him running away and happily starting over in PA. He's probably already picking up a pretty new reporter at the DMV . . . or maybe not.

Maybe he's sitting in a session with a new depressed girl with a dead dad. And maybe she's noticing that amazing jawline and the little temple depressions.

Fuck. Maybe Elle is right and I need to report him to the cops or some board of something or other. Maybe I will. Or maybe I will talk to V about it . . . or even Mom, someday.

All I really know is that for the first time, I'm glad Glen Brooks is out of the great state of Florida. As I pedal home on Old Montee, I feel . . . free.

DAY 90

∘∘∘

Scrumptious Carrot-and-Apple Cake

Her hair twisted up in another impossible braid, Mom is peeling roughly seven hundred apples in the model-home kitchen.

Plopping down at one of the bar stools at the island, I pick up an apple and a peeler and start adding to the pound of red skins. That nervous don't-scare-the-woodland-creature look from Mom again.

"So why *didn't* you tell me?" I say, out of nowhere, picking up the conversation where I left it eleven days ago. "About Dad, I mean."

Mom puts down her apple and wipes her hands on her apron.

"Maybe I should have told you. My mother always said I need to let you girls know 'exactly what kind of man he was.'"

Mom imitates Gram's little old lady tone, and suddenly all those conversations I remember hearing when we were staying at my grandmother's make more sense. You can tell Mom is thinking about those, too, and it clearly still bothers her.

She takes a breath. "I love my mother, Molly, but she has no clue what kind of man your father was. She was always furious that we eloped, and she saw him maybe ten times total. To her he's just some guy who drove his car into a tree and screwed her daughter out of life insurance. I didn't want him to be that to you girls."

How perfectly fake.

Perfect for V and Mom and me, ambling around this huge house decorated by stagers for some aspirational family, where people cook and sew and give their kids the most amazing toys. Where a giant portrait of the four of us hangs in the dining room, even though it's a giant lie and we never really were that family.

"So, what, it's better to mislead us?" Even as I'm asking it, I realize that's exactly what I did to Dr. B. and Gina and Tina, and everyone, mostly to me. I built a dad—two parts family sitcoms, one part old photographs. Much easier than the truth.

"Molly, your father was sooo much more than the way he died—more than some screwup in his brain that made him do what he did. He loved us very much."

"How can you say that?" I ask, frustrated that Mom is still protecting him. If I can't have my *Family Ties/Growing*

Pains fantasy father, let's do this no-holds-barred. "You don't show your family how much you love them by choosing *not* to be with them. That's a dick move."

"I felt that way for years." Mom exhales. "I was so angry that I would sometimes turn up the volume on the TV and scream. But then I finally realized that one really bad thing didn't invalidate everything else."

No, it shouldn't. But this is a pretty monumentally bad thing. And . . .

"It wasn't one bad thing, though, was it?" I ask. "People don't just wake up and decide to drive into a tree. You had to suspect something."

"Yes, and no," she says. "I knew he wasn't happy all the time, but neither was I—we had two young kids and no money. After it happened, I sifted through everything over and over, trying to find the evidence. That day when he didn't want to go out to dinner with our friends, was that a sign? Or how we talked about Kurt Cobain the night we met—should I have known then? It's impossible not to apply hindsight to history. Finally I just realized I'd never get to know exactly what he was thinking.

"But then when things started going bad for you, it brought back all that craziness. I just kept thinking, *How could I have missed this again?* So when V found me going over the accident report, I got this idea that she could be my ally. That maybe if Bill and I hadn't been so far away from our families, someone else would have noticed. And if I told V, we could keep an eye on you together."

Being the big sister: my job.

"But she was barely fourteen, and it was probably too much to ask," Mom says.

After saying so much, we don't say anything for a while.

My sister, who's beautiful and popular and talented, and my mother, who's perfect and independent and successful— the kind of people other people assume have it so easy. Heck, I've assumed they have it so easy—have been living with this big stupid secret that was eating away at them.

"And the cakes?"

Mom utters a bittersweet semi-laugh. "I know that it sounds really dumb, but I did want you to have that cake you never had. The week before your birthday, we went to the bakery to pick it out—you wanted one with the fish from *Finding Nemo*—and for days you stopped total strangers to tell them about it. I'm sure you don't remember this, but after the accident—you had no idea what was going on—people kept bringing over food, and every time you'd ask if that was your 'berday' cake."

"But I do remember there being a cake."

"At some point I had Gram run to the corner store, but all they had left was this stale Entenmann's crumb cake two days past the sell-by date. And we could only find two candles, but you were turning three.

"So," Mom continues, "when I saw that 100 Days of Cake challenge, I figured maybe I could give you some great cakes to make up for that cruddy one, and that it might give you something to look forward to every day."

"*Mom.*" I'm going to cry . . . again. Because it is so sad and sweet that a day after her husband up and killed himself, my mom loved me enough to worry that I had only two candles on my cake. Because that is a kind of love that I can only hope to one day comprehend. A love that I am beyond lucky to have. So many people—people with both parents living—never get anything close to that.

And I remember that dream episode of *Golden Girls* where Blanche found out her husband had faked his death. With all those commercials in syndication and the time to resolve the dream plot at the end, it probably really only took Blanche fifteen minutes to forgive him. I'm not sure I can ever forgive my father for doing what he did, for giving me fucked-up genes and crappy hair. For putting Mom through this. Putting V through this. But I can easily forgive my mom for doing what she thought was best. And I can try to understand.

"Do you think sometime you could tell me about Dad? Like, what he was actually like? Not the Disney version."

"I'd like that."

So I ask her to tell me about the night they met in Miami. And while we bake, she does.

DAY 92

Mocha Madness Cake

The picture of our family in the dining room looks the same as it always has. Mom is still so impossibly luminous that she almost doesn't seem real but like some goddess slumming it down on earth with us. V is still all eyes peeking from a blanket. I'm still wearing my jumper, still holding the doll the photographer gave me to make me smile. And Dad is the same too. His hands are still ginormous and one of them is still holding my shoulder.

For some reason I thought that he might have changed since I found out the truth. That he might have morphed into something sinister or that I'd suddenly be able to detect something that I never noticed before. A can't-keep-your-shoelaces-tied sadness in his eyes. Some pain or longing in Dad's smile. But no, he looks the same.

Maybe Mom is right and he really did love us even if he chose to leave us. Maybe, at least in this moment forever frozen in time, Dad wanted nothing more than to protect me.

DAY 95

⚬⚬⚬

Hummingbird Cake
(No Hummingbirds Are Harmed in the Making of This Cake)

Elle, Jimmy, V, Mom, and I are baking together in the model-home kitchen, because this is apparently something we do now.

Okay, it's pretty awesome. Even if Elle does require that everything we use *must* come in containers that don't leave a carbon footprint, and Jimmy sometimes feels compelled to turn the bowls and spoons into a drum kit.

"This next song is for Veronica my love," he announces before an impromptu performance.

"Sorry, kid," says V. "The whole rocker thing is the way to your sister's heart, not mine."

"And Mom's," I add. Toupee Thom told Mom he was so impressed with Alex's band at the FishTopia event that he decided to re-form his law school group—the Legal Eagles. Oh yeah, Mom and Thom are back on.

Curling up his lip, Jimmy proclaims, "You guys are weird."

The glossy picture in *A Baker's Journey* shows a brown spice cake, topped with a white frosting and chopped nuts, so it makes perfect sense that Jimmy asks if we can make it purple.

"Jimmy," Elle whines.

"You know." Mom has her magical-idea look again. "I bet we *could* do that with food coloring."

The suggestion seems highly suspect, but it actually turns out pretty badass—I mean, as much as any baked good can be badass.

"Is it okay if I take some over to Mark's later?" Elle asks, and Mom assures her there is plenty to go around. "His band is practicing tonight, and they're always starving afterward."

His band . . . Alex. Elle's eyes nervously flick to me. Because she is sooo ooey-gooey *The Fault in Our Stars* in love, for a second she forgot about the whole me-Alex debacle—and that makes me happy. I don't want the people I love keeping their good news from me.

"How is the band?" I ask. I do not ask if Alex is with one of the Hot Topic girls or Meredith Hoffman. "Did they come up with a name yet?"

"They did, actually." Elle looks at me as if I'm the world's most delicate blown-glass figurine. "They decided to call themselves FishTopia."

"For serious?"

"Yeah, the drummer couldn't believe that was the name of the store and thought it was really cool."

V rolls her eyes. "What is it with you people and that place?"

"That's awesome!" I say.

"I wasn't sure how you'd feel about it," says Elle. "But I thought it was kind of nice."

"Jimmy"—V nods at him—"would you please tell Elle and Molly what they are?"

Throwing off sun rays from V's attention, Jimmy says, "You guys are weird!"

"Thank you." V gives him a high five and comes away with a hand full of purple icing.

"You know, V," Mom says, "there should be plenty left if you want to invite *your* boyfriend over for a piece tonight."

At the mention of Chris, Jimmy scrunches up into an angry emoji.

"Does this mean I'm no longer grounded?" V asks hopefully.

"It means I'd like to meet this guy," says Mom. "I've heard some good things."

Everybody's paired off, but it's okay.

I wonder if Dr. B. is in Philly yet. And then it occurs to me that this is the first time I've thought of him today. Maybe a few days. And I haven't had any desire to watch *Say Anything . . .* even though Dr. B. gave it to me as kind of a grand romantic gesture. In fact, hearing Elle and V talk about their boyfriends, I realize just how ridiculous my crush on Dr. B. really was, and I chuckle under my breath. Yeah, and he was telling me Alex was the one with maturity issues.

So I guess it's just Jimmy and me forever. He thinks I'm weird, and I think he's a rabid possum. We could both do a lot worse.

DAY 99

New Day Cake
(with Optional Icing Drizzle)

FishTopia isn't really on the way home from Dr. Frankel's, but it's not that out of the way, so I bike past it sometimes. Today is one of those days. Slowing down, I notice two things. First, there's a bunch of balloons and a sign that says GRAND OPENING. Second, Alex is there. Leaning his back against the side of his car, staring at the building. In his jeans and that really faded Doors T-shirt that used to be his uncle's, he just looks familiar.

Almost without thinking about it, I ride over. For a fractured second I'm so excited to see him that I momentarily forget all the stuff that happened, forget that he told me he was through with me and that the best part of Charlie closing the store was that I'd be out of his life forever.

Apparently he forgot all that too, because when I pull up next to him, he gets this lottery-winner glow. "Molly!"

"Alex!" I hop off Old Montee.

Then things return to awkward when we shuffle around trying to determine the appropriate gesture of greeting. Handshake? Cheek kiss? Fist bump? We settle on this limited-touching back-pat thing.

"FishTopia is sleeping with the fishes." I gesture toward the diner, which does seem pretty fun. Through the window there are red-and-yellow-stripped booths and a long counter with a row of those bar stools on silver poles like in Norman Rockwell paintings. It's the middle of the day, but the place is already crowded. What do you know, central Florida really was clamoring for chicken-fried steak.

"The end of an era," Alex says. "Good times."

"Yeah, I've really gotten behind on my *Golden Girls*. I don't think I've seen the one where Blanche gets jealous of Dorothy's lounge singing in at least three weeks."

"I really do miss this place." Bowing his head, Alex gets this weird sheepish expression. "Actually, do you remember that redheaded woman with the two kids, who came in that last week?"

"Sure."

"Well, ever since she made that comment about marine biology, I can't stop thinking about it."

"Really?"

"Crazy, right?" he says. "Don't laugh, but I've been looking into schools and everything. The University of Tampa has a really good program, and I could still minor in music, so I could still piss off my dad at least a little."

"That is so cool!" I say, and mean it. For once I'm not freaked out about senior year and college and stuff. Dr. Frankel and I just spent part of our session talking about how I might start looking into colleges or internships for graphic design.

"And to think," Alex says, "I only took the job because it paid more than Walmart."

We talk a little about Elle and Mark and how they're practically ready to move in together after just a few weeks. Alex assures me that Mark is a great guy as long as you don't buy a plastic bottle of soda around him. "Take it from someone who's made that mistake on more than one occasion."

He asks about V. "Chris said she was grounded for life."

"No, just till her seventy-fifth birthday. Otherwise she's good. We're actually getting along petty well—that whole listening to each other thing."

"Yeah, that." He laughs. "I'm really glad."

"Oh, do you know whatever happened to JoJo?" I ask. "The diner people said they offered her a job, but she turned them down."

"You didn't hear?" Alex is super-excited. I shake my head. "She sent an audition tape to *Wheel of Fortune*, and they loved her. She's going out to Cali to film her episode next week!"

"Way to go, JoJo!"

"I know, right?"

Then I remember that Mr. K. wanted to hire Alex as well, and I was supposed to let him know about the job, so I do. "I'm sorry I didn't tell you earlier."

Of all the crappy things I've done to Alex, *this* is what I'm apologizing for? The thing that legitimately borders on "not really my problem"?

"Actually, I'm sorry for a whole lot of things," I add.

"Me too, Molly." He nods. "Me too."

It seems sort of important, like we're both covering a lot of ground with these words.

After a while he asks, "School start for you guys on Monday too?"

"Yeah, back to the grind, bleah." But I'm not dreading it quite so much. V and I have that art class, and I signed up for driver's ed. Also, I'm weirdly excited about the final day of cake and Mom and V's sewing thing. I've been helping out a little with the "Posh Pelts." (It's a working title. We're also considering "Plush Pelts," "Cutie Kills," and "Haute Hunters.") We've decided that if anyone ever buys one, we should put a chunk of the money away in some sort of Jimmy college fund, even though he'd probably think that was weird.

"Well, it was really great seeing you, Molly." Alex pats my arm and reaches into the front pocket of his jeans for his keys. "Hopefully we'll run in to each other again before Elle and Mark's wedding."

I can't just let him go again, without trying.

All those times that he put himself out there to ask me out; all those times I played dumb or brushed him off because I was scared. But like Elle says, he already knows I don't shit rainbows.

I guess this is my turn.

Taking a here-goes-nothing breath, I step in front of him before he can get back into the car. Confused, Alex cocks his head.

"So, you know how once upon a time you wanted us to go out for dinner, on a proper date-date?" I ask hopefully. "Well, if you're still interested, there's this new restaurant in town that has a killer chef named Mrs. K. It just opened, and I'm dying to try it."

"I don't believe you." Alex shakes his head incredulously in a way that's hard to read. Optimistically, it might be a head shake of amusement, but it could very well be one of exasperation and/or disgust because I'm the world's most frustrating cock tease. "After everything that happened, you're asking *me* out on a date?"

"So I take it that's a no?"

"I didn't say that. I mean, I hear this place has the only chicken and waffles in all of Coral Cove."

I laugh, and he reaches for my hand—those calluses on

the pads of his fingers—and for the first time, I don't pull away. Instead I squeeze back and smile. My guts are fluttery and twisty, but not in the spiral way, just in an excited, who-knows kind of way.

Maybe this will be the single greatest thing that ever happens to me, or maybe it will implode and suck worse than what happened with TJ. I guess sometimes you have to just take chances—send a shuttle out as far as you can, even if it means you might find out that Pluto isn't a planet. Maybe you'll find something else great.

"And if you're still hungry after," I tell him. "I know a great place we can go for cake."

Acknowledgments

Jessica Sit, this book is really just as much your baby as it is mine. Thanks for tirelessly working with me to make it a reality.

A hearty thanks to Alex Glass for wheeling and dealing for me all these years. I'd also like to give a shout-out to Andrea Mason for legal advice; Terri Goveia for an early read; and Eric Hollander for agreeing to go in to the office early for weeks.

Thank you, as always, to my family. Nancy and Bob Wall, who provided crucial childcare and Cherry Coke Zeroes. Nancy and Michael Goldhagen, for always offering support and encouragement and forgiving me repeatedly for deadline-induced bitchiness. And of course to my Bobwall and Victoria—my greatest distractions and my absolute everything.